IRIS
IN
THE
DARK

ALSO BY
ELISSA GROSSELL DICKEY

The Speed of Light

IRIS
IN
THE
DARK

a novel

ELISSA GROSSELL DICKEY

LAKE UNION PUBLISHING

Text copyright © 2022 by Elissa Grossell Dickey
All rights reserved.

Published by Lake Union Publishing, Seattle

www.apub.com

Amazon, the Amazon logo, and Lake Union Publishing are trademarks of Amazon. com, Inc., or its affiliates.

ISBN-13: 9781542037822
ISBN-10: 1542037824

Cover design by Faceout Studio, Tim Green

Printed in the United States of America

For my parents, Bill and Elaine Grossell.
Thank you for loving me unconditionally and teaching
me the importance of family.

Either the Darkness alters,
Or something in the sight,
Adjusts itself to Midnight,
And Life steps almost straight.
—*Emily Dickinson, "We Grow Accustomed to the Dark"*

Rural Minnesota
Eight years ago

I creep across the parking lot of the aging gas station, eyes adjusting quickly to the darkness. We go out only when it's dark because it's easier to hide. I don't mind anymore. I'd rather hide now, rather tuck away the parts of myself I have left.

I'm almost to the door, beckoned by the glow of fluorescent light, the promise of air-conditioning. But a low whistle makes me turn back—he's watching, always watching. I shiver as I push the door open, stepping into soft music and crisp air, like entering another world.

"Evening," the attendant calls from behind the red counter.

The greeting jolts me, and I turn quickly down an aisle, remembering his warning: *Don't take too long.* I rub my tender wrist—proof of my last mistake—then absently pull down the sleeve of my ratty flannel.

I cross to the back corner, then walk the perimeter, staring intently into each cooler as if deciding which soft drink to purchase. In my peripheral vision, though, I'm scanning, checking, as I've been taught.

Suddenly the bathroom door creaks open behind me. A giggling toddler bounds out, followed by a frazzled-looking brunette, who lunges for his hand—but not before the little one knocks into a display of chips, sending blue bags of Doritos cascading to the floor. The mom clings to the child with one hand while reaching for the scattered bags with the other. A pang of something foreign tugs at my chest, and I hear myself say, "I got it." I'm crouching to pick up the bags before I can stop myself.

"Thank you." She smiles in relief. "Someone is up *way* past his bedtime."

I smile faintly as I watch her carry him out the door. The feeling within me lingers, a far-off hope I can't name. I glance out the window, where Mitch waits in the car with his best friend—I shudder again, then sigh as I walk to the checkout counter.

The old man working tonight scratches his salt-and-pepper beard. I clear my throat. "Can I get a pack of Marlboro Lights?" I ask softly.

His face twists into a "gotcha" grin. Poor guy. If he only knew. "Let's see some ID," he says gruffly.

I make a show of patting my pockets as my eyes dart behind him for cameras. Finally, I say, "I'm sorry, I must have left it in the car." He smirks at me, but then his brow furrows. I look down and see my sleeve has pushed up, revealing the large purple-black bruise on my wrist.

He glances outside, then back at me. "You okay?"

I freeze, unprepared, then quickly tug at my sleeve. "I just need to go get my ID."

He nods sadly. "Sure, kid."

Back out into the sticky heat, trapping me, not letting me go. At the car, Mitch is leaning against the trunk, passing a cigarette to his friend. "Well?" he says.

I open my mouth, and my tongue is thick. Mitch steps toward me, his hand clasping around my wrist, and the words come out: "No camera," I say. "He's alone."

"Good girl."

They grab their guns and walk back the way I came. I'm sick to my stomach as I scramble into the car.

Then I stare into the night as if looking for hope, or forgiveness. Only darkness stares back. I start the car and wait for them to return, wait for the light to come.

CHAPTER ONE

The night is dark and quiet and I welcome it, like an old friend. The blanket of inky-black sky. The glow of a watchful moon. It's not that I don't fear it—fear is my constant companion, my mind ever spinning its spidery web of potential dangers. And yet there's something about the cover of darkness that gives me peace, lets me rest. When the world sleeps, I can pretend there's nothing to fear.

I can pretend the worst hasn't happened and never will.

I click the door shut behind me carefully, lest I wake my little monster. The heat of the summer day has evaporated into a blessedly cool night. Traffic hums across town, proof of life at a comfortable distance, the way I like it. Out here in the night air, the gentle breeze, I can let myself relax.

Until a muffled shout comes from behind the house. Ripples of laughter and cheerful greetings follow, then a burst of music. My body tenses as I creep across the lawn and around the side of my house. The darkness and my ample rosebush help to conceal me, but I have a full view of my neighbors' son and his delinquent friends drinking beer in the adjoining alleyway behind our houses. The glint of a lighter, then a pungent aroma in the air. I dig my cell phone out of my pocket because I have to. Someone has to do the right thing, even when it's hard. *Especially* when it's hard. It took me way too long to learn that.

My fingers punch the nine and two ones as if by muscle memory.

"911. What's your emergency?"

"I'd like to report a disturbance, please."

"What sort of disturbance, ma'am?"

"A group of teenagers are drinking and smoking pot in the alley on Baker Street."

"Can I have an address, please?"

"An address?" I blink.

"I need to know where to send the officer, ma'am."

"Uh, of course . . ." *Damn.* I scramble to calculate the number of calls I've made to dispatch lately. Technically this is my third noise complaint this summer against my teen terror of a neighbor. Plus, there was that suspicious vehicle I called in two weeks ago that turned out to be a rental car for a family down the street.

As I'm deliberating, a twig snaps in the grass behind me, and I whirl around. My monster has found me, big blue eyes narrowed in confusion. "Who are you talking to, Mom?"

I place a hand over the phone. "None of your business—but why are you out of bed?"

Finn blinks over my shoulder. "Are you spying on Johnny Pike?"

"No," I say quickly. *Busted.* I huff out an annoyed sigh and bring the phone to my ear. "Sorry, never mind—they left. Thanks anyway." I end the call and turn to my son. "Go back to bed."

"But I can't sleep," he says. "Can I play on my tablet?"

"No way. It's bedtime."

"But it's *summer,*" he whines.

"It's midnight, and you're seven years old."

"Seven *and a half,*" he mutters.

"Finnegan Charles." I draw out the syllables, my classic warning.

"Fine." He stomps away, and I hear the door slam.

With a sigh, I follow in his footsteps before locking the front door—knob and dead bolt, checking twice—then I sneak down the

2

hall to peer into Finn's room, making sure he is in fact back in bed. Because I have to. I always have to.

I'm weary when I retreat to my own bedroom, where I pour myself into bed and pull the blanket up to my chin. The whir of the ceiling fan isn't enough tonight, so I click on my old DVD player, let the muted sounds of my favorite old Italian movie, *Nights of Cabiria*, play in the background—careful to keep the volume low so my son will have no more reasons to get out of bed.

But I don't go to sleep, not yet. Even exhaustion can't rob the night-time from me. I stare at my phone, completing a crossword puzzle to squeeze out every last moment of blissful freedom before drifting off.

In the morning the sun peeks through the curtains, and I'm half-awake as a small figure, warm and soft, wriggles in under the covers. "I'm sorry for the way I acted." Finn's hair is askew, his sweet breath warm on my cheek.

I smile. "I'm sorry, too."

He snuggles in close, and I wrap an arm around him. I savor these moments when I can be absolutely certain nothing bad will happen because he's right here next to me. I let myself drift off until my alarm squawks. Finn shimmies away, scrambles out of bed. "It's six thirty—I can have screen time!"

Moment passed. I roll out of bed and pad to the kitchen, where I pour a cup of coffee from the pot I preprogrammed the night before. Steaming mug in hand, I head for the shower, stopping to poke my head into Finn's room. "Twenty minutes—then you need to get dressed."

He nods, eyes not leaving the screen, and I sigh as I shut the door.

Forty-five minutes later, we're on our way to work and summer day care, and I'm emitting the appropriate number of "mm-hmms" as, from the back seat, Finn tells me all about every character of the Marvel action game he's been engrossed in on his technological babysitter.

We're about halfway there when suddenly he asks, "Mom, where are we from?"

My eyes widen at the abrupt subject change. "Uh, well, here of course. South Dakota."

"But who are my grandparents?"

A familiar alarm beeps in my head, but I keep a light tone. "You mean besides Papa Lowell?" I say, referring to his nickname for my beloved boss.

"Do I have real grandparents?" he asks quietly.

The alarm blares louder—I can't handle this today. "Why did you bring this up? Did somebody ask you about it?"

I glance back, and he's frowning out the window. "At day care they want us to bring in pictures of our family and talk about them."

My heart breaks for the millionth time, but I force a cheery smile. "Well, we have photos." Selecting which photographs were safe to keep was a tricky, painful process—choosing enough pieces that the puzzle would appear complete while keeping the full, terrifying picture hidden. I scramble to deflect. "Hey, what do you say we eat at the diner tonight?"

His eyes light up. "Chicken nuggets?"

"And french fries, if you want." I smile, grateful that I was able to throw in my own smooth subject change.

I pull the car into a parking spot in the potholed lot behind the large brick building that has housed my employer, the *Prairie Daily News*, for almost a century, distracting Finn with more exciting talk of the diner meal that awaits us tonight as we walk inside. In the corridor, we enter the door that leads to the day care, its bright colors and soft music welcoming us in. I triple-check that Finn's EpiPen and Benadryl are in his backpack before handing the pack over to his day-care teacher. He's already bouncing toward the toys, but I catch up to him, showering his cheeks with kisses until he giggles and swats me away; then I slip back out the door as he brags to a little friend about the chicken nuggets that await him.

Back in the corridor, I lean against the door, breathing slowly, struggling to compose myself.

It's a fragile thing, this life we live.

At once tenuous and treacherous, like my rosebush. Most days I can nurture it to perfection, coax out beautiful blossoms. Yet without warning a rogue thorn can attack, vicious and sharp, creating a painful mess that spins out of my control.

It's going to get even harder as Finn gets older. But I can't worry about the future yet. There are already so many dangers lurking beneath the soil right now.

If I'm not careful, they could resurface at any moment.

CHAPTER TWO

Mornings in the newsroom are quieter than you might expect. Deadlines are still hours away, so there's only the clack of a solitary keyboard and the drone of a morning news show from the flat-screen mounted on the wall of the vast open space. This early it's usually only the agriculture editor and me. But as I cross the faded brown carpeting toward my chair at the main information desk, I see light peeking out from underneath the office door of the editor in chief, Lowell Gordon. Odd. He's never in before nine.

Right now, though, I have more pressing concerns. I plop my purse down on my impeccably clean desk, casting a scornful gaze at the ag editor, Frank, hunched over his nearby workspace. He sighs, silently handing over the remote, and I swiftly change the TV from national cable news to a local news channel.

Frank harrumphs, scratching his bald head. "You said I could watch what I want before eight."

I cross my arms. "Well, it's 8:01, and this is an unbiased newsroom."

"So we watch these clowns instead?"

"It's this or the weather."

"Bah." He swats his arm, turning away.

I revel in this one small victory as I sit, moving my small potted succulent just so and straightening the nameplate on my desk: IRIS JENKINS,

ADMINISTRATIVE ASSISTANT TO THE EDITOR IN CHIEF. The glue of the news-room, keeping all the journalists in line, as Mr. Gordon—Papa Lowell to Finn, just Lowell to me—once said. A fitting description, I think, as I sip my coffee and prepare to wade into the cesspool that is a newspaper email in-box on a Monday morning. Much can be eliminated immediately—like scams, or a well-intentioned PR firm that decided, God bless them, we might care about their new branch opening in Rapid City. Our state's population may be small, but physically it's a pretty massive area, and we don't have the staff to cover that much territory.

Then I move to the next ring in this circle of hell: angry readers. It's amazing how, in one email, a subscriber will rant about how a story clearly showed a reporter's "liberal agenda"; then, the very next email will be from someone claiming that same story showed obvious bias toward conservatives.

I smile. Lowell likes to say if both sides are angry with you, you're doing things right.

My objective with these emails is twofold: identify any potential threats and alert Lowell immediately, and locate any news items of interest from people within our eight-county region for him to assign to reporters. It's a job I take seriously, and I'm proud to say nothing has gotten past me.

I'm finished with the in-box and ready to shift my attention to snail mail when I look up and see that a couple more reporters have trickled into the newsroom. Natalie, our new high school intern, scowls at her computer. When she glances up, I offer a small smile. She doesn't return it, her eyes sliding back to her monitor, and by God, I admire her the more for it. She keeps to herself, gets here on time—and, most important, gets shit done. What more can you ask?

The main phone line rings, and I clear my throat before answering: "Newsroom, this is Iris; how may I help you?"

"Brayden Barnes, please," the deep voice booms. I glance over to assure he is in fact the other reporter who has arrived, then transfer the call. Brayden "Big City" Barnes, as Lowell jokingly calls him, with his slick blond hair and even slicker smile, makes it clear every day that he is above the rest of us. I wrinkle my nose. I wish Brayden, unlike Natalie, would keep to himself *more*.

A few minutes later, though, Brayden walks up and stands next to me. He's clearly waiting for my attention but says nothing, so I make him wait. Only after he huffs indignantly do I look up from the sweet, handwritten thank-you note an eighty-eight-year-old reader sent in about our recent coverage of the city's Memorial Day ceremony. "Yes, Brayden?" I ask slowly.

"If it's not too much trouble, could you *please* alert me when you're going to be transferring a call?"

I frown. "You were at your desk, ten feet away. You heard the call come in."

He sighs, pinching the bridge of his nose as if he's the most patient person on earth. "Yes, Iris, but it's more *professional* if you place them on hold, let me know, and then take them off hold to let them know you're transferring the call. Then, you know, transfer it. It's how we did things back at the station in Minneapolis."

I blink. "Gee, that's a lot of steps, Brayden. You'd better write that down."

Frank speaks up: "Uh, you know, Iris, I think I'd prefer that, too." I shoot him a death glare, and he shrugs. "Hey, if my man Brayden here says it worked for Minneapolis, then I'm with him . . ."

Frank trails off, and I'm left glaring at the two men and fighting the urge to let loose a string of obscenities. Then, a small voice speaks from behind a large computer. "Yeah, because when I think of the height of knowledge and professionalism, I *definitely* think of Brayden and Frank."

I snort in surprise and catch the small smile on Natalie's face as Brayden and Frank stare at her in shock. Then her phone rings, and she flashes them a smirk before picking up the receiver and answering in an impressively professional voice.

Damn, I like this girl.

Behind me, a throat clears. "Iris? You got a minute?"

I turn into the crinkled smile of Lowell Gordon, and I smile back. "Sure, boss."

Brayden snaps into suck-up mode. "Morning, Mr. Gordon. I'm here bright and early, interviewing sources." But our editor has already retreated into his office, and I, too, ignore Brayden as I follow him in.

"Shut the door, please, Iris, will you?"

I comply, but I notice the uncharacteristic worry on his face. I settle into the soft chair in front of his desk, watching, amused, as he makes a show of shuffling his scattered papers into a haphazard pile—as if after over seven years of working here I don't know that he thrives on this constant state of disarray.

At last he settles down, wraps a hand around his coffee mug, and brings it to his lips. "Now," he says as he sets the cup down again, "I'm just going to get to it. We both knew I wasn't going to be around forever."

I gasp, eyes widening. "You're sick?" God, I knew he was moving more slowly lately; I should've done something, said something.

He holds his hands up, chuckling. "No, no. What I meant was, I wasn't going to be leading this newspaper forever. I'm talking about retirement."

My shoulders sag in relief. "But you said you had a few more years left in you."

He rubs the back of his neck. "I said a lot of things. But the truth is, I'm getting older, and the time is right—financially, I mean."

I raise my eyebrows. "Stratus contacted you again?"

Stratus Communications has been trying to buy us out for months now. It's amazing we've lasted as long as we have, with the state of newspapers in general shifting over the past few decades, plus the recent push of antijournalism and government officials trying to sow mistrust in the media.

"Yes. And this time they made it clear they won't be offering again. I have until the end of the year to make arrangements."

I freeze. "You've already made the deal, then."

"I trust you'll keep this between us, for now." I nod, and he sighs heavily. "Look, Iris, we've always been honest with each other. I need to tell you—Stratus will most likely be making some changes. They don't run things like we do. The news is not their top priority. And neither are the people who deliver it. They're interested in turning a profit at any cost."

"Layoffs." My voice shakes.

He nods grimly. "The fact of the matter is, a lot of people will have to go. And first in line will be people whose employment papers might not exactly be in order."

I rock forward, wrapping my arms around myself as if it will cushion the blow. I squeeze my eyes shut, and suddenly it's eight years ago and I'm that terrified young woman again who rolled into town with nothing. "How long do I have?" I finally manage to whisper.

He shakes his head. "Now, hold on. I don't know what they're planning for sure. But no matter what, Ivan and I made you a promise, and I intend to keep it, young lady."

I nod, fighting back emotion thinking about all the Gordons have done for me. Eight years ago they found me crying over a coffee cup at the truck stop at the edge of town—the spouses were about to leave on a weekend getaway; I was newly arrived, pregnant, scared, and alone. They sat and listened to my story—and before I knew it, they were coming to my rescue. They gave me this job at the newspaper where they were coeditors; as property owners, they rented me a nice little starter home for next to nothing. They became the fathers I never had—and soon, the grandfathers Finn never had.

Now, I glance at Ivan's photo on Lowell's desk, and the pain of missing him takes my breath away. It's been three years since cancer stole him from us, and yet the loss is raw, a wound that won't heal.

Lowell's eyes glisten as he follows my gaze. "You're not alone, Iris."

"Thank you," I whisper, swiping at my eyes. "I just don't know what I'm going to do."

He smiles. "How do you feel about a career change?" My brow furrows as he continues. "I've been selling a lot of my properties, but I'm not quite sure what to do with Windy Acres."

I blink. "Your bed-and-breakfast?"

"More of a hunting lodge now. It's not quite as up to snuff as it was when Ivan ran it. He really loved that place." His smile is wistful. "It'll be hard to let it go, but I can't live out there like I used to. I need a caretaker there year-round."

He looks at me pointedly, and I stare back in shock. *"Me?"*

"I've been considering other options, but you're my top choice."

"But I don't know the first thing about hunting. Or lodging, for that matter."

"You're a fast learner. I believe in you."

His kind words wash over me, and yet the weight of responsibility is suffocating. "Would it really be *just me?*"

"I have a groundskeeper who does some odd jobs around the property. And if you have questions, I'm only a phone call away."

"But what if I can't do it?"

"What if you *can?*"

Windy Acres. The massive old farmhouse is way out in the country, with a huge yard. Finn loved it when Lowell held the employee picnic there last year, with its tire swing, firepit, even a fort in the woods, according to coworkers who explored the grounds—which honestly creeps me out a little bit, but it's not like I'll let him go out there alone.

I'm lost in thought, but Lowell says, "Why don't you try it out? I'm going to be spending the week after next in Minneapolis with my

11

brother's family. He's celebrating his eightieth birthday. You and Finn can stay out at the lodge while I'm gone. Make yourselves at home."

He slides a key across his desk, and I stare down at it, shiny and beckoning, as my brain tries to catch up to all these rapid changes. My mind spins with the anxiety of a new career, a new life. I'm not sure I can do it again. But Lowell has given me so many chances over the years, and here he is giving me yet another one. I don't want to let him down.

And if I'm likely going to be laid off, what choice do I have, really?

I glance again at the picture of Ivan, who seems to be smiling encouragingly at me, his eyes saying, *You can do this*.

I look up at Lowell with what I hope is a confident smile. "Okay. I'll give it a try."

CHAPTER THREE

I'm already having doubts about this new adventure Lowell has proposed for me—but either way, my first step has to be getting my tiny copilot on board. Tonight's diner meal will provide the perfect opportunity to bring it up to Finn.

When we step inside the diner, we're greeted by friendly faces and the clatter of cutlery against plates. My own stomach rumbles at the intoxicating smell of grilled burgers and crispy fries. We slide into a cushy, high-backed booth, awaiting our server. I'm grateful that, at age seven, Finn doesn't get tired of always going to the same place—his peanut and dairy allergies make it difficult to go anywhere at all, and it took much deliberation with an online allergy parents' group to even try. Chain restaurants are more likely to have information online, they said, but a local place is more likely to have a caring staff.

All Finn's little friends at school love the local diner, so that's what we tried. And it was a great choice. On our first visit I peppered our server with questions, and she patiently fielded them and even spoke to the cook, assuring me he would be using separate cookware and utensils for our meal. Now we're at the point that the servers know us by name and know to automatically accommodate Finn's needs. And let me tell you, the peace that comes with knowing, for that moment in time, I am not on my own in keeping him safe is an amazing thing.

But tonight a new server is approaching us, which triggers my anxiety alarm. The young girl—Kelsi, according to her name tag—smiles as she sets down menus. "What can I get you?"

I swallow. "Uh, well, my son has allergies, but usually when we come here we're able to get chicken nuggets made special for him?"

"No risk of cross contamination," Finn says solemnly. I smile—people often comment that Finn seems younger than his seven years, and I'll admit my overprotective nature and worry over his allergies make me coddle him. But his awareness of his own dietary needs has also given him a vocabulary—and a sense of empathy—beyond his years.

Kelsi narrows her eyes, concentrating. "Wait a minute . . . are you Finn?"

His eyes widen. "How did you know that?"

She beams. "They told me about you." Then she turns to me as she writes on her notepad. "We'll get those—no problem at all."

"Thank you," I say, letting out a breath.

She takes my order and whisks away, and at last I face Finn. "So." I plaster a big smile on my face. "I have some exciting news. How would you like to take a vacation?"

His eyes light up. "Where?"

"A really nice big house out in the country. Remember Mr. Gordon's lodge, with a big yard and a tire swing and stuff? He asked us to stay there."

He nods, mirroring my excitement, though his smile quickly fades. "But, Mom?"

A twinge of anxiety as I remember his earlier line of questioning. "Yeah, buddy?"

"Does he have a TV there?"

I laugh, relieved. "Yes, Finn. He definitely has a TV."

14

Now that Finn is excited about the lodge, of course it's all he wants to talk about—and let me tell you, when seven-year-olds want to talk about something, they are relentless. He chats endlessly for the next few days, asking me all kinds of questions about Papa Lowell's lodge. *How many TVs does it have, really? Will I have my own room? Do I have to bring my own toys?*

I'm corralling him into bed one evening when he says, "Can we just call and ask him, Mom? *Please?*"

"It's late, honey." But genius strikes and I pull out my phone. "Let's write all these questions down, and we'll ask him tomorrow."

Satisfied at last, Finn recites the questions again as I type them on my phone. Then we say prayers and I kiss him good night and walk to the living room, where I stare through the blinds of the front window into the darkness. As much as Finn's excitement fuels my own, a small part of me is still nervous to take this leap. My job at the newspaper isn't anything special, but it's mine, and I've been doing it for seven years. It's comfortable. Safe.

Lowell said he didn't know for sure what the new owners at the newspaper would do—maybe staying right where I am is the best choice right now.

The thought rolls around in my brain during a fitful night's sleep, and it's there when I wake the next morning. It's now Saturday, which means I only have to make a quick stop at the newsroom. After promising Finn we'll make allergy-friendly muffins when we get home—and, of course, call Lowell to ask him pressing questions about the lodge—we set out for the *Prairie Daily News.*

Only one set of fluorescent lights is flipped on in the newsroom, and it's illuminating the news editor's desk. Kallie Horn holds up her coffee mug in a one-handed salute, and I wave back as Finn runs ahead. He knows the drill—he can play with the bobblehead sports figures on Frank's desk as long as he is *very* careful and puts them back where he found them afterward.

Then I sit at my desk and weed through the email in-box.

"What are you doing here this early on a Saturday, Jenkins?" Kallie calls across the newsroom.

"I could ask you the same thing. Weren't you here until press run last night?"

She laughs. "I'm just using the printer. Had some time to kill during my daughter's soccer practice."

Kallie stands, stretches, and walks over to my desk. The fifteen-year veteran news editor is the closest thing I have to a work friend, and the only person in the newsroom besides Lowell whose opinion I actually care about. Right now she's giving me a look she usually reserves for young reporters who have no respect for AP-style usage, and it makes me a little nervous. "So *why* are you here on your day off?" she asks.

"The Saturday reporter is supposed to check the main in-box when they come in, but they never seem to," I say, trying to keep the defensive edge out of my voice. "So here I am."

"Have you mentioned it to Lowell?"

Honestly, that's the last thing I want to do. I feel enough animosity from Brayden already without being labeled a tattletale—it's amazing how similar workplaces are to middle school when it comes to drama and grudges.

There's also the fact that I'm no longer capable of letting something go once I know it's wrong. I don't know if I can explain that, or if I want to.

I force a smile. "It's just easier to do it myself, I guess."

Kallie smirks. "I hear you. But be careful about donating your time. I've heard . . . Well, I've heard things." Our eyes lock, and I know she's talking about the sale. Of course there are already rumors—this is a newsroom; it's what we do. Kallie sighs. "Remember this is just a job. You need to do what's best for yourself and your family."

Before I can respond, the door whooshes open across the newsroom. We both look up as Natalie walks toward us, eyebrows raised. "What? I'm not late."

Kallie puts her hands up in defense. "You're fine. I actually need to go, so I'll see you all later." She winks at me and then turns for the door.

Finn looks up from his pile of bobbleheads. "Mom, can we go, too? I'm bored."

"Put those all back first," I say warningly.

When I turn back to Natalie, she sets her purse down on my desk and crosses her arms. "I need to check the main email account," she says, looking annoyed.

"Oh." I stand up quickly. "Sorry."

She slides into the seat, and I stand, awkward, unsure. Finally, Natalie sighs. "You can go now. I got this."

"Right." I grab my purse and motion for Finn to follow me to the door. When we pass Kallie's desk, her words come back to me. *You need to do what's best for yourself and your family.*

In one bold, decisive move, I whip out my phone and text Lowell: What day should Finn and I head out to the lodge?

CHAPTER FOUR

Friday is the big day, and by that morning we're all packed up and ready—I've watered my plants, turned down the thermostat, and sent out a newsroom-wide email at work letting everyone know I'll be gone. There's a certain satisfaction in getting your own auto-reply reminding yourself it's time to leave the office. And leave I do, striding out and picking up a giddy Finn from day care.

Now, the filmy hue of twilight dances across the prairie as we make our way out of town, the highway flanked by fields of corn and soybeans freshly sprouted in neat green rows, scant trees and farmhouses dotting the hazy horizon. Rounding a corner, I spot the skeletal brown remains of an early nineteenth-century home, its sad, sagging form a reminder of time gone by.

Up ahead, an agricultural sprayer ambles along the highway, and I brake gently, easing around the massive piece of farm equipment. As we pass, the farmer waves from his perch high up inside the machine atop enormous wheels, and I return the friendly midwestern gesture automatically. Traffic is otherwise sparse this evening, though we also meet a semitruck carrying a wind-turbine blade from the nearby plant—the long white monstrosity filling the length of the trailer.

There are places in South Dakota where you can drive for miles upon miles seeing nothing but flat prairie—no houses, no signs of civilization, almost like you're driving off the end of the earth into nothingness. There are patches of prairie grasses, too, untouched by humankind all these years. It was all disconcerting when I first moved here from tree-filled Minnesota. But I soon discovered there's a beauty in the openness, nothing lurking that you can't see, the vast sky bursting with color and with freedom. It made me feel grateful and safe.

That's how I feel tonight. It's a ten-minute drive down the highway to our destination, and Finn passes the time with near-constant chatter about what he's going to do first once we arrive. I listen in silence, interjecting the obligatory parental exclamations when required, and then at last we turn down the gravel county road that will lead us to the farmhouse.

Scatterings of tree groves crop up here and there, but otherwise we're surrounded by nothing but golden fields, and we're chasing the dwindling sunlight as we carve our dirt path down the roadway. At last, a pop of trees opens up, and we see it—Windy Acres. Unexpected warmth and excitement surge through me, and Finn cheers in delight as we pull into the driveway and stop in front of the massive white farmhouse-style lodge. For a moment we sit and stare.

"Is it really a hundred years old?" Finn whispers.

"A hundred and twelve, actually." His eyes widen and I smile. "They remodeled quite a bit of it, though. It's like new on the inside."

"And you said they *do* have a TV, right?"

I laugh. "*Yes*, I think there are several TVs, buddy."

He whoops in excitement again and scrambles out of the car. I step out as well, still smiling. "Don't go too far!" I call after him as he races across the wide green lawn toward the tire swing. I inhale a deep breath, the air crisp and fresh as it fills my lungs; then I open the trunk and pull out our bags. For a moment I think about making Finn help, but he's swinging away, and I'm oddly okay with it. I don't feel the need to hover over him out here like I do in town.

Rolling my large suitcase behind me, I climb the porch steps, my eyes landing on the quaint porch swing. I smile. I'd forgotten they had this. I hurry to unlock the door and roll the suitcase into the entryway, then force myself to make the two more trips required to get everything into the house. Then at last, I ease down onto the padded seat of the smooth wooden swing, let it glide gently beneath me, each muted creak a beautiful melody carrying away my remaining traces of fear and doubt.

From this cozy perch I have a perfect view of Finn, who has apparently discovered a brand-new attraction in Lowell's yard—a trampoline, complete with safety netting. He races toward it, and I let my eyes shift to the side of the house, smiling in delight when I spot a burst of fuchsia—the peony bush is positively thriving. I make a mental note to take a closer inspection of the flower garden in the morning.

Still smiling, I turn my gaze to the field beyond the house and the cluster of trees, dark and mysterious, that border the field's edge, a symphony of frogs serenading as dusk deepens around us. The wind has picked up—as it tends to do in South Dakota—and it blows across the prairie, grass dancing and waving to its airy rhythm. The vast sky has exploded into a purply-pink display, and I lean back, wondering if this is what contentment feels like. I'm not sure I've ever truly felt it, not in these eight years in hiding, and certainly not before then.

But maybe contentment, even peace, is something we can find here. Maybe Lowell is right—this might be the change I need.

Maybe this, at last, could be a home for us.

Home. I close my eyes. The prairie wind seems to carry my grandmother's laughter, the smell of the chocolate chip cookies she used to bake every Saturday, the pleasure and pain of long-ago memories, gone but never forgotten.

I stay this way, lost somewhere between this moment and my past as Finn jumps and giggles on the trampoline, until my peace is broken by the hum of an approaching vehicle in the distance. I brace myself as it nears, but my inner alarm remains dormant as the vehicle rumbles past without slowing.

But then I hear it stop abruptly, gravel and rock spitting up against steel.

My eyes fly open and land on the cloud of dust out on the county road. It's a truck, dark colored, I can make that much out, and it looks like it barely passed the driveway before lurching to a stop. Now it's backing up, and suddenly any sense of peace I had is gone.

I clutch the edge of the swing, heart thumping, and push myself to my feet. "Finn!" I cry, but he keeps jumping.

The truck is coming into the driveway now, a little too fast, and I race down the steps and across the grass toward Finn. *It can't be him it can't be him.* The words race through my mind but do little to calm me because bad things happen—bad things *have* happened—and I can't let my guard down. When I reach Finn, I hear the truck door slam shut behind me. I whirl around, blocking the entrance to the trampoline. "Who's that, Mom?" asks Finn, still jumping.

I have no idea, but a man stalks toward us, and I clutch my phone in my pocket, the only defense I have. "Stop right there!" I call out as he nears us, willing my voice not to shake. "What do you want?"

The man stops several feet away, hands on his hips. It's getting dark, and even though the porch light is on, I can't make out much except that he's tall and menacing. "I want to know who you are and what the hell you're doing here."

I bristle at his rough words, but he's not coming any closer. So I steel myself, straighten my shoulders. "I think I should be asking who *you* are, rushing in here and scaring us like this."

"I'm not scared," Finn calls from behind me.

I shoot him a look, though it's too dark for him to notice, so I turn back to our visitor. "I think you should leave."

"Lady, I'm the caretaker of this property, and I think *you* should leave."

Before I can respond, a buzzing fills the air, followed by a faint glow as the man apparently lifts his phone to his face to answer.

"Yes, Lowell. I'm actually here right now, and I—" He pauses, and I wish I could make out his face. Several seconds go by before he speaks again. "I see. No, no, it's no problem." His voice is quieter—dare I say, defeated. "Right. Yes, of course. I'll help in any way I can."

He ends the call, and for a moment we stand in silence, the sound of Finn bouncing and giggling behind me blending with the frogs in the distance. I wait, arms still crossed, trying to stop the small smile from tugging at my lips—though not trying all that hard, honestly.

Finally, the man sighs. "That was Lowell."

"And how *is* Lowell?" I ask smugly.

"Look, I'm sorry, I had no idea you were coming. Usually he tells me these things."

I nod, happy for the small victory yet suddenly tired, all the adrenaline and energy sapping out of me. I turn to my leaping son. "Come on, Finn." He doesn't answer at first, so I pull out my ace in the hole. "Let's go see how many TVs Mr. Gordon has. I'll make some popcorn."

"Woo-hoo!" he calls as he bounces onto his bottom and scoots toward the edge of the trampoline. I help him wriggle through the net and down to the ground, where he slips into his shoes. We turn, hand in hand, and the man is standing awkwardly behind us. "I should get him inside," I say quietly.

"Right." He steps back, out of the way. "I'm, uh, I'm Sawyer, by the way. Sawyer Jones. Like I said, I'm the caretaker here, and I live next door."

I nod again. "Iris."

"I'm Finn," Finn chirps. "It's short for Finnegan."

The man—Sawyer—chuckles softly. "Nice to meet you, Finnegan."

"You can call me Finn."

"Well, okay, then." He turns to me and his smile fades, though it's too dark to see whether he's embarrassed or annoyed. "Sorry again if I scared you."

"My mom is scared of a lot of things," Finn says, and I shush him, though not before catching the twitch of amusement on Sawyer's face.

Dammit. I'm humiliated and I want to clap back somehow, yet I'm too tired to do anything but sigh. "Inside, you," I say to Finn, and we set off toward the house as Sawyer walks silently to his pickup.

We're up on the porch when the truck rumbles to life, and I allow myself to peek back over my shoulder from the doorway, watching him drive away. Then I click the door shut, lock it tight, hoping that's the last I'll see of Sawyer Jones.

CHAPTER FIVE

One Pixar movie and three bowls of popcorn later, my boy is fast asleep in the bedroom he picked upstairs—right down the hall from the master suite, where I'll be sleeping. Now I'm free to explore the house. The stairs creak under the weight of my footsteps as I descend into the living room. I'm a little creeped out, so the first thing I do is double-check the dead bolt on the front door.

In the kitchen, the luscious scent of popcorn still hangs in the air. I walk across the white-tiled floor and into the mudroom to make sure the back door, too, is locked, and I feel a little safer. On my way back through the kitchen, a glowing orb catches my eye through the window—an outside light illuminating the detached garage. Damn. I should've shut that off, but there's no way I'm going out to do it now.

I squint, my eyes making out a smaller gravel path winding around the side of the garage and what might be another building beyond it, though it looks like nothing more than a black mass in the darkness right now. Hmm—something else to check out tomorrow. I wrap my cardigan tighter around myself and continue my tour into the living room, my cozy gray slippers scraping against the hardwood floor. I remember when the Gordons remodeled this room into its current outdoorsy state—wooden beams crisscrossing the vaulted ceiling, knotted wood paneling and faux fireplace. Ivan felt it was a little clichéd, yet it's homey—and the exact look people expect when hunting in the Dakotas.

My gaze falls down the dark hallway leading to the guest rooms, and that homey feeling fades. Ivan had ambitious plans to keep remodeling these guest rooms, each with its own theme—nautical, western, and tropical—but then he got sick. Lowell hasn't touched the rooms since. A pit of grief wedges inside me, but I make myself walk down the hall, where three large rooms sit behind closed doors.

When I open the first, I'm greeted with the thick, hot smell of sealed-off must. I flick on the light and take in a mishmash of decades—orange shag carpeting, a peeling wallpaper border, and a tall glass-encased corner cabinet displaying various porcelain knickknacks, including a pale baby doll whose white-frilled dress and bonnet do a poor job of hiding a battered body and matted blonde hair. I shudder—the Gordons went through a vintage-toy phase as part of their antiquing days a few years ago, and I find myself wondering what other creepy treasures await. As I close the door, I vow never to open that cabinet—and to possibly have this room saged.

Fortunately, the next two rooms are more neutral. The first has two sets of bunk beds with childlike bedding—though, thankfully, no more creepy toys. The final room has a soft blue-and-pink-checkered quilt covering a double bed and a simple wooden dresser against a beige wall. It actually looks like it's been used more recently. I narrow my eyes at the dresser, then walk across to view the small framed picture on top. It's a picture of the Gordons.

I frown in confusion. *Lowell was sleeping in here?* The master suite upstairs is the nicest room in the house, which is why he encouraged me to stay there. It hits me then—he probably hasn't slept up there since Ivan died.

I pull the door gently closed and lean against it, suddenly exhausted by this day filled with newness and excitement mixed with familiar grief. I trudge back the way I came and up the stairs, check on Finn, then head straight for the master suite. Bleary eyed, I slide into the massive king-size bed, rubbing my eyes and smiling at the touches of Ivan's decor. Sky-blue walls with artsy black-and-white photos of dilapidated old farmhouses dotting the prairie landscape. A big wooden dresser painted white, with a large mirror on the wall behind it and a white-cushioned bench in front of it.

I smile, grief seeping away and hope filling back in, feeling tired but content.

Maybe I am exactly where I belong. Maybe this adventure will work out.

I click on *Cabiria*—cued up and ready in the DVD player—and fall asleep to her adventures as I dream of my own.

I wake the next morning to small hands cupping my face and a little-boy stage whisper: "Mom, get up, they want breakfast!"

"What?" I mutter, rolling over deeper into this luxuriously thick comforter. After staying in the master suite this week, it's going to be difficult to go back to my own barely adequate bedding. "Who wants breakfast?"

"Both of them!" Finn says.

I grumble. "Both of *who*?"

"The hunters."

"What hunters?"

"The ones downstairs."

My eyes fly open, and I bolt up to a sitting position. "What?" It's all I can say, my sleep-fogged brain trying to catch up to this news. We were alone last night—the house was empty, and I walked through all the guest rooms. Didn't I? "Where did they come from?"

"They stayed in the outhouse last night."

I stare in horror, certain I'm caught in some ludicrous stress dream. "The *outhouse*?" Then it hits me—the *outer* house. It's what Lowell

calls the barn he converted into secondary lodging. I'd completely forgotten about it, but surely it was the building I saw behind the garage
last night. I thought he only rented it out during pheasant season in
the fall, when the lodge was all booked up. Now the thought of some
strangers coming into the house this morning while I slept—talking to
my unaccompanied seven-year-old—makes me shudder.

I jump up, shove on my slippers, and scramble to pull on my bath-
robe, smoothing and twisting my bedhead of hair into a bun and hoping to God I look presentable as I follow my Batman-pajama-clad son
down the stairs. As he skips blissfully into the living room, I tread slowly
into the dining room.

There, the feeling of being in an awkward nightmare returns as two
camouflage-clad men turn from their spots at the table and grin in amusement at me. My face flushes instantly, and I clutch my robe tighter. "Um,
good morning," I say. "Can I ask . . . uh, could you please tell me—"

The older man, bearded and jolly, chuckles. "I'm guessing Lowell
didn't tell you we were staying an extra night, or that we usually just
let ourselves in?"

He holds up a shiny silver key and I smile thinly. "No, he didn't,"
I say. "I didn't realize he gives guests house keys."

"I don't think he usually does," the man says quickly, "but Lowell
and I go way back. I'm Kirk Blackwell. I come every year from
Colorado."

The name rings a bell somewhere in my memory—an old college
friend of Lowell's, I think—and I feel slightly more at ease. "Nice to
meet you. I'm Iris. I understand you gentlemen would like breakfast?"

"Yes, ma'am. If it's not too much trouble. Then we'll be out of your
hair. Heading home today."

I nod and glance around the table, where their coffee mugs sit,
empty and expectant. "Uh, I can put some coffee on first, if you'd like?
I know I could use some." God, that was an understatement.

"That would be great," Kirk says.

"Be sure to put extra sugar in mine, sweetheart." I finally look at the other man, a little younger than his counterpart and significantly smarmier, with hawkish eyes and close-cropped salt-and-pepper hair buzzed in an apparent attempt to hide a receding hairline. He winks, and I swallow back the irritation at both the gesture and being called *sweetheart* by a stranger when I'm in my midthirties.

"Got it," I say with a tight smile.

Kirk chuckles awkwardly. "This is my business associate, Dave Donnelly. It's his first time visiting South Dakota."

"Welcome," I say, forcing a smile.

Dave smiles back, his eye contact unwavering. "Thank you, Iris. Kirk has been showing me all the sights, trying to entice me to move some of my business enterprises into this area. I have to say, some of the establishments we visited last night were very promising indeed."

A shiver ripples through me. There is something positively unnerving about this man—like behind his soft words and pleasant smile lies something else entirely.

Kirk breaks the silence with a nervous chuckle, his face a deep crimson. "Well, now"—he clears his throat, turning to me—"about that coffee?"

"Right," I say, then escape into the adjoining kitchen and make an immediate beeline for the coffeepot. If I don't get some caffeine pumping through these veins soon, there is no way I'm going to be able to speak to them again, let alone serve breakfast, without risking stabbing someone, literally or figuratively—take your pick at this point.

My fingers drum on the granite countertop as I listen to the pleasing sound of percolating coffee, willing the scent to calm my nerves.

I can't cook. There, I said it.

I mean, I can put meals together. I can feed myself and my son. But bed-and-breakfast-level cooking—no way. What does one even serve guests at a bed-and-breakfast? I can feel panic rising in my chest, but suddenly there's a knock at the door. I jump—the sound is closer than

I expected. I walk across the tiles of the kitchen floor and into the mud-room, which leads to the back door that I locked last night.

I blink through the window—the man standing on the other side looks vaguely familiar, but it takes a moment to recognize him because it was dark last night.

I swear under my breath. *Are you kidding me?*

I whip open the door, fire in my eyes. "Back already to yell at me?"

To his credit, Sawyer Jones winces. "I guess I deserved that."

We stand in awkward silence, and my irritation grows. "Can I help you with something? I'm a little busy here."

"Uh, well, can I come in?"

I sigh but step aside. To my utter shock and annoyance, he shrugs out of his coat, slips out of his shoes, and strolls into the kitchen like he owns the place. I'm positively shaking with rage as I follow him in. "Well, *make* yourself at home," I say with all the sarcasm I can muster.

He snorts. "Do you want me to make breakfast or not?"

I blink. "You're . . . you're here to make breakfast?"

He shakes his head in exasperation. "It's part of what I do around here. Believe it or not, my job is not to irritate you."

"Oh. Well. I mean, sure, if you want to." Then I give up, sinking onto a stool and lowering my head onto my hands. "Actually, that would be really wonderful."

There's a pause and I shut my eyes, waiting for the biting reply. I hear him shuffling around, and soon there's a gentle thud as he sets down a cup in front of me. I look up at the full coffee mug in all its beautiful, steaming perfection, and take a greedy sip. "Thank you," I say softly.

His back is turned to me as he reaches into a cupboard for a pan, and as he works, I'm safe to study him more closely here in the light of day. Wavy brown hair that should probably be cut, stubble with flecks of gray, muscled forearms reaching into the fridge, pulling out eggs. His hand hovers over the soy milk I brought, and he glances over at me with an expression I can't read. I quickly drop my eyes.

"So, Lowell didn't tell *me* about *you*. He also didn't tell *you* about *me*, or about the fact that you have guests." Sawyer shakes his head. "I'm a little worried about the old guy."

"He's just a little forgetful, is all," I say quickly.

"Hmm."

I clear my throat. "So, you cook for him?"

He shrugs. "It's kind of my thing."

I'm about to ask what he means when Finn bounds into the room, announcing, "I'm hungry." He looks at Sawyer. "Oh, it's you. What's for breakfast?"

"Finn," I say, "be respectful."

"It's fine," Sawyer says. "How about eggs?"

Finn's face lights up. "Can we have scrambled eggs? My mom never makes them because they're too hard."

I cringe—apparently my son is determined to list all my winning qualities in front of this stranger. Sawyer's mouth twitches as he glances at me again. "It's all about the timing."

Isn't that the truth, I think as I watch him. When he heads for the fridge again, I say, "Oh, use the soy milk. I mean, please."

Sawyer looks at me with that same unreadable expression, then turns back to Finn. "Do you ever eat at the diner in town?"

"Uh, *yeah,*" Finn says as if it's the most obvious thing in the world, and Sawyer chuckles. "We were there last Friday night, weren't we, Mom?"

I nod, but I'm still looking at Sawyer, whose eyes are twinkling as he looks from me to Finn. "Well, so was I. I work there."

I suck in a breath. "You cook there," I whisper.

He meets my eyes again and smiles, nodding, but I can't say anything. I only stare at him.

Suddenly the door to the dining room opens again, and a head pops in—Dave Donnelly. "Say, darlin', could we get that coffee?" He winks again, and I suppress another shudder. "Don't forget the sugar, now."

He walks out again, and Sawyer frowns at the doorway. "Mr. Blackwell usually brings his grandkids." He turns back to me. "I'm not sure what I think of that guy."

"You and me both," I say, standing. "At least they're leaving today."

I walk over to the coffeepot, but Sawyer beats me to it. "I can do it," he says.

"Okay. Thank you." Our eyes meet, and I will myself not to blush.

"*Then* you'll make me breakfast?" Finn asks.

"I will," Sawyer assures him. "I promise."

He walks out of the kitchen, and I watch him go. When he returns, I can't tear my eyes away as he makes my son breakfast—in a different, uncontaminated pan, with only safe ingredients, as he apparently does every time we visit the diner.

Before I can feel too much about this, I pour another cup of coffee, take a big slug, and stand. "Okay, Finn, after breakfast we both need to get dressed." He whines, and I add, "Hey, remember we need to explore the rest of the property today? We promised Mr. Gordon we'd take care of it." Sawyer clears his throat, and I turn to see him twirling the spatula in his hand. "Oh, I'll clean this up first—I didn't mean we'd leave you with a mess or anything."

He sets down the spatula, shaking his head. "No, I was thinking . . . I don't have to go into the diner today." Is it my imagination, or is his face a little red? "I could show you two around, if you want. We could talk about how things work around here, some of the events coming up. Maybe even take a four-wheeler ride."

He looks over at Finn, whose eyes widen in excitement, but I shake my head. "Absolutely not." Sawyer winces, but I hold up my hand. "I mean about the four-wheeler ride. But it would be great if you could show us around."

"Okay," he says, breaking into a wide smile.

It's such a nice smile, dammit, but I take a giant slug of coffee, pretending not to notice.

CHAPTER SIX

A half hour later, I'm dressed and ready to face the day. Out the living room window, I can see Sawyer helping Kirk and Dave with their bags, so I join them in the driveway, feeling obligated to offer a polite goodbye.

"We'll see you next spring for goose hunting," Kirk says jovially.

"Sounds great, sir," Sawyer replies, shaking the old man's hand.

Dave turns to me with the same creepy, over-the-top eye contact as before. "I have a feeling I'll be back sooner than that. I think South Dakota will be perfect for my business venture."

"And what business is that?" I ask.

"It's sort of a hybrid model, you could say—hospitality and enter- tainment." He smiles broadly, and for some reason it almost makes me feel sick to my stomach.

"Well"—Sawyer claps his hands, stepping next to me—"if you need a reservation, let us know." He reaches for the car door, pulling it open with a smile. "Have a nice flight."

Dave nods briskly, then eases into the passenger seat as Kirk starts the vehicle. Soon, they're driving away, and I let out a breath. "Are guests always that . . ."

"Weird? No." Sawyer shakes his head. "I have no idea what's up with that guy. And I *really* don't want to know what kind of business he's running."

He turns to me with a smile. I smile back at him, and there's a flutter within me threatening to throw me off guard, so I quickly say, "I'd better check on Finn." Then I jog up the porch steps and into the house, where I find my son sitting on the soft carpeted living room floor, a cardboard box turned over in front of him. "What are you doing?" I ask.

He turns with a grin, two action figures in his hands. "I found some old toys!"

For a moment I freeze, remembering the creepy toys from last night. But as I walk over for a closer look, I see these aren't as ancient as the disheveled doll. Finn is holding an old He-Man and Skeletor. The rest of the box's contents—including an old Rainbow Brite doll, a stuffed Care Bear, and other toys that come from my own childhood era—are spilled out onto the floor. "Where did you find those?" I ask.

"In the closet," he says without looking up.

I'm about to scold him for snooping when I hear Sawyer from the doorway. "Lowell wanted to have toys for families who stay here, but clearly he hasn't updated them in a while."

I smile back. "I think there's a lot he hasn't updated in a while—besides here in the living room, I mean," I say, surveying the open space, sunlight flooding through the large windows.

Sawyer smiles. "I take it you've had a look around the house, then?"

"Just a quick sweep."

"Okay, well, how about we head outside?"

I nod. "Ready, Finn?"

"Can I bring these guys?" He holds up He-Man and Skeletor.

"Sure," I say. "But when we come back in, you're picking all this up, okay?"

"Okay, Mom." But he's already skipping ahead.

Sawyer chuckles and I shake my head. "It's like I can see the thought already leaving his mind."

"Well, it doesn't get any better when they get older." I look at him quizzically, and he smiles. "My daughter's at home, still asleep. Teenagers."

I smile as we walk out the door. Outside the wind is blowing, but it's a beautiful day. I scan the yard for Finn and see he's back out on the trampoline. Then my eyes are drawn to the flower garden. I turn to Sawyer with a hopeful smile. "Can we start there?"

"Sure," he says.

I walk among the billowing hostas that blanket the rocky landscaped path. I soak in the bright-yellow daylilies framing the edge of the house, the stately weigela bush that will soon pop with delicate red blooms. My eyes land on the bursting fuchsia magnificence of the peony bush—Ivan's pride and joy.

It's like he's still here, with us.

They were his precious gems, and being here in his flower garden makes me ache with bittersweet memories. Ivan is the reason I can grow any flowers, the reason *I* grew at all. The first day I worked with him in this very garden, the scars of my old life were still visible, outside as well as in. When he and Lowell rented the house in town to Finn and me, their housewarming gift was the rosebush that now thrives there. Ivan helped me plant it, even though I was scared I'd fail. *You have to take the first step, Iris. You have to move forward, take care of it the best you can, and trust that it's enough.*

"Are you okay?" Sawyer asks softly.

I wipe at my eyes, embarrassed. "I'm sorry, I just miss him."

"Ivan? You two were pretty close, huh?"

I nod. The truth is, he saved my life, like the father I never had. I take a deep breath. "He taught me about flowers." I smile. "Well, he tried to. I picked up what I could. I helped him plant a lot of these."

"Do you have a favorite?" Sawyer asks. Then he smiles. "Wait—irises, right?"

I laugh, shaking my head. "Actually, we never planted any. He said, 'You don't need to share your name with anything. You're one of a kind, Iris—remember that.'"

I glance at Sawyer, embarrassed, but he's still smiling. "He sounds like a smart guy," he says softly.

"He was. I could barely keep a plant alive before I met him. I'm still not that great at it, but . . . he gave me the confidence to try, if that makes sense."

Sawyer nods. "My mom was like that. With cooking, I mean. She used to let me make whatever concoction I could think up, and then she'd even pretend to like it."

I smile. "I bet she's really proud now that you're a cook."

He looks off into the distance. "She passed away." I open my mouth to say I'm sorry, but he holds up his hand. "It was a long time ago. She was one of a kind, too. Tough but soft, and always there for me when I needed her." He turns to me with a sad smile. "I would like to think she would be proud, though, so thank you."

The breeze picks up, carrying the intoxicating scent of the flowers, and I close my eyes, let my sadness turn to gratitude. Ivan was the kindest man I've ever known—you could tell it about him, the way you can tell that sort of thing about some people. Like they radiate warmth and safety.

My eyes fly open, and I glance at Sawyer again and understand my feelings toward him. But I shove it down, look away, because that ship has sailed—it sank, actually, into the depths of the sea, and I will never again step foot in the water.

"Mom!" Finn calls from the trampoline. "Watch me!"

It's the distraction I need as Finn shows us some sort of ninja jump kick. "Wow, buddy," I say in that practiced way mothers do when they pretend their child's feat is more impressive than it actually is.

Finn keeps jumping, and I turn back to the flowers, hands itching to dig in the dirt, but Sawyer shifts his weight. "So," he says, "you ready to start chores?"

One more longing look at the flowers, then I nod. "Okay, sure. Let's do it."

He claps his hands together. "First, of course, we need to clean up after the guests who just left."

My nose wrinkles automatically, and he chuckles, motioning me forward. We walk toward the *outhouse*, as Finn so charmingly called it. As we round the garage, I glance back and realize my view of Finn on the trampoline will be obscured, especially once we're in the building cleaning.

Sawyer looks back, too, and seems to understand. "Do you want to call him over?"

Finn giggles loudly, and the sound carries easily to us.

"I should be able to hear him. Maybe we can keep a window open?"

He nods and we walk into the house. The door whooshes open, and I don't brace myself in time—the warm musty smell, damp garbage, and tang of empty beer cans. *Run,* my insides command, as memories flood back.

Rural Minnesota
Eight years ago

We step into darkness, a funky damp stench I can't place flooding my nostrils as the door creaks open, and I cover my nose and mouth instinctively.

"What do you think?" Mitch asks, clearly excited. He's in his happy state, frantic and loud, where it's kind of contagious and kind of scary, a spark that might blow up without warning.

I squint in the dark, and it makes my eye hurt, a reminder from the last time I disagreed with him. He loves me, and he swore it won't happen again—I believe him, but still, I keep the nagging ache inside me, the one that feels dangerously close to regret, to myself. "I can't really see anything," I say carefully instead.

Mitch bounds across the living room—it takes him two steps in this cramped trailer house—and pulls back a curtain to let in sunlight. Somehow, it makes things worse. Peeling olive-green wallpaper. Faded brown carpeting—at least I think it's supposed to be brown. An ancient couch with cigarette burns. Eventually, I stop looking around and focus on Mitch, forcing a smile. "I love it," I say.

His face falls. "You hate it."

"No, baby." I reach for his hand—I hate when he's upset with me. "Let's look at the rest of it."

His smile is back as he takes my hand, leading me down the narrow hallway. "You and I get the biggest bedroom, of course—nothing but the best for my girl."

He leans in for a deep kiss, and for a moment it's almost like our early days of dating, those fleeting weeks when he was almost always nice to me, not only sometimes. Those are the times I'm desperate to believe we can still get back to, somehow.

See, Grandma? I'll be okay.

I want to tell her, even though she never got to meet Mitch. When she found out she was sick, she was so scared of leaving me alone. I just wanted her to get better. But the cancer took her so fast, and I could barely get enough hours at the diner to keep our apartment. I had to sell most of Grandma's stuff and mine to have any money at all. And I was not going to take any of the donations from people at church, or from my old school—those people always treated Grandma and me like we were invisible, forgettable.

But not Mitch. He told me I was pretty the first time he came into the diner. Sure, he said so just as he was being thrown out by the cook for being too drunk and rowdy, but he remembered me the next time he was allowed to come back, and he even asked me out. No one had ever asked me on a date before.

To Mitch, I was never invisible. Now we're in love, and we're starting our lives together. I won't be alone anymore.

Mitch kisses me again and then pulls me down the hallway. "There's the bathroom, of course." He stops by one door but then keeps going without saying anything.

"What's that one?" I ask.

"And the kitchen is back that way."

"Mitch," I say, pointing to the door he skipped, "what's that room?"

He turns to me, his face impassive. "That's Rex's room."

I freeze. "What?"

"You heard me," he says coldly.

"Mitch, we never talked about him living here with us."

"He's my best friend, and we're in business together. What the hell do you expect?"

I squeeze my eyes shut, picturing creepy Rex down the hall, day in and day out. "I thought you were going to get away from all that," I say softly. "The . . . drugs and stuff."

"Shit, Iris, I said I'd think about it—isn't that enough? How else are we supposed to get money, huh?"

"But we paid for this with my grandma's money—I sold almost all her stuff to get that." The words come out before I can stop them. His eyes go wild, and for a moment I think he's going to lunge at me. Instead, he screams at the top of his lungs and punches the wall repeatedly with his fist.

When he finally stops, we stand in silence. Mitch pants in exertion as tears stream down my face. "God, you make me so fucking crazy sometimes," he says. "Why do you do that?"

"I'm sorry," I say softly.

"The money is gone, okay? Is that what you want to hear? We're gonna need to make more if we want water and electricity in this place. Rex said we should sell everything that's worth anything so we can buy more product and make more money. He's living with us, and I don't want to hear another goddamned word about it."

He stalks away before I can say anything else. Not that I would have. I've learned enough lessons for today. I hang back, giving him time to calm down because then he'll say sorry and everything will be okay again.

It also gives me time to quietly take off the diamond necklace my grandma left me—the one thing I couldn't bear to sell—and slip it safely into my purse, out of sight.

CHAPTER SEVEN

I pull myself back to the present, place a steadying hand on the wall for support. I'm here. I'm not back there. I will never again be back there.

Behind me, Sawyer clears his throat. "You okay?" he asks softly.

I nod quickly without making eye contact. He shuffles past me, crossing to the living room to push open the window. "Sorry, I should've warned you about the smell—these guys tend to leave quite a mess." He turns to face me. "Okay if I take the bathroom, and you start in the kitchen?"

"Sure," I say, my tone light as I force back a wave of nausea while walking toward the large, boxy refrigerator. Damn the fact that one memory leads to another, sending me spiraling into self-doubt. I fight to shove it all down, but these memories are stubborn, taunting. *She's worthless.* "I can do it." I say it quietly, as if to myself or the person in my past who first said that to me.

But it's Sawyer who answers: "Okay. Let me know if you need help." He retreats to the bathroom as I face the kitchen, willing myself to handle any disgusting mess that awaits me.

I can do this.

I repeat the phrase to myself until I believe it.

The laughter of my son through the window is the only joy carrying me through the gross parts, like the crusted brownish-red spill I can't identify on the bottom tray of the fridge. I scrub the entire kitchen until it shines, all bright white and gleaming, and I'm filled with a deep satisfaction.

I use my arm to swipe at my sweaty forehead; then, after locating the broom and dustpan, I make quick work of sweeping the checkered linoleum. I hum to myself as I hear the distant roar of the vacuum down the hall. I'm gliding the mop across the floor when Sawyer returns.

"Looks great in here," he says, smiling.

"Thank you." I smile back, taking one last swoosh with the mop. "So, we're done?"

"In here, yes. But I can show you some of the outside chores if you'd like."

What I'd *like* is to sit down in front of a fan with a glass of lemonade, but I'm determined to do this right. "Okay," I say, nodding.

Outside, we walk back toward the house, and I smile across the yard at Finn, still bouncing with all his might on the trampoline. Sawyer motions me to the side of the garage, where a large red riding lawnmower sits parked. "We don't need to mow today, but do you want to try it out to familiarize yourself with the lawn equipment?"

"Uh, I'm not sure I feel comfortable driving that," I say.

He shrugs. "You could always run the push mower. Have you done that before?"

"Of course I have," I say quickly. I mean, the truth is, it has been a very long time—Lowell pays a neighborhood teenager to mow my lawn in town.

"Okay, go for it." Am I imagining things, or is there a spark of challenge in his eyes?

I straighten my shoulders and stride toward it, placing both my hands hesitantly on the black handlebar. Ah—there's the second, movable bar. I grab that as well, keeping them pressed together because if I let it go, the mower will stop. That much I remember. Then I locate the pull cord, reach down, and pull it. The cord whips up easily, and yet nothing happens. Frustrated, I yank it again, harder. And again.

"Wait," Sawyer says, and I turn. "You have to push that little black button down there, five times. It primes it."

You could have said that. I bite back the reply and do what he says, only to pull the damn cord and once again get nothing. I turn to him, exasperated, and he quietly steps forward and places a hand on the handlebars. With his other, he gives one easy tug on the cord, and the engine roars to life. I stare at him in a mix of shock and irritation, and he offers an apologetic "It takes some getting used to." I frown and he quickly adds, "I can keep doing the mowing; it's no problem."

Stubbornness flares past my embarrassment, and I stalk toward the rider. "I'll try this one instead."

"You really don't have to," Sawyer says, but I ignore him. The grass is lusher near the garage, longer and thicker—and apparently, easy to hide in. Because as I step my foot onto the sideboard of the mower, there's a flash of movement in the blades below me. I see it and leap back, screaming.

There, slithering in the grass, is the largest snake I've ever seen in my life. At first I can't speak as I stumble backward, unable to tear my eyes away, but then for a split second I see its little tongue flicking about. "Rattlesnake!" I cry out. Those are only supposed to be west of the Missouri River, not here in eastern South Dakota. I whip my face to Sawyer, wide eyed. "It's a rattlesnake!"

He puts up a hand, shaking his head. "Not a rattlesnake," he says as he steps forward.

"How are you calm right now?" I shriek, but he's already reached for a large stick from the nearby firewood pile, then uses it to nudgingly fling the scaly beast on its way.

I watch in horror as it slithers away, and when I turn back to Sawyer, he's smiling. "It's a regular old garter snake," he says. "Just a little bigger than usual."

42

I continue to gape at him, my pulse slowly settling back to its normal rhythm, and it occurs to me that he is so at ease out here, capable and confident. Suddenly I realize how out of my league I am.

That old word comes back again, the one that followed me around most of my life. *Worthless.* My shoulders sag.

Sawyer eyes me, concern in his gaze. "Really freaked you out, huh?"

"No. I mean yes, it did. But . . ."

"But?"

I sigh. "But it's more that I don't know what in the world I'm doing here."

"It's your first day." He shrugs. "Don't be too hard on yourself."

"I'm not . . . I'm not sure I can do this." My voice cracks slightly, and I turn away, squint into the yard, willing the tears not to fall.

There's a pause, and then Sawyer sighs. "The first time I helped Lowell clean one of those cabins, we found some rotting fish in the garbage can. I threw up right on top of it."

I turn to him, grimacing. "Ugh, I'm sorry."

He nods. "Compared to that, you're doing great."

My mouth twitches into a smile. "Thanks. Sorry that I took my frustration out on you, by the way."

He scoffs. "I live with a teenager, remember? That was nothing."

We both chuckle, and when I meet his eyes fully, we linger a little too long and I have to turn away. Across the lawn, I see Finn skipping toward us. "I'm bored, Mom," he announces the minute he reaches us.

I sigh, but before I can say anything, Sawyer speaks brightly: "Hey, how about that four-wheeler ride?"

Finn flashes me his doe eyes. "Can we, Mom? *Please?*"

"I don't think it's a good idea, buddy."

Sawyer clears his throat. "I do have helmets, you know. And we'd go very slow."

Finn grins in excitement, and they both look at me expectantly. Dammit, I'm not used to having two of them to gang up on me. I sigh in resignation. "Fine. *Very slow*," I warn.

I feel like I'm having an out-of-body experience. My head is stuffed inside a helmet, and I'm sitting behind Sawyer on a four-wheeler, my tiny, fragile son in front of him. "Are you sure your helmet's all the way on, Finn?" I ask nervously.

"Yes, Mom," he says, annoyed.

Sawyer looks over his shoulder, grinning. "You ready?"

"No," I mutter. "Why aren't you wearing a helmet, by the way?"

"I only have two—it's usually just me and my daughter." He shrugs. "I'll be fine."

Men. The ATV roars to life, and I scream, which makes Finn burst out laughing.

"You okay back there?" Sawyer asks.

I huff. "I'm fine. Do you have ahold of him?" I can see for myself that he does, his strong arm wrapped protectively around Finn, but I'm very much trying to deflect attention away from my own irrational fear.

"I got him." He winks. "Better hold on."

No time for a snippy comeback—the four-wheeler lurches forward, and it's all I can do not to scream again. Instead, I cling to Sawyer, my arms wrapping tightly around him. It's an instinct, and when I come to my senses, I'm mortified yet still too scared to let go because—as I feared—our definitions of *very slow* are quite different.

My eyes are squeezed shut as I endure this windy, bumpy ride, but then Finn squeals, "Mom, look!"

I open my eyes, and we're rushing across the golden field. I see where Finn's pointing—a deer stands in the distance, near the tree grove lining the edge of the field. It bolts away as we near it, and when at last we reach the trees, the ATV slows to a stop. I quickly release my viselike grasp on Sawyer and slide down, helping Finn down as well. We both take off our helmets, and Finn cries, "That was so cool!"

I smile at Sawyer. "Thank you."

"Not so bad, right?" He disembarks and takes the helmets from us, then sets them onto the back of the ATV. "Finn, you want to see something really cool?"

This kicks Finn into overdrive, and he bounds ahead as we make our way into the trees. "Careful!" I call out to him, hurrying as my feet crunch over twigs and leaves.

Sawyer jogs to catch up to Finn, whose hand slides easily into Sawyer's. Sawyer looks down at him in surprise, then smiles as they walk forward.

My poor heart skips, but I squash it out, calling, "So *where* are we going?"

"There," Sawyer says, pointing ahead to a massive elm tree. Specifically, about five feet up, to a sprawling tree house. A wooden ladder leads to a miniature front deck with a small entry door.

Finn gasps. "Whoa."

"Is that roof *shingled*?" I ask.

Sawyer looks down, rubbing his neck. "It's nothing fancy, really."

"It's amazing," I say quietly.

He smiles, obviously pleased. "It's a few years old now. But it's safe, I promise."

I believe him. And when a wide-eyed Finn asks if he can play in it, I nod. He whoops as he rushes over and climbs up the ladder. I fight the urge to follow him, stand underneath as he crawls up, arms outstretched lest he fall, but I let out a relieved breath when he reaches the deck. Then I turn to Sawyer. "Thank you."

"I figure somebody might as well enjoy it. Natalie hasn't used it in quite a few years."

I blink. "Natalie?"

My brain has barely had a chance to connect the dots before I hear the crunch of footsteps behind us.

"Dad?"

I turn at the familiar voice and see the shock on the young newsroom intern's face when she spots me and says, "What are *you* doing here?"

CHAPTER EIGHT

Sawyer's eyes narrow in confusion. "You two know each other?"

My face flushes. I'm not sure I've ever seen a fellow staffer outside the office besides the Gordons—especially not after I've been out on a four-wheeler ride with said coworker's father. "I, uh, I work at the newspaper. I guess Lowell never told you?" Before he can respond, I turn to Natalie, smiling awkwardly. "Hi. It's good to see you."

She raises her eyebrows and doesn't respond, just turns back to Sawyer. "Ms. Simpson called for you. About their stupid party today or whatever."

Sawyer sighs, turning to me. "That was one of the events I was going to talk to you about—I don't suppose Lowell told you about it?" I shake my head in confusion. "He sometimes rents the place out for special events. This evening is the Literary Ladies' Luncheon."

"Luncheon?" I look down at my phone. "It's eleven thirty. What time will they be here?"

He holds up a hand. "They've turned it into an evening thing over the years, but Sherri wanted to keep the old name."

"Sherri?" I ask.

Sawyer looks embarrassed, and for some reason it bothers me. "Yeah, she's the one who organizes it every year. She calls a lot when it's getting close."

Natalie smirks. "I think she likes what's on the menu, Dad."

Now he's *definitely* embarrassed, shooting his daughter a look, and I feel a little bit like a fool. "Oh. Well, then, I guess we should probably get back."

Sawyer shakes his head. "No, it's fine—let him play. It's not until this evening."

My smile is forced. "But you have to call Sherri back." Before I can see his reaction, I call up to Finn. "Come on, bud, we have to get going."

"But I just got up here," he whines, poking his head out the door. He spots Natalie and is suddenly shy. "Mom, who is that?" he stage-whispers.

"That's Natalie," I say brightly. "This is actually her tree house you're playing in."

"Is it okay that I'm playing up here?" Finn calls.

I turn, and to my utter surprise, Natalie breaks out into a wide smile. "Sure. Did you see the toys in there?"

Finn's jaw drops in awe. "Toys?"

"I'll show you." Then she turns to me, her smile sliding away as she resumes her look of bored indifference. "I can play with him for a while if you need to get ready or whatever."

"Thank you, Natalie," I say in surprise. Then I add a hasty, "Uh, how much do you charge for babysitting?"

She shrugs. "It's fine. You don't have to pay me."

As she climbs up, I turn to Sawyer, impressed and grateful.

"She loves kids," he says, beaming proudly. "Used to want to be a teacher, but then suddenly she was all about this journalism internship. Probably because Lowell suggested it—he was as excited as she was, and once she went into the newsroom to try it out, she was hooked."

I smile. "Well, I guess I'll go get ready. But I don't really know what I'm supposed to do at this party. Do I decorate or something?"

He shakes his head. "Nah, they bring all that stuff. And I do the cooking, of course, so don't worry about that. You're kind of the hostess, I guess—you don't have to hang out with them or anything; just be there in case they need anything."

From the top of the ladder, Natalie calls back, "You do have to wear something fancy."

"I do?"

"You don't *have* to," Sawyer says quickly.

Natalie glances back, and I can't read her expression, but I take a guess. "Do Sherri and her friends wear fancy clothes?" She nods, and I sigh. "Then I guess I need to go home and look through my closet."

"I can give you a ride back across the field," Sawyer offers.

I shake my head. "It's not far. I can walk." I glance up at the tree house, where Natalie has disappeared inside with Finn. "But you two are sure you're okay with watching him?"

"Of course," he says. "He's safe with us."

I smile. I believe him and make my way through the trees and across the field.

I pull my car into the driveway in the alley behind my house, stop outside to water my flowers—cooing compliments at my beloved rosebush—then hurry inside and up to my bedroom to find something suitable for this party.

On my dresser, my eyes land on my jewelry box, so I push it open gently and run my fingers over the silver chain that used to belong to my grandma. A wave of bittersweet memories washes over me—my grandma, the only family I ever had as a child. The only family that mattered, at least—the only one who truly cared about me. Her daughter, my mother, was nothing more than a ghost who floated in and out of my life whenever she pleased. My dad was long gone, a soldier who'd died at war, Grandma said. She never admitted it was a lie, but I always knew on some level she'd made it up to cover up the fact that my mom never knew who he was.

And I was so young—not even in school yet—when my mom came over late one night, stumbling and high. I crept downstairs to listen to my mom and grandma argue in the kitchen, Grandma pleading for Mom to be quiet so she wouldn't wake me. *Do you really want your daughter seeing you like this?*

What the hell do I care? She's a worthless little shit.

I want to force the words away, yet they're etched into my soul. Those words, and the aching loneliness after Grandma died, made me vulnerable. Easy prey for a terrible man.

But there's no changing the past. It's gone, and it's never coming back.

He's never coming back.

I look down at the necklace one last time; then I kiss my fingertips, tap the necklace gently, and shut the jewelry box.

No more looking back.

It's after three when I pull back into the driveway of Windy Acres. I walk in looking as fancy as I can—meaning I've put on a dress and makeup, which for a mom on a Saturday is no small feat. In the kitchen, my eyes zero in on Finn, who sits at the table chewing on something— my inner food-allergy alarm goes off. "What are you eating?" I cry.

"Chicken nuggets," he says happily.

Sawyer turns from the stove, mouth open as if to speak, but he freezes, staring long enough that I smooth my dress self-consciously. Then he apparently recovers, saying, "I made them exactly like I do at the diner—is that okay?"

I nod. "That's perfect."

Finn pipes up: "We're having a late lunch, Mom, and then Natalie's gonna make pizza for supper with my special cheese!"

I smile. "Well, that sounds fun."

"We were going to ask you first," Sawyer says quickly. "Nat said they can watch movies upstairs during the party, and she'll come down and make him a pizza—maybe you can write down some instructions for her?"

"Of course. Thank you," I say, overwhelmed by their kindness, the way they've taken us in. "Are you sure I can't pay her something for babysitting?" I bite my lip, no idea what the going rate for sitters is these days but quite certain my meager bank account can't afford it.

Sawyer waves a hand dismissively. "No, don't even worry about it. I told her if she helps out, I'll give her money to see a movie with her friends. Bribery is the only way I can get my teenager to spend time with me." We both chuckle; then he claps his hands. "Well, if it's okay, I'm going home to get ready—we've got about an hour before they'll be here."

After he leaves, the first thing I do is tidy up the living room—and almost trip over the box of toys, which Finn shoved aside rather than actually put away. "Finnegan Charles," I growl. He bounds in from the kitchen and flashes a sheepish smile. Before I can issue another command, there's a knock on the front door. Great—they're early. I frown at Finn, who has already moved to the couch with his tablet, then kick the box hastily under the coffee table and hurry to the door, fixing a smile on my face as I open it.

Standing there is a woman I can only describe as a middle-aged Barbie doll, blonde and poised and glamourous. Her eyes dart behind me. "Oh, I was expecting Sawyer. Is he here?"

Ah. "Sherri?" I say, and she nods. "Please come in. He'll be here soon."

The scent of expensive perfume wafts in the air as she breezes past me, gazing into the kitchen as if she thinks I'm hiding Sawyer somewhere. I clear my throat. "Um, I'm Iris. I'm helping out here while Mr. Gordon is out of town."

She smiles and then, spotting Finn on the couch, peers at me more closely. "Iris *Jenkins?*"

I cross my arms. "Do I know you?"

Her smile is sweet but sharp. "You sent me quite a lengthy email last spring asking why we allow peanut products at the elementary school's family-fun night." My eyes widen. Sherri must be short for Sherrilyn, as in Sherrilyn Simpson, PTA president. I've only seen her in person a few times, and I almost didn't recognize her with such heavy makeup. But she doesn't give me a chance to respond. "I sure hope we can put that all behind us. My friends and I have a lovely evening planned. I just got here a little early to spruce the place up a bit. Can you help me?"

I want to say no, ask her why her only response to my email was a dismissive *Thanks for your opinion but we can't accommodate everyone; we need to be fair to all the kids.* But right now I am doing my job, and she is the customer. So I nod, ignore her smug smile, and pray this party is as quick and painless as possible.

CHAPTER NINE

We make quick work of Sherri's decorations, stringing up white lights in the dining room and spreading an intricately designed silver cloth along the long mahogany table. It turns out that Sherri is surprisingly hard working—and talkative.

"So I told my ex, 'Next time you think about buying tickets to Jamaica with a twenty-five-year-old, why don't you put that money toward braces for our *fifteen*-year-old instead?'" Sherri says, finishing the story as we lay out the place settings. "Men, am I right?"

I nod automatically. "How many kids do you have?" I ask.

"Three kids at three different schools this year, which makes morning drop-off a pain. Plus, they're all on traveling soccer teams this summer, so scheduling is a nightmare." She cocks her head. "What about you? Is Finn in any sports?"

"Uh, he played peewee baseball last summer, but I'm not sure if he will this summer. It was tough leaving work to get him to practice every day."

She nods sympathetically. "I hear ya, girl. I'm lucky my job at the dental clinic is flexible. Where do you work?"

"At the newspaper."

"Oh, right—for Lowell Gordon. Now, how do you know each other, again?"

I smile. "Lowell and Ivan are like family to Finn and me." My smile fades. Three years on, and I still refer to Ivan in the present tense.

"Oh, honey," she clucks. "I'm sorry. Cancer is a bitch. It leaves people destroyed—physically, emotionally, financially."

"Thank you," I whisper, though a thought pricks in my brain at her last word. *Financially.* Lowell has never mentioned anything about it, but then again, I've never asked.

Sherri's phone beeps and she picks it up, then sighs as she taps at the screen, apparently sending a text. "My oldest is supposed to be watching his little brother and sister, but all he wants to do is play video games."

"Trying to control screen time is a nightmare," I say sympathetically.

She nods, eyes wide. "Especially when they have free rein at their dad's house. The real nightmare is when they come home from there, and I have to try to get them back on an actual schedule." She laughs, but there's a sadness in her eyes, and I'm hit with a wave of sympathy. In the end, we're all moms just doing our best to get through each day.

And honestly, in terms of girlfriends, Sawyer could do a lot worse. Not that it's any of my business, anyway. "So," I say, "how long have you known Sawyer?"

With that, a smile spreads across her face, and she fluffs her hair. "Oh, quite a few years now—ever since he moved here with Natalie and started showing up at school functions."

"He's divorced, too?" I say casually as I straighten a butter knife—because, again, it's not that I care. I've barely known him for one day.

Sherri leans in, whispering as if sharing a secret: "He's a widower, honey."

My eyes widen. "I had no idea. I'm sorry to hear that."

I want to ask more questions, but then I hear the back door open, and soon Natalie peeks in from the kitchen. She looks from me to Sherri and smirks, then asks, "Is Finn upstairs?"

"Yes, thank you," I say, smiling. "Oh, and he was making a blanket fort for you two to hang out in, so if you wouldn't mind acting impressed, that would be great."

She flashes a thumbs-up, then disappears. Then Sawyer pokes his head in, and his eyes dart nervously from me to Sherri. "You're early."

Sherri lets loose a tinkling, flirty laugh. "I had to make sure everything looks perfect." She bites her lip. "Well, don't you look handsome."

Sherri's right. He's freshly showered, his wavy hair much more tamed, and the navy-blue sweater fits him nicely. "You ladies need any help?"

"Ooh, will you help me carry in the place settings?" Sherri asks. I pretend to be focused on smoothing the corner of the tablecloth, diligently avoiding eye contact.

"Uh, yeah. Be right there," he says. When she hurries out, he walks over to me. "I'm sorry, I would've gotten here sooner if I'd known she was going to be so early."

"No problem." I smile, looking up at the twinkling lights. "It's beautiful, isn't it?"

"Yes," he says, and when I turn he's looking at me.

My neck warms, so I say quickly, "Sherri's nice."

He scoffs. "Nice like a barracuda." I frown in surprise, and his smile fades. He looks at me quizzically. "Hey, I know Natalie likes to tease me, but just so you know, there's nothing—"

"Yoo-hoo, Sawyer?" Sherri's voice rings out, and he cringes. She pops her dazzling blonde head back into the dining room. "Are you coming?"

He flashes me an apologetic look, then forces a smile. "On my way."

He follows her out, and I go back to smoothing the tablecloth, pretending I didn't desperately want him to finish that sentence.

The rest of the Literary Ladies filter in, and Sawyer gets busy cooking as I open the bottles of chardonnay Sherri had chilling. I bring the glasses out, then set them down carefully in front of each of the chattering women.

I've set down the last glass and am about to make my escape when the woman at the end of the table speaks: "Excuse me, could you please let Mr. Jones know that I can't have gluten?"

"Of course, ma'am," I say, nodding. "No problem at all. My son has allergies, too."

"I actually avoid it for my autoimmune disease—but thank you so much for understanding." She smiles. "You're Finn's mom, right?"

I look down in surprise. "Yes, I am."

She smiles warmly. "My son was in his class last year. Dante." She nervously tucks her black hair behind her ear, and I recognize a kindred spirit in shyness. "I'm Jane."

"Iris," I say, smiling back.

"Do you want to join us?" Jane asks. "Technically we're discussing the latest Tana French novel, but it pretty much always devolves into gossip and complaining about mom stuff."

I laugh. "I can't, I'm sorry. I'm filling in while Mr. Gordon is gone. Thanks, though." In a burst of bravery, I add, "Maybe some other time?"

She beams. "That would be great. I know Dante would love a play-date with Finn."

I turn to go, but Jane says, "Oh, and Iris?" I look back, and she says, "Thanks for making us feel so welcome. This is a really great party."

I nod as graciously as possible, then walk back into the kitchen feeling grateful and exhilarated and a little bit proud, like maybe I can handle this job after all. My eyes settle on Sawyer in front of the stove, his earlier words floating back into my mind: *Just so you know, there's nothing . . .* I square my shoulders and stride over to him. "Hi."

He glances up. "Everything okay in there?"

"Yeah. I was wondering . . ." He turns back to the multiple pans in front of him—tender strips of sirloin, sizzling slices of peppers and mushrooms—completely concentrated on stirring a creamy sauce that

56

smells spicy and divine, and I lose my nerve. He's way too busy for me to pester him about what he was going to say—best to stick to relaying the crucial news. "I was wondering if you knew that Jane can't have gluten."

"I know," he says, eyes not leaving the stove.

"Oh, okay. Great." I stand awkwardly for a moment, then turn away.

"Iris?" I turn back, and he smiles. "Thank you."

I smile back, then walk over to load the dishwasher.

I'll tell you one thing—those Literary Ladies sure know how to party. They eat their dinner and dessert, laughing and talking and singing Sawyer's praises. Sherri continues to bask in each compliment as if claiming ownership, and I'm as confused as ever.

And exhausted. The sun is dipping low, and the party finally seems to be winding down—some guests have already left, and others are gathering up their purses by the door. It occurs to me that I have not once checked on Finn, so I hurry up the staircase and over to his bedroom door, which is ajar. It's dark inside, except for the faint glow of a laptop screen. He's curled up inside the blanket fort, leaning against Natalie as they watch the latest Pixar animated film. He's engrossed in it, but she looks up. I give her a hopeful thumbs-up, and she nods, smiling slightly. "Thank you," I mouth before slipping away.

Downstairs it's quieter, and I hear car engines rumbling to life outside. The dining room is empty, but voices murmur from the kitchen. I walk silently to the door, feeling like a creeper but leaning in anyway when I hear Sawyer's voice, sounding tense. "I just don't think it's a good idea."

"And why not?" It's Sherri, sounding playful, though her tone is forced.

"I'm not really looking for anything right now, okay?"

"But you never really know what you're looking for until you take a chance."

There's a pause, and I lean so close that my ear grazes the door. Finally, Sawyer sighs. "Look, Sherri, I'm just . . . I'm not interested. I'm sorry."

My hand flies to my mouth. Despite the small soar of happiness within me, I can only imagine the gut punch Sherri is feeling—I, for one, would want to make a fast exit without being forced to make small talk. So I slip back through the dining room as quickly and silently as possible, then ease open the front door and retreat to the corner of the deck, away from the glow of the porch light.

Sure enough, the front door soon swings wide, and Sherri stalks out, slams the door behind her, and rushes down the steps. As she drives away, I walk across the thick wooden planks of the deck and ease down into the porch swing. I take a deep breath, close my eyes, and listen to the frogs in the distance.

The door opens again, but I keep my eyes closed until Sawyer speaks. "Mind if I sit down?"

I look up at him and smile, scooting over so he has more room. He sits, and we're shoulder to shoulder in the dark night. I stare up at the stars, feeling nervous adrenaline from being so close to him but also a contented peace at Sawyer's calming presence.

Finally, he sighs. "Quite a night."

"I think it went well," I offer.

"You did great," he says. "Thank you for all your help."

We're silent again, and I glance over. "Are you okay?"

He shakes his head. "I don't like being the asshole."

"You were just being honest."

He looks at me, eyes narrowed. "You heard us?"

Busted. "I'm sorry, I didn't mean to," I say. "I was coming in to see if you needed help, and I heard you talking . . ." I trail off, mortified.

"Spying on me, huh?" My cheeks blaze, but he chuckles. "Well, that's what I was trying to tell you before, anyway. There's nothing between us." He rubs his face, and I wait silently for him to speak again. "It's not that I never want to date again—it's just . . . Natalie was still little when she and I moved back here. I had to get out of that city. We needed a fresh start. I really haven't had much time for anything else."

"I understand. It's been just Finn and me for so long," I say. Emotions battle within me—I open my mouth to say more, but nothing comes out.

Sawyer looks at me, and I meet his gaze. "I also wanted to tell you that you look beautiful tonight," he says softly.

My entire insides warm. "Thank you," I whisper. Then, summoning my courage: "I really enjoyed today. I mean, with Natalie, and . . . with you."

The door creaks open again, and I lean away from Sawyer as I turn to the door. Natalie stands in the doorway, arms crossed. "Finn's asleep," she says to me. Then she turns a pointed gaze to her dad. "Time to go?"

He stands quickly, rubs his neck. "Yeah, I suppose so. Oh—" He looks down at me in concern. "After we help you clean up, of course."

I swat a hand toward him. "Don't even worry about it. Honestly, I'll probably leave everything until tomorrow."

"Well, then, we'll be over tomorrow to help," he says, smiling down at me.

"That sounds great."

They start down the stairs, and I stand. "Natalie, thank you so much for watching Finn. He really adores you."

She almost looks sad, though her face is half shrouded in darkness, so I can't be sure. "He's great," she says.

I wave goodbye, then head inside, exhausted but filled with an unexpected joy from being so close to Sawyer—so close to letting him in, to feeling something I swore I'd never feel again.

CHAPTER TEN

I complete my first-floor sweep—shutting off lights, triple-checking locks—then climb the stairs and peek into Finn's room. I watch his little back rise and fall once, twice, three times, to be sure. Then I blow him a silent kiss and say a quick prayer of protection before shutting the door.

In the master suite, I slip into my pajamas and snuggle up under the covers. My nighttime movie is cued up, and even though I'm exhausted, I'm still coming down from the thrill of the day—plus, this is my time, my nightly ritual. So I turn on *Cabiria*, then scroll on my phone until my eyelids droop.

As I drift off, I'm in that half-awake, half-dreamlike realm of sleep. Cabiria is walking along the street, smiling at the youth around her, ready to be strong again—but suddenly she also gets the man of her dreams. He's walking toward her, looking surprisingly like Sawyer, and all is well.

Until a scream pierces the night.

My eyes fly open. I blink into the dark room, the DVD home screen glowing from the TV, the movie long finished. I grope along the bed for my phone. Two in the morning. What woke me? I rub my face—whatever it was must've been a dream. I ease back onto my pillow, close my eyes.

And then I hear it again—a scream, shrill and muffled, coming from outside my bedroom.

Finn.

I leap out of bed, heart hammering. It's happening.

He's alive and he's found us.

I race down the hall, all my imagined scenarios evaporating, replaced by cold fear. I burst into my son's room with no plan—nothing but the primal need to protect him.

"Finn!" I cry into the darkness.

He rustles on the floor, his tiny body exactly where I left him. I switch on the light, and he groans in annoyance. My eyes sweep the room, seeing no dangers. But I tear through the closet, peer under his bed, even overturn his pile of stuffed animals. Nothing.

"Did you . . . did you hear that?" I ask him, but he's asleep.

I flip off the light and ease his door shut again, still trembling but doubting myself now. The scream seemed so real. Did I dream it? I stand still in the hallway, staring into the darkness until my eyes adjust, black blurs forming into objects—the bathroom door, the stairway banister. I wait what seems like an eternity, but there's nothing but buzzing silence.

Finally I walk slowly back toward my room. But as I take a step, another scream bursts out—a word. *"Help!"*

I freeze, my eyes darting to the banister—the voice came from downstairs.

Without thinking, I slink down the stairway, one hand grasping the banister, the other clutching my phone, my mind racing.

At the bottom of the stairs, the voice calls out again. *"Please, help me!"*

It chills me to the bone, high pitched and childlike, but unnaturally so. And now that I'm closer, it sounds oddly muffled, almost scratchy. I shine my phone into the living room, sweeping side to side. "Hello?" I whisper. "Who's there?" God, I've always wondered how people can make such foolish mistakes in horror movies, yet I have never felt that cold fear, that confusing terror.

I feel it now.

I stagger forward until I reach the coffee table, and my foot thumps against something—the cardboard box of toys. Reaching down, I spill out the remaining contents and see an old black walkie-talkie. Hand shaking, I pick it up and stare at it for a moment, then push in the side button until it clicks. "Hello?" I whisper.

"Please, save me!"

The handset vibrates with the force of the shriek, and I almost drop it. But I regain control and clutch it tight, pressing in the button again. "Who is this? Do you need help?"

In the pause, I hold my breath, my mind spinning in the darkness. Who could this be? Is it someone nearby? The walkie-talkie is so old I don't even know how it's working. But I don't have long to wait before the voice speaks again—quieter, but with a hint of menace. *"You didn't help me before."*

A chill seeps through me as I stare in confused horror at the walkie-talkie. Then a flash of thought—I look around frantically, dig through the box, but there's no matching handset. I race back upstairs and burst into Finn's room, where I switch on the light and drop to my knees in front of him. "Finn, wake up—I need to ask you about the toys!"

He groans again, shielding his face from the light. "Can't I put them away tomorrow?"

"No, Finn, I need to know: Where is the other walkie-talkie?"

"What?" He blinks up at me.

I wave the handset in front of him. "Where's the other one?"

"There was only one," he says, rolling back over.

My eyes widen, and I drop the walkie-talkie on the floor like it's blazing hot. Then I stare at it, my mind clouded with fear and confusion and exhaustion.

You didn't help me before. That's what the creepy voice said. I shudder. There's no way it could have been truly talking to *me*.

And what could I even do about it? It's not like I can call the police for something like this. I wince—I've called them way too much lately anyway; they'd never believe me.

But there's no way I'm going back to bed tonight. So I stand up, flick off the light, and lock myself inside the room with Finn, who has fallen back asleep. Then I sit in the darkness, waiting for the chilling scream to return, praying that it doesn't.

CHAPTER ELEVEN

I jerk awake, blinking in confusion at my unfamiliar surroundings. I'm on the floor, but this isn't my room. The dusky light of early morning filters in, displaying a scattering of stuffed animals, LEGOs spilled in the corner. Finn's room.

The terror from last night rushes back with force, and I grope around until I find the walkie-talkie. I stare at it, and it stares back silently. My foggy brain struggles to wake fully, to decide whether last night was nothing but a dream.

Then I remember the haunting voice, the chilling words. I swallow the lump in my throat and press the button. "Hello?" I say hesitantly.

"What are you doing?" I startle, turning to see a sleepy Finn peering at me. "Why are you in here so early?" he asks.

"I, uh, couldn't sleep." I lower the walkie-talkie, bracing for more questions.

He rubs his eyes. "Can we have pancakes?"

I sigh. Duty calls. "Sure, buddy." Standing, I drop a quick kiss on his forehead, then walk downstairs, dropping the walkie-talkie in the pocket of my robe and shoving down any lingering dread.

In the kitchen, I get coffee brewing, then scour the cabinets for a griddle. As I walk toward the fridge, I hear a knock on the back door, and I freeze. I totally forgot that Sawyer said he'd come over to help clean up.

Instinctively, I cinch my robe tighter and pat at my hair, which I'd swept up into a wild bun, and try not to grimace as I open the door. But it's not Sawyer—Natalie stands facing me, wearing a hoodie and her usual cool expression.

"Oh. Good morning," I say with forced cheeriness.

"My dad got called to the diner, so he told me I had to come help clean up." She makes no effort at hiding her annoyance, and I bite back a smile. At least with Natalie, what you see is what you get.

"Thank you," I say, ushering her inside. "I started a pot of coffee, if you want some."

"Okay," she says, then shrugs. "So, what do you want me to do?"

"Honestly, Finn asked for pancakes, so I was going to start with breakfast." I smile. "I'm not as good of a cook as your dad, though."

She offers the faintest glimmer of a smile. "I can make pancakes."

"That would be great!" My enthusiasm is too much—I see it in the slight raise of her eyebrows. So I tone it down, adding, "You cook, I'll clean, okay?"

Natalie nods, then turns to the fridge, and I start cleaning. We work in contented silence, me whipping the kitchen and dining room into shape and Natalie flipping pancakes on the sizzling griddle. As I'm tidying up, I bump into her backpack, and three books fall out—how to make origami, the history of feminism, and a sci-fi novel.

"Oh, I'm sorry," I say, picking them up off the floor. "Wow, though, you are well read. I'm impressed."

Her face flushes as she takes them from me and stuffs them into her backpack. "I'm a fast reader. I just like learning about new things and trying out different kinds of books." She shrugs. "I actually thought Finn might like origami."

I nod, smiling. "He would love that. Your dad said that before you took the newsroom internship, you used to want to be a teacher—is that something you're still thinking about?"

She rolls her eyes. "I said that one time in seventh grade. I mean, I *do* like working with kids." She smiles softly. "Finn is really great."

My insides warm. "Thank you."

"But I kind of wanted to work with kids a different way. Like a pediatrician, or maybe a speech therapist or something." For a moment, she's open and vulnerable, but it's like she catches herself caring too much and quickly turns back to the griddle.

I smile. "That would be a great career," I say as I go back to cleaning.

She says nothing but soon taps at her phone, and soft music wafts through the kitchen. It's nothing I've heard before—I'm too old to know what's popular—but it sounds lovely, adding to this peaceful moment.

When my tasks are finished, I shift to setting the table. But as I reach into the cabinet for clean plates, my robe bumps against the counter with a soft thud—the walkie-talkie. I'd slipped it into the pocket of my robe, and now the dread of last night comes crashing back.

"Everything okay?"

I look over, and Natalie is eyeing me with raised eyebrows. And it's no wonder—I'm standing here, holding plates and staring fretfully down at my robe. I force a smile. "It's nothing." Then, in a surge of trust and companionship from this shared morning—or, probably, a burst of sleep-deprived recklessness—I blurt, "Well, actually, it is something. Or it might be." Natalie's eyebrows raise even higher somehow, but she says nothing, and I pull out the walkie-talkie sheepishly. "So last night, in the middle of the night, I heard something. A voice."

She frowns. "Was it Finn?"

"He was asleep. The voice was coming from this. And when I woke Finn up, he said there was only one of these in the box."

Natalie's eyes widen, but only briefly. "Whoa."

Unexpected relief floods through me—saying it out loud and having someone take my fears seriously for once is so validating. "Weird, right?"

"So, like, what did it say?"

"Just screamed at first. Then, 'Help me,' or something."

"Holy shit."

I nod, ignoring her language—I'm not her parent, so I'm off the hook. "I have no idea where it came from, or whether I should be freaked out or not."

Natalie flips fluffy golden-brown pancakes onto a plate, then turns to me, eyes narrowed in thought. "When I was little, my grandpa in the city had a police scanner running, like, all the time. It was so weird, but I feel like he said something once about frequencies getting crossed?"

My eyes widen. "Really?"

"Yeah, like, so you could just randomly hear a voice from somewhere else."

"Ah, like with baby monitors." Of course. I flash back to years ago when Finn was an infant—the nurse jokingly warned me that we might accidentally pick up our neighbors' conversations. (The joke was on her because I never actually used it; I kept the crib in my room until Finn was almost eighteen months old.) Tension seeps from my shoulders as the weight of this fear slips away. It was probably someone far away just messing around, and I was too scared and exhausted last night to think clearly. "That makes so much sense. Thank you, Natalie."

She turns away, like she's trying to hide any sense of pride at my praise. I press forward, clapping my hands. "Well, you have made a delicious-looking breakfast, so I am going to summon the seven-year-old pancake-eating monster, if that's okay."

Natalie nods, still not meeting my gaze, and when I call for Finn, I hear a whoop from upstairs before he bounds down into the kitchen. "Natalie!" he cries, lunging at her for a hug.

"Whoa, buddy, don't knock her over," I say with a chuckle.

But she's smiling now as she returns his hug.

I smile, too. "Make sure you thank her for these yummy pancakes, Finn."

"Thank you!" He skips over to the table, and I set a plate in front of him, along with a glass of soy milk.

I turn back to Natalie, who's picking up her backpack. "I should get going."

My brow furrows. "You're not going to eat?"

"Nah," she says, already moving to the door. "But my dad said he'll be over later to talk about more events coming up."

I nod. "Got it. Thank you again for all your help."

She steps out, and when she closes the door, I lean against it and take a deep breath. I'm grateful that the creepy voice was explained away yet apprehensive about hosting more events. As I stare around this big, strange house, doubt seeps in. Maybe it was a mistake thinking I could handle this.

For now, we finish breakfast, and I get Finn settled in his room playing so I can retreat to the bathroom for a shower, hoping the hot water will wash away my lingering unease.

As I scrub my hair and body, my eyes fall to the red scar on my upper arm, faded but permanent, a lasting reminder of why I'll always jump to the worst possible conclusion, why I'll always be a little afraid. I shut off the water with a sigh, step out carefully, and wrap myself in one of the thick, puffy towels from the stack in the bathroom cabinet. Then I rub my pink face in the mirror, take a deep breath, and turn to the door.

But when my hand touches the knob, I freeze—I hear voices on the other side.

I hold my breath and lean into the doorway, but it's silent again. The sound must've come from whatever game Finn is playing on his tablet. I'm wary nonetheless, the strange voice from last night playing in my mind, but as I ease open the bathroom door and peek around, I see no one.

Then I step out and turn toward my bedroom—and scream in alarm when I see a large figure standing before me.

Sawyer's hands fly up instantly, an automatic defense mechanism. "Oh shit, I'm sorry," he says quickly.

I clutch my towel, flustered. "What are you doing here?"

"Finn let me in," he says quickly, dropping his eyes.

My smiling son walks up next to Sawyer, and I glare down at him. "What have I told you about not letting people in the house?"

Finn shrugs. "But we know him. I wanted to show him my room."

I'm ready to launch into a lecture about boundaries, but before I can say anything else, he leans in with a stage whisper: "Uh, Mom, shouldn't you put your clothes on?"

I swear I see Sawyer's mouth twitch, though I refuse to look at him again. "Working on it." I stalk past them into my bedroom, then slam the door behind me.

Twenty minutes later I venture out and quietly make my way downstairs. Sawyer probably ran straight out of here and didn't look back, and I can't decide how I feel about that. Downstairs it's silent, and I'm about to let my anxious nature get the best of me when I see a flash of movement out the window. My eyes widen, and I walk to the front door, then step outside to make sure of what I'm seeing.

They're on the trampoline. As in, Sawyer is up there, jumping with Finn. It's so goofy looking, this huge man and my tiny son, bouncing around, that a laugh escapes me. Sawyer looks over and waves, and I walk across the lawn toward them.

"Mom, we're seeing who'll fall over first!" Finn calls out excitedly.

"Can't believe I let him talk me into this," Sawyer says, but as he's talking, Finn bumps into him, and Sawyer topples over quite ungracefully, bursting into laughter as he does so.

Finn laughs, too, crying out, "I won!" before plopping down on his butt next to Sawyer.

I join in their laughter, my heart threatening to burst at the cuteness. Sawyer's words from last night come back to me—*You look beautiful*—and I feel the same in this moment.

They scoot to the edge, and I help Finn down. Sawyer follows, leaning against the trampoline to steady himself. "Haven't done that in a long time," he says, grinning.

"Mom, I'm thirsty," Finn announces.

"Your water bottle is in the fridge." He sprints toward the house, and I glance at Sawyer. "Thanks for playing with him."

"He's a great kid." He rubs the back of his neck. "Look, I really am sorry that I scared you. I promise I'm not usually in the habit of walking into houses unannounced."

I wave my hand dismissively, eager to change the subject. "So, Natalie said something about another event?"

He nods. "It's the day after tomorrow. Lowell called this morning. Apparently he's found a few potential buyers for the lodge, and that date will work for them to take a look."

"Oh." I take a deep breath. "I didn't expect this to happen so soon. I honestly didn't think he'd actually sell this place."

"Nothing is set in stone," Sawyer says quickly. "He said he wants to put on a dinner to hear their proposals, make sure they're a good fit."

I frown, remembering Sherri's words about cancer ruining people financially. "Do you think Lowell wants to sell because he's in financial trouble?"

Sawyer shrugs. "I think he's ready to take a step back, and he wants to make sure this place continues to be secure."

My eyes trail over the expansive grounds. Worry and guilt collide within me—Lowell is trying to look out for Finn and me, but he's the one who might need help. Glancing at the house, I see the small wooden Windy Acres sign the Gordons nailed to the porch when they first moved in, and I stand up straight. "What do we need to do?"

"Lowell said he'll be home in time for the dinner, but we need to get everything ready for it. I was going to start by doing some shopping today and thought you might want to join me. But if you're not up to it, I understand." I glance over at him, and he's watching me closely. "Natalie mentioned you had some sort of scare last night?"

"It was nothing," I say quickly, embarrassed.

"Are you sure?" He motions to the house. "I can take a look around, if it'd make you feel better."

His offer is sweet, but I don't want to be known as the jumpy neighbor here like I am at my place in town. "I'm sure. Sometimes I let my imagination get the best of me." I laugh, hoping it doesn't sound forced. "I'm happy to help with the shopping."

Then the screen door slams, and Finn comes skipping back across the lawn. I add wryly, "You know it's a two-for-one deal, of course."

Sawyer smiles warmly. "I wouldn't have it any other way."

CHAPTER TWELVE

Finn hops out of the truck before I can stop him, but I slink out with the catlike speed only moms possess, slipping my hand protectively into his as I scan the packed parking lot of the home-improvement store for speeding vehicles. Sawyer doesn't notice, or at least he pretends not to, as he eases out of the driver's-side door, whistling a soft tune as if he has no cares in the world.

Finn practically pulls me forward, skipping as he sings, "Save big money at Menards!"

Sawyer snorts. "Did he really just sing the Menards commercial?"

I cringe. "He, uh . . . he might watch a little too much TV sometimes."

Sawyer holds up his hands, signaling he's not judging me. "I guess it *is* practically the Midwest national anthem," he says, eyes twinkling.

We reach the store entrance, and the double glass doors whoosh open before us, welcoming us into the massive air-conditioned space.

"Where are we headed?" I ask.

Sawyer nods to the right, and we walk that way. Finn eyes the aisles of light fixtures, gawking up at the sparkling chandeliers hanging from the ceiling. "Is that what rich people have in their houses?" His voice is a little too loud, and an older couple standing at the endcap glances our way.

I look down in embarrassment, but Sawyer laughs. "Yeah, buddy, I think so. Maybe we should get something like that for the lodge someday, huh?"

Finn nods excitedly, and I ignore the flip in my stomach at Sawyer's use of *we*.

Looking ahead, I gasp when I finally realize where we're going. "The garden center?"

Sawyer grins. "I thought you'd want to come along."

We reach another set of glass double doors leading us out into the partially enclosed space, and I breathe it in—fragrant flowers colliding with potting soil and sunbaked earth—while my eyes scan the rainbow sea of foliage before me. Finn tugs away from me to run over to a trickling mini stone waterfall, and I let him go, at peace in these surroundings.

"So," Sawyer says at last, "do you have any ideas of how we should decorate the porch?"

A giddy feeling envelops me, and I cross my arms. "Okay, let's start with hanging baskets all along the porch. Some lighting will make an impact and add a touch of elegance. Ooh, and maybe some succulents as centerpieces." I stop, noticing he's smiling at me. "What? I saw it on Pinterest."

"Nothing." His eyes twinkle again. "I just like how excited you are about it."

I blush, and there's an awkward beat of silence; then Finn runs back over to us, and we get started. Sawyer pushes one of the oversize carts, its wheels rumbling along the bumpy pavement, as I point to a hanging basket bursting with bright yellow, white, and purple blooms spilling over the sides. We continue on until the cart is overflowing.

I'm ticking off my mental list of items we need when Finn groans: "I'm bored. Can I go look at the toys?"

"No toys today," I say sternly.

"But I just want to look," he whines. *"Please?"*

Sawyer leans in. "I can take him over there for a few minutes," he says conspiratorially. "I have to grab some light bulbs for the lodge anyway."

I turn to Finn. "Five minutes—no complaining, okay?" He nods, and I smile at Sawyer. "Thank you."

He winks, then looks down at Finn. "Come on, bud." I stand by the cart, watching them go with a contented smile.

Then I shake myself back to reality and the task at hand. "Potting soil."

With a heaving push, the loaded cart rolls forward, bumping across the pavement to the pallets of potting soil. I grab the largest one I can lift, and as I'm turning back around, a little girl, maybe three years old, stares back at me. "Oh!" I say. "Hi there. You surprised me."

She giggles, and just as I'm glancing around for her parents, an older man with dark sunglasses comes around the endcap and exclaims, "There you are, Mya! Time to go."

She shakes her head, but when he holds out his hand, she takes it.

As they walk away, a shiver runs down my neck. I grip the shopping cart, a familiar panic rising within me.

Something doesn't feel right.

Someone has to do something.

I can't just let them go.

In a split second, I grab my purse and abandon our loaded cart, walking quickly in the direction they went. The garden center has an exterior gate, and as I expected, that's where they're headed—in fact, he's picked her up, and now they're walking through it. I quicken my pace, already memorizing their descriptions just in case. *White male, sixties, balding, sunglasses, gray T-shirt and cargo shorts. White female, about three years old, blonde ponytail, pink T-shirt and shorts.*

I step through the gate, eyes wildly scanning the parking lot until I spot a silver sedan. The man is opening the back door and ushering the girl inside. My pulse pounds, and I rush across the parking lot, about to say something.

But then the driver's door opens, and out steps a young blonde woman who looks quite a bit like the little girl. As I reach the car, in fact, I'm pretty sure I hear a little voice say, "Mama."

Mama is now looking at me with a mixture of concern and confusion. "Do you need something?"

The man looks up in surprise from helping the little girl.

I scramble to think as fast as I can. "I . . . uh, I was just making sure . . ." Quickly, I stuff my hand in my purse, digging around and pulling out a crumpled five-dollar bill. "Did you drop this?"

The man pats his pockets, taking out his wallet and peeking inside. "No, I don't think so."

I force a smile. "Never mind, then."

The woman raises her eyebrows at me before getting back in the car. As they drive away, I turn back, where a confused-looking Sawyer stands at the gate with Finn and the cart. My shoulders sag in humiliation, but I smile and wave at Finn as I walk back toward them. "Ready to go?" I ask brightly.

We check out, and when we're loaded up in the truck, Sawyer hands Finn his phone. "I think Natalie put Angry Birds on there a few years ago, if you want to play it." We drive in silence for a while, and then he glances at me and asks softly, "What happened back there? We came back and you were gone."

I wince. "I'm sorry. Was Finn scared?"

"No. Just confused. We found the cart; then we saw you standing out there with that family. Did you know them?"

I shake my head. "I . . . sort of followed them out to their car."

Sawyer raises his eyebrows. "Why?"

Such a loaded question. I stare out the window at the golden prairie rushing by, trying to decide how to answer, how far into my past to dig. "Because the little girl was by herself at first, and when the man came to get her, I wasn't sure if she was supposed to go with him. I just wanted to make sure she was okay."

There's so much more I leave unspoken. How I spent so many years of my life saying nothing, letting so much pain and harm go. Now that I've found my voice, I can't be silent. I will never be silent again.

Sawyer nods thoughtfully. "I'm sure the family understood you were just trying to help."

I smile sadly. "That's very kind of you to say, but no, I'm pretty sure they think I'm bonkers. And I get it." I shrug. "Most people think I'm over the top, overprotective, overzealous, overbearing . . . just too much in general. But it's okay; I'm used to people not liking me." I look out the window again, and we're quiet as peppy music plays from Finn's game in the back seat.

"Well, I like you."

Sawyer's voice is so soft I'm almost not sure I really heard it. But when I look over at him, he smiles. I smile back, feeling a little lighter than before.

Back at the lodge, the sun is shining brightly, warm and restoring. As Sawyer starts unloading items from the truck bed, Finn bolts for the trampoline. I'm about to call after him to help, but my eye catches movement on the porch. I take a few steps forward and see a man sitting on the swing. Oh no—were we supposed to get guests today?

I catch Sawyer's attention, point to the man, then hurry toward the porch, smiling as I ascend the steps. "Hi there. Can I help you?"

The man removes his sunglasses, revealing piercing blue eyes that leer at me. "What kind of help are you offering?"

Before I can respond, Sawyer growls from behind me, "Dammit, Cole."

The man bursts out laughing, and I turn, confused. Sawyer shakes his head apologetically, then turns to the man. "What the hell are you doing here?"

He feigns offense. "Wow, is that really the way to welcome your only brother?"

CHAPTER THIRTEEN

My eyes widen, but Sawyer is still shooting daggers at this man—his *brother*. Finally, he sighs, turning to me. "Iris, this is Cole. Cole, Iris."

"Nice to meet you," I say, extending a hand.

Cole shakes it vigorously, grinning. "And you." He raises his eyebrows wickedly at Sawyer. "Maybe if you returned my calls once in a while, I would know you had a new girlfriend."

I open my mouth to correct him, but Sawyer beats me to it. "We work together here at the lodge, Cole. Now, what are *you* doing here?"

Cole shrugs, running a hand through his messy blond hair, the picture of innocence. "Can't a guy visit his big brother?"

"Not without asking for money, in my experience."

"Ouch." Cole leans back in the porch swing. "Well, this time I only need a place to stay. I'm here on business."

"Cole," Sawyer warns.

"Just some deliveries."

"I don't want any of that shit in my house." Sawyer's voice is low.

Cole eases into a mischievous smile. "Well, I could rent a room here at the lodge. Get to know Iris a little better."

Sawyer's jaw hardens. "That's not happening."

The brothers stare at each other, and the strained silence is excruciating. But then Finn bounds up the steps, panting from his sprint across the yard. "Who's that?" he whispers loudly to me.

Cole laughs before I can answer. "The name's Cole. And who are you, my good sir?"

"Finn." But he has already lost interest, turning his back on the stranger. "Mom, I'm thirsty."

"Let's go in for a juice box," I say.

Cole jumps up. "Mind if I join you?"

I blink, caught off guard, politeness winning in the end. "Sure."

Sawyer glowers but says nothing. Inside, he refuses to sit with the three of us at the kitchen table, instead putzing around the kitchen and sneaking glances at his brother, as if he's going to steal something.

After a long swig of the Budweiser he found in the fridge, Cole sets his bottle on the table with a thud. "Where's my favorite niece?"

"Out with friends," Sawyer mutters.

"Can't wait to see her. God, how old is she now?"

"Sixteen."

"*Sixteen?*" Cole shakes his head. "If she's got her license, I think I found my new designated driver." A look of horror crosses Sawyer's face, and Cole bursts out laughing. "I'm *kidding*. Jesus, you really think I'm the worst asshole ever, huh?"

Finn giggles, and Sawyer rubs his forehead. "Just *stop*, Cole. Stop."

Cole drains his beer and stands. "Fine. If you need me, I'll be outside, not offending anyone." He winks at me. "Thanks for the beer."

He strides out, and Finn flits over to the living room, where he scoops up some action figures and plays a make-believe game. I glance at Sawyer, who's leaning against the counter, deep in thought. "Do you want to talk about it?" I ask softly.

He turns to me, his eyes pained. "I'm sorry about all this. I didn't mean to speak for you outside when I said he couldn't stay here. It's just that I know my brother. Wherever Cole goes, trouble follows. He's an addict and a terrible influence on Natalie." He scoffs, rubs his face, then sighs. "But he's my brother, so I can't just turn him away. I'll figure something out."

"Let me know if I can help," I say.

"Thanks." He smiles at last. I've already missed seeing it. "But we really should get started with dinner preparations. We can at least get the porch decorated. Tomorrow I'll get started on a menu."

I smile. "That sounds like a great plan to me."

Outside, Cole is thankfully nowhere to be found. Sawyer retrieves the stepladder from the garage, and I climb carefully. We make quick work—a great team, if I do say so myself—hanging the flower baskets one by one along the porch, followed by the string of lights. The sun is still high in the sky, but when Sawyer plugs the lights in, I clap and cheer admiringly.

A low whistle sounds from across the porch. We both turn our heads to find Cole walking toward us. "Looks like you're planning quite the party. Do I have an invitation?"

"Only if you're looking to buy a lodge," I say, forcing a laugh.

Cole smirks at me, but I hear a soft chime, and he looks down at his phone.

"So," he says, looking up at Sawyer, "Nat sent me a Snap. She's on her way home and says we should meet her there. She says you should take her super-cool uncle out to dinner."

"Wait." Sawyer narrows his eyes. "She sent you a *Snap*?"

"Uh, yeah. Snapchat." Cole laughs. "You are one old son of a bitch."

Sawyer glares at him. "Well, I suppose you need a ride from this old son of a bitch?"

"Why get my own car when these good looks get me free rides all the time?" Cole flashes a cheesy smile. Then he clears his throat. "So yeah, a ride. And, uh, you think you got a place I can crash, after all?"

There's a hint of vulnerability, like he wants his brother's approval, and when Sawyer grunts his okay, Cole relaxes into a smile.

Sawyer turns to me. "Okay if I go meet Natalie at home?"

I wave him off. "Of course."

He sighs. "I guess we're going into town for dinner, but we'll stop back on our way there to see if you need anything."

I smile. "Okay. Have fun."

He flashes me an uncertain smile, then follows Cole to the truck.

Back in the house, I decide a bowl of cereal in front of the living room TV is an acceptable lunch option for Finn—not exactly a stellar parenting choice, but it gives me time to clean up the kitchen. It also might be the perfect opportunity to explore a little more inside the home.

This creaky old farmhouse was built way back in 1911 and used to sit even farther out on the vast prairie. About thirty years ago, it was moved onto a new foundation here, the location that has become its forever home. When the Gordons bought it, they added on substantially, transforming it into a massive lodge.

On the outside, the sheer size and uniform appearance—bright-white steel siding and black shutters, with the stately columns lining the front porch—make it a perfectly beautiful, welcoming lodge. Inside, it takes a while to determine which sections of the house are original and which are add-ons. Walking around, you can feel a soft dip in the carpeting, a shift in the floorboard, a crease where linoleum squares have moved. There's a rich history in this century-old house, and I'm glad the Gordons attempted to keep some of the authentic fixtures—mahogany doorframes, intricately carved wooden mirrors—that add to the house's historic charm.

Climbing the stairs now, I set my sights on the one upstairs room I haven't yet entered: Lowell's office. I tell myself it's perfectly acceptable; Lowell left me in charge, and I wouldn't be doing a good job if I wasn't thorough about checking to make sure there isn't some sort of calendar or schedule of events posted in the office that I need to know about. Plus, a part of me is concerned about Lowell, who's seeming a little more forgetful these days.

And yes, a part of me has the compulsive need to snoop, the urge to find out everything I can, because if I don't, something could go wrong that I could've stopped if I'd only paid better attention. They say listen to your gut—to that voice in your head telling you when something is off. But for me, that voice is *always* there, relentlessly warning me of potential dangers. It's why I've learned to always err on the side of caution, no matter what—like with the little girl at Menards.

And this is exponentially more true when it comes to my own child. Doing otherwise is such a potentially catastrophic risk. Parenthood comes with the most all-consuming love you've ever known, but with it, the most all-consuming fear, the possibility of the greatest loss imaginable. And I can always imagine it, in every scenario. So I always play it safe.

Because I know that bad things happen. They have, and they might again.

Halfway up the staircase, I pause and stare out through the large living room window and into the wide expanse of prairie.

There's nowhere you can run that's far enough.

I shake the words away, focus on one foot in front of the other until I'm at the office door. It's unlocked, the wooden door swinging open silently and displaying a surprisingly tidy office. Sunlight filters in from the window on the opposite wall, illuminating a wooden desk flanked by a steel file cabinet.

I sit in the desk chair, swiveling back and forth, and smile at the candid framed photos of the Gordons, taking in Ivan's kind smile. I reach absently for the top file-cabinet drawer. It rolls open quickly, thudding to a stop. A quick scan of the files lined neatly along the drawer reveals taxes, titles, deeds, a map of the property. No calendar that I can see, but I pick up a stack of business-size envelopes and flip through them.

They're all from Atlantis Health System—opened but with their documents still inside. Carefully, I take the first paper out, unfold it, and my eyes widen. It's a bill for over $50,000. I narrow my eyes as I read it and see that it's for various procedures related to Ivan's cancer treatment three years ago. The next in the stack is a second notice of the same bill. The next, though, bears the phrases *Final notice* and *Collections agency*, phrases that cause bile to rise in my throat.

Lowell *is* in financial trouble, after all—this could be the real reason why he's willing to sell his properties, including the newspaper. But he's never said a word to me about any of this. I set the letter down with a sigh, making a mental note to find a gentle way to ask him about it when he comes back.

For now, I turn to the second drawer. Inside, instead of neat rows of files, there's one haphazard pile of black-and-white photographs. I pick them up delicately, marveling at the stoic faces, the old-fashioned dress. It's a man and a woman, holding a baby in front of this very house—the original version of it, at least. On the back of one in faded handwriting, slanted and elegant, is written *Jacob and Emma Miller with Baby Reuben, October 1913.*

This must be the original family who lived in this house way out on the prairie. I try to imagine life in October 1913 with a tiny baby, miles and miles from the nearest town, with a harsh winter on the horizon. I glance outside the office window and watch the trees sway, whipped by the unforgiving Dakota wind, wild and relentless. Somehow the grass doesn't seem like it's dancing anymore—it's thrashing about in a violent frenzy.

"Mom?"

I jump, dropping the pictures back into the drawer before turning to see Finn standing in the doorway. "What's up, buddy?"

"Can I have a cookie?"

"I don't think we have any cookies."

He grins. "Can we make some?"

I smile. This kid is too smart for his own good. "Okay, sure. Let's do it."

Finn whoops in victory, then runs back downstairs. Before I stand, I look down at the drawer again, locking eyes with Emma Miller one last time; then I gently shut the drawer.

CHAPTER FOURTEEN

Forty-five minutes later, the heavenly scent of chocolate chip cookies—dairy- and nut-free, of course—wafts through the house. As I'm scrubbing the dishes, exhaustion from the day's events and my lack of sleep sets in. But when I glance out the window over the sink, I see the ladder still lying on the deck. After a check that Finn is engrossed in building LEGOs on the living room floor, I rush out and give the hanging baskets a quick but thorough watering. Then, I heave up the clunky ladder before lugging it down the porch steps and over to the garage.

"Need a hand?"

The unfamiliar deep voice startles me, and I almost drop the ladder, but when I turn, Cole stands behind me.

"Uh, sure," I say lightly, glancing behind him to see Sawyer's truck parked in the driveway. "I didn't hear you drive up. Where are Sawyer and Natalie?"

"In the house—looking for you." He takes the ladder from me, and I open the garage door for him. "I think Sawyer wanted to check on you."

I smile before I can stop myself. "Well, that's nice of him."

"That's my big brother," Cole says wryly; then his smiles fades. "So, Iris . . . where are you from?"

"Oh, we just live in town."

"No, I mean originally."

Something in his tone makes me freeze. I glance toward him, and he's eyeing me with curiosity. I swallow. "Why do you ask?"

He sets the ladder in its place. "You look familiar for some reason."

I scoff and move to step around him, but he blocks my path. "Did you ever live in the Twin Cities?"

Somehow I manage a stiff laugh. "Well, sure, me and millions of other people."

He laughs, too, but his eyes don't leave mine. "I don't suppose you used to party in the West Metro area? It's been a long time, but it was quite the, uh, circuit of partygoers, if you know what I mean."

My hands shake now, but I hold his gaze, force my face to stay neutral. "You must have me confused with someone else."

He takes a step toward me, leaning in. "Oh, I don't know. You've got a pretty distinctive face." His voice dips low, and I don't know if he's trying to rattle me or hit on me. Maybe both. "It's the eyes, I think. Very . . . expressive."

A chill runs through my body, and I feel like I'm about to crack, like my past is about to come spilling out, but then I hear footsteps scuff to a stop at the garage door. "Uncle Cole?"

I turn, and Natalie is eyeing us strangely. I force a smile as Cole slides away from me easily, grinning at his niece. "Hey, you ready to go?"

"Yeah." Her eyes flick to me. "Dad's in the house with Finn."

"I'd better get in there." I rush toward the house, sucking in deep breaths of air to try to slow my racing pulse. Inside, I find them in the kitchen, Sawyer fixing Finn a sandwich.

"Finn," I say, hands on hips, "really? We just made cookies."

He smiles sheepishly. "I was still hungry."

I turn to Sawyer. "I swear I do feed the kid."

Sawyer chuckles. "I really don't mind."

"His sandwiches are better than yours," Finn says. "Sorry, Mom." He smiles; then his eyes focus past me. "Hi, Natalie and . . . uh . . ." Finn trails off. "I can't remember."

Behind me, a deep laugh. "Cole."

I bristle, focusing on a spot on the floor.

"Ready, Dad?" Natalie asks.

Sawyer hands Finn his sandwich, and as Cole and Natalie walk out the door, he looks at me quizzically. "Is everything okay?"

I wave a hand dismissively. "I'm fine. Have fun."

"You can call if you need anything, and I can stop over again later tonight after dinner. Check in."

"You don't have to check on us. I know you're busy."

"I want to," he says simply.

"Okay," I say, smiling as I watch him go.

That evening it's Finn and me while the others are at dinner, and I relish the one-on-one time. We play games of go fish and charades, and he even talks me into a lightsaber battle. After dinner, we curl up on the couch for a movie night, giggling together at the antics of the animated cat and mouse on the screen. He nestles into me, and I lean my head on his, breathing in his scent and thanking God for this moment, for this boy who has my heart, for the second chance at life.

I'm feeling so grateful that when the movie stops and Finn turns his hopeful doe eyes to me, asking if we can jump on the trampoline before bed, I cave. Outside, as we walk across the grass, the sun is dipping low on this summer evening—Finn is up past his bedtime, but I've eased up on our schedule since I'm home with him this week.

Home.

The thought catches me off guard, and I peer back over my shoulder at the vast white house, the setting sun glinting off its windows. I'm not sure I've ever felt at home, not really. Yet it's all I've longed for—home and family, a place to belong and feel loved and accepted—since losing Grandma all those years ago. Finn takes my hand, and warmth spreads through me. He and I are the only family I need. Maybe we've found our home at last.

A car rolls by on the gravel. They keep going—it's totally normal, just someone driving by—yet I tense up, always on alert. Suddenly my thoughts drift back to earlier, my unsettling encounter with Cole inside the garage. Logically, the odds that he knows me, that he truly recognized me from an encounter years ago in a huge city, seem unlikely. And yet, most people from around here have connections to the Minneapolis metro area. It wouldn't be too implausible for us to have been at the same party once.

And the thing is, I know the party circuit he was talking about. If he truly hung with that crowd—my former crowd—he might be as dangerous as they were.

I stare out over the darkening prairie. Deep down, I've always known this was inevitable. That someday I'd cross paths with someone from my past. I've planned for this, like I plan for all worst possible outcomes. But I don't yet know his intentions, so I don't know if I need to enact one of those plans.

All I can do is be ready.

"Mom, come on," Finn calls out, already scrambling up onto the trampoline.

I heave myself up and attempt to stand while he bounces, only to fall forward onto my knees, rolling down onto my side. Immediately, we both erupt into laughter, and we keep laughing as I get up and we jump together. We bounce and bounce until we're both panting with laughter. Finally, when it's fully dark, I bounce down onto my bottom, encouraging him to do the same. Then I lie back. "Look up," I whisper.

Finn lies back as well, and in the dark I see the saucers of his eyes. "Wow."

Above us, the stars dazzle across the sky, scattered spots of light in the dark, some clusters of brilliance, others shining brightly on their own. "Should we wish on one?" I ask softly.

"Yeah!" Finn says.

Together we recite the "Star light, star bright" rhyme. "Close your eyes and make your wish," I say. And I do it, too, silently reciting my usual plea for a long, happy, safe, healthy life for my baby, my miracle, my Finnegan Charles.

After a moment of silence, Finn whispers, "Do we say our wish out loud?"

I shake my head. "You keep it secret, so it's more likely to come true."

He nods solemnly, but then I have a sudden moment of parental panic. I told him to break a cardinal rule—never keep secrets from Mama. "Uh, unless you *want* to tell me," I say lightly. "You know, since I'm your mom."

He looks back up at the stars, and I hold my breath, wait. "I wished to find my dad."

My breath catches, and for a moment I'm frozen—we've never talked about it; I've been so careful to talk around it, hoping to fend off specific questions until he's older. Now I don't know what to say, so I take his hand, give it a gentle squeeze, and offer, "That's a great wish, buddy."

"Let me guess—it'll come true when I'm older?"

His wry tone catches me off guard, so beyond his years, and I smile sadly. "Something like that."

We stare up at the vast canopy for a long time, and eventually, Finn's breathing slows. I'm debating how I'm going to get my sleeping boy into the house when the hum of an engine approaches, and head-lights soon illuminate the yard.

I prop myself up on one elbow with a smile, not at all worried anymore.

He said he'd come. That he wanted to.

"Sawyer?" I call into the darkness. It's a half whisper, trying not to rouse Finn but loud enough that he can hear me. "We're on the trampoline."

Soon his tall figure materializes in the darkness, and when he reaches us, I can see that he's smiling. "You guys went for a late-night jump, huh?"

"He talked me into it." I smile. "It was a lot of fun, actually. The stars are amazing tonight."

Before I know it, Sawyer has kicked off his shoes and is climbing onto the trampoline.

"Shh," I caution. "He's asleep."

Sawyer crawls slowly toward us. He eases down on the other side of Finn, and we both lie back, looking up, as Finn curls into me.

"You're right; they are amazing," Sawyer says.

We're silent, content; then he rolls onto his side, looking at me over Finn's sleeping head. "How did tonight go?"

"Finn and I kind of took the night off," I admit, turning toward him. "How was dinner?"

He sighs. "I forgot how much Natalie eats up everything my brother says. I'm just the uncool dad, I guess."

I laugh. "Well, I think you're cool."

"Likewise." His eyes lock on mine. "I think you're pretty amazing, actually."

In the dark, our faces inch toward each other until they're almost touching. I'm aching to close the distance, but I hesitate, my breath hitching in the unmet space between us. I've known him such a short time, and as much as this electricity between us feels real—as much as I *want* it to be real—I don't know how to be sure. I don't know how to open myself up again after all that I've been through. And I don't know what he could possibly see in me anyway.

"What's wrong?" he asks softly.

"I don't know," I say honestly, then take a deep breath to compose my thoughts. "I guess I'm nervous, since we just met."

Sawyer flashes an apologetic smile.

"What is it?"

"We did just meet . . . but that wasn't the first time I saw you." He squeezes his eyes shut, and when he opens them he faces me, eyes earnest. "I saw you at the diner."

"When? I don't remember seeing you there."

"You didn't. I kind of, uh, saw you from afar."

"What do you mean?" Then, in a flash of surprise and understanding, I smile coyly. "Wait, were *you* spying on *me*?"

He winces, his words thrown back at him. "No, no—I wasn't being creepy or anything, I swear."

I chuckle. "So what were you doing?"

He takes a deep breath. "At first, preparing for an argument, honestly. I'd never had a customer make such specific requests—a detailed list of ingredients, confirmation of what type of oil we used in the fryer."

"Oof, my first night at the diner, huh?"

He nods. "You scared the hell out of your server, you know."

I cover my face with my hands. "I did not!" Then I peek through my fingers. "Did I?"

He chuckles. "Let's just say she was a bit intimidated. So I definitely wanted to get it right, and I wanted to see who this person was who was making all these demands."

My defenses flare, and I open my mouth to speak—those were completely reasonable accommodations for someone with food allergies—but he holds up his hand. "Please let me finish explaining?" I sigh, nodding as he continues. "I expected to see someone angry or arrogant, or something. But then I saw you. You were talking to the server, and you didn't look angry—you looked . . . scared. At first I didn't understand, but when she walked away from the booth, I saw Finn. The moment you looked at him, your face changed, like you were completely lit up and happy, and so was he. You looked like a really good mom, and I realized you were just trying to protect your son."

I blink back a tear at the validation, the acknowledgment of how hard I work to keep Finn safe. Sawyer smiles. "I also realized what a jerk I was for questioning your requests. So I decided right then I would do whatever I could to help. And every time you came in, I peeked out to make sure it was you—not in a creepy way, I promise. And then, when I saw you here, up close, and figured out who you were—I realized something else."

"What did you realize?" I whisper.

"How beautiful you are." His voice is husky, and I draw in a shaky breath. "So," he continues, "to me, it doesn't seem like we just met because it kind of feels like I already know you. Is that strange?"

I shake my head. "I already feel so comfortable with you, too. Maybe that's what scares me."

"Don't be scared," he whispers.

Sawyer reaches out in the darkness, placing his warm hand gently against my face, and it sends a shiver through me. I lean into him, closing my eyes and inhaling his musky scent. Our lips touch at last, and it's the softest, sweetest kiss I could ever imagine.

Between us, Finn stirs, murmuring, "Mom?"

Sawyer and I pull back. "I'm right here, buddy," I say softly. "Sawyer's here, too."

Finn rubs his eyes as he turns to Sawyer. "Did you make a wish?"

Sawyer looks at me. "It already came true."

CHAPTER FIFTEEN

The night is crisp now, and Finn cuddles into me, falling right back to sleep. I kiss his head softly, then smile at Sawyer. "I think it's time to go in."

Sawyer carries Finn all the way inside and upstairs into his bed, and my little guy snuggles under his blanket as I give him a soft kiss, cross his forehead, and whisper, "Sweet dreams."

Out in the hallway, Sawyer and I stare at each other, and I am acutely aware of how close he stands, how close we are to my own bedroom. But I take a deep breath, whisper, "Thanks so much for coming over."

"Of course," he says.

I follow him downstairs, smiling up at him as he turns to me in the doorway, clearing his throat. "Look, about earlier . . . I'm sorry. I hope I didn't come on too strong."

I shake my head. "No, I'm very happy about . . . earlier." God, that was so awkward. "I just . . ." I glance up the stairs toward Finn's room. "I don't know how to do this. Dating, I mean." I drop my eyes, embarrassed.

Sawyer puts a hand under my chin, lifting gently until we're looking into each other's eyes. "Maybe we can figure it out together," he says softly.

I stand on my tiptoes, reaching up to place both of my hands on the sides of his face, pulling him down until his lips meet mine. Our kiss is sweet again, but it's deeper, longer, and when we pull back, I'm breathless.

Sawyer leans his forehead against mine. "I could get used to that."

Me too. But instead I say, "I should get to bed."

"Right," he says quickly, straightening up.

"But you're coming back tomorrow?" I bite my lip, hoping I didn't sound too needy.

"Absolutely." He grins. "Someone has to make breakfast."

As he drives away, I lean against the doorway, watching until his taillights disappear into the night.

I'm girlish that night, lying in bed curled up in my blankets wondering what it would be like to have Sawyer lying next to me. To be wrapped in his arms, feeling his heartbeat against me.

For our bodies to be entwined.

I flip over in bed, grasping the pillow. It's been so long; I wouldn't even know where to begin. But something tells me that with Sawyer, it would come naturally. I sigh as I drift off dreaming about this unexpected man who seems to be everything I always wanted but never thought possible.

I'm jolted awake when the first scream comes, and it's almost like I was expecting it. Like I can't imagine things actually working out for me. Because I don't deserve that.

The second scream wrenches me out of bed, trembling with terror. I blink around the room, the lightening predawn sky helping my eyes adjust.

This is really happening. I didn't imagine it.

Pawing through my desk drawer, I pull out the walkie-talkie with a shaking hand.

"Help me!" the high-pitched voice screams, and I jump.

My mind spins back through the day to my talk with Natalie—this could be some kid far away somewhere—and my fear turns into frustration. I press in the side button, barking, "Who is this? What do you want?"

There's a pause, the old house silent except for my own pulse throbbing in my ears.

Then the voice speaks again.

"You didn't save me, Iris. You ran away and left me behind."

CHAPTER SIXTEEN

I stare at the walkie-talkie in my hand as if it's going to come alive and bite me.

It said my name. *My name.*

And it knows what I did.

I freeze, terror squeezing my insides. Then I drop the handheld radio as if it were on fire and leap into motion—lurching across the room and grasping under the bed for the canvas backpack full of necessities. Go bag over my shoulder, I race down the hall to Finn's room and scoop him up, adrenaline on my side as his sleep-heavy body shifts in my arms; then I rush to the staircase.

Something catches my eye down the hall—the office door ajar—but I keep going down the stairs, hitching Finn onto my other hip when I reach the front door so I can grab the knob.

But my eyes fall to the floor, where Sawyer keeps a pair of work boots. Next to them, I'd carefully placed a soft blue sweater Natalie had accidentally left behind yesterday.

My breathing slows as I pause, pained. I can't leave them like this, with no explanation. And Finn will be devastated if he wakes up and we're miles away, with no chance of coming back.

But we can't stay if it's not safe—I have to do *something*. Without thinking, I take out my phone and punch in the familiar three numbers my fingers have memorized.

"911. What's your emergency?" a woman's voice asks.

"There's . . . uh . . . I need help," I sputter. I hadn't thought this out. What can I say—my kid's toy walkie-talkie is threatening me? "I heard a voice . . . in my house."

"You have an intruder in your house, ma'am?"

"Um, yes," I say quickly. At least she's listening.

"Where are you?"

"My son and I are downstairs in the foyer. He's asleep."

"And is the intruder still in your house?"

"I . . . I don't know." My voice cracks.

"Ma'am, it's going to be okay," she says, taking my address and promising to stay on the line with me.

I push the speaker button so I can set the phone down as she continues talking, her tone calm and assured. Then I lay Finn gently on the couch. He murmurs, but I remain still until his breathing slows again, then cover him with a blanket and walk to the living room window. Outside, dawn is breaking over the horizon now, its faint orange glow promising calm. But inside I'm a storm of fears and doubts.

It can't be him. The voice on the radio can't be my ex.

I close my eyes, recall the words I read online all those years ago: Mitchell Charles Wheeler, age twenty-nine, died August 3rd, 2014, in rural Hennepin County, Minnesota.

I shudder, my thoughts drifting from the obituary to images of his body, mangled and bloody. I fight back a wave of nausea, force my mind to move past it. He's gone—that's all that matters.

Suddenly I flash back to my rush down the stairs—the open office door. I'm sure I closed it earlier. Didn't I? I rub my tired eyes, and an even more ludicrous thought strikes. The photos I unearthed, the chilling gaze of those stoic black-and-white faces. *You ran away and left me behind.*

Could this century-old house be haunted?

I shake the thought away. That's as implausible as Mitch still being alive. But I can't shake the cold fear, the chilling feeling that I'm being watched—but from inside or outside, I'm not sure.

I step away from the window, slink back down in the chair, close my eyes, and rack my brain for a logical explanation besides my dead ex-boyfriend or the ghost of a pioneer woman.

My eyes fly open. Mitch's friends.

It's been so long, and I've shoved those terrible memories down so far that I can't really recall their faces—they all form one ghoulish mob in my mind. And I didn't even know most of their names . . . except Rex. I shudder again. The most vicious of all. When moving drugs was no longer enough, it was Rex who suggested arms. Then, when that wasn't enough, it was his idea to dabble in pure evil: human trafficking.

People moving, he called it. Like it was some sort of joke. A wave of nausea hits me.

In the end, it was Rex's truck that got me to freedom—that brought me here, that helped me find the Gordons, and a second chance at life.

But he's still in prison . . . isn't he? I was so diligent about checking online those first few frightening years, but once I'd read he'd been arrested, then convicted, I got lazier about it. Now, I can't remember the last time I checked.

The silence is oppressive now, closing in upon me. I'm sweaty but chilled to the bone, weary but restless, like I can't think, can't breathe.

"Ma'am, are you still with me?" the operator asks calmly.

"Will the police be here soon?" I ask.

I don't hear her reply. Instead, I rush to the door and throw it open to breathe in the fresh air. But the wind has picked up, gusting now, massive and relentless like a freight train barreling toward me, ready to pulverize me, bury me deep in the earth. Is this wind—this terrible, unforgiving wind—what Emma Miller heard, night after night, a century ago?

I quickly shut the door, more panicky than ever. Desperate, I fall back on a prayer from my childhood. Grandma took me to church when she could, but she had me say prayers every night. My favorite was Angel of God.

Angel of God, my guardian dear
to whom God's love entrust me here.
Ever this day be at my side
to light, to guard, to rule, to guide.

I need an angel now more than ever.

Outside, at last I see the lights of the police SUV, and I relax a little. "They're here," I say, ending the call and letting myself believe that maybe, just maybe, this was the right decision.

The door opens a crack. "Police!" a man calls.

"We're in the living room," I call out weakly.

The door swings open, and two police officers walk cautiously toward me. "Ma'am, you called about a possible intruder?" says the younger man. I nod, and he adds, "Is someone in the home?"

"No. I mean, I don't know."

The second police officer, an older man with a permanent scowl, steps forward. "You don't *know*?"

"I'm not sure where the voice was coming from," I say quickly.

The officers exchange a quick look, and my stomach drops. The younger man clears his throat. "Ma'am, I'm Officer Barnes. Why don't we sit down, and you can tell me what's going on?"

I shake my head, arms crossed. "I don't want to sit; I want to stay here by my son." I gesture to Finn, somehow still asleep on the couch. "But I'll tell you what happened."

"Please do," the older man—Watson, according to his name tag—says gruffly.

"I . . . I heard a voice over a walkie-talkie, and I don't know where it's coming from."

Watson's eyes narrow. "A *walkie-talkie?*"

Barnes's eyes flick to his counterpart before settling on me again. "What did the voice say?"

"It . . ." I stop, suddenly unsure if I'm ready to say the words out loud. "It said I didn't help them, or something. It's happened two nights in a row now, but tonight it said my name."

Barnes's eyebrows raise. "Your name?" I nod, and he leans forward. "Did you recognize the voice at all, or get any sense of gender or age?"

I shake my head. "It's oddly high pitched, like maybe they're using something to distort their voice."

He nods. "Do you have any reason to believe someone is targeting you?"

"Whoa, okay, easy now, rookie," Watson says. "*Targeting* is a strong word. We don't even know if she heard anything at all, and even if she did, it could be some kids playing a prank."

I frown at him. "I know what I heard."

He crosses his arms. "You do? Tell me, is it the same thing you heard on May thirtieth at your residence on Baker Street? Or on June fifth, for that matter? Should I look up the other dates as well?"

My eyes widen, and he nods. "That's right, Ms. Jenkins, we did our jobs. We looked you up on the way over here, and we know this isn't your place of residence."

"I'm house-sitting for my boss," I say quietly.

"So now you're going to start making a bunch of false reports here like you do at your house?"

I stare in shock, blindsided by this good cop–bad cop routine. To his credit, Barnes seems a bit blindsided as well, shooting a look at his partner I can't quite read. He turns to me. "Look, let's stick to the matter at hand. Ma'am, where is the radio—the one you heard the voice on? Can we see it?"

My eyes dart to the staircase. "I dropped it upstairs." I glance apprehensively at Finn. "Can I leave him here with you?"

Barnes nods. "Of course."

I race upstairs and retrieve the walkie-talkie from my room, then hurry back down, holding it away from me as if the voice will call out at any minute.

But no, quite the opposite. There's no voice at all once I want there to be one.

"Hello?" Watson says time and again, pressing the side button over and over dramatically, then turning to me in mock consternation. "Well, golly gee, Ms. Jenkins, the mystery voice seems to be gone now. Guess there's nothing we can do."

"That's it?" I look between the two of them, embarrassment and exhaustion bubbling inside me. "Can't you guys, like, trace the call or something?"

Watson bursts out laughing. "Yeah, let me call my buddies over at *CSI: Miami*, and they'll get right on that."

"But what am I supposed to do if it happens again?"

"Ignore it. Nothing but kids messing around." He turns to go.

"You didn't *hear* it." My voice breaks. "It's . . . disturbing."

Watson shrugs. "No law has been broken. There's nothing we can do."

"Then I want someone who can do something." I raise my voice against my better judgment, but I'm desperate and terrified and tired of his bullshit. "I want to talk to your supervisor."

There's no smirk now, only a glower. "Go right ahead and call the chief." He nods to the window, where the sun brims pink light over the prairie. "I'm sure she would *love* to get a call bright and early, especially from a frequent caller like you."

Tears of frustration build within me, but I'll be damned if this bastard sees me cry. I turn to Barnes and detect an ally in his sympathetic gaze. "We can file a report, ma'am," he offers.

Watson shoots daggers at his partner, but the young man holds his gaze. "Fine," he growls, "but this bitch has to come down to the station to do it."

I wince, and just then Sawyer steps through the door. "What's going on?" My face crumples at the sight of him, and he rushes over, wrapping me in a hug before turning to the officers with narrowed eyes. "What the hell did you just say to her?"

Watson scoffs, his face red. "All I'm saying is, if she wants to file a report, she needs to come down to the station."

"Is that so? You can't do it here?"

Watson's jaw tightens. Barnes speaks quickly. "We, uh, we actually can do it here. I can take her statement."

"That would be great," Sawyer says, eyes not leaving Watson.

"I'll wait in the squad car," Watson grumbles, stalking out, Barnes staring after him.

Sawyer turns to me and cups my face with his hands. "Are you okay? Is Finn okay?"

"We're fine," I say shakily.

"What happened?"

I take a deep breath. "It was the voice again."

"The voice?" Recognition hits his eyes. "Is that what you told Natalie about?"

I nod. "It was scarier this time. It said my name."

"Jesus," he whispers. "I'm sorry you had to go through that alone." He glares at the door. "And deal with that asshole."

I manage a smile. "I'm so glad you're here."

"Me too. I was on my way into the diner and saw the cops here. I didn't know what to think . . ." He lets out a shaky breath, then leans down and plants a soft kiss on my forehead. "I'm just glad you're both okay."

Barnes clears his throat, and we all retreat to the kitchen, though I keep Finn in my line of sight. The rookie is patient as I recount as much of the story as possible, already doubting myself when I can't recall exact times, precise phrasing.

Finally, he leaves us with a grim "We'll do what we can, but I can't promise anything."

Sawyer locks the door behind him, and suddenly the house is silent. Finn is still sleeping peacefully, oblivious to the chaos of this night. But inside me, fear and frustration threaten to bubble out. Calling the police was a mistake. I should've known that.

I stare out the kitchen window, the colorful flowers we hung yesterday now looking dull and lifeless somehow.

Someone is after me. I can feel it, almost as if they're out there now, watching. And they know about my past. I drop my head onto my arms in despair.

Sawyer clears his throat, and I startle, looking up at him. He's leaning against the counter, watching me with the same worried look he's had since he got here. The kiss we shared seems so long ago now, a fairy tale in the harsh light of this frightening morning. "I suppose you need to get to work." I close my eyes, steel myself for him to walk away, physically and emotionally.

"I'm not going anywhere," Sawyer says. "Already texted my boss to let her know."

"Really?" It's so needy—I can hear it, but I can't stop it. I'm so damn tired, crashing from the adrenaline, the sleep deprivation, and the exhaustion of constant anxiety.

He walks over and places a gentle arm around my shoulder. "How about you go up and lie down for a while?"

Panicked eyes flash to the living room. "Finn."

It's irrational; I know that. But in this moment, despite the locked door, despite Sawyer's presence, the thought of letting my son out of my sight makes my hands shake. Wordlessly, Sawyer walks to the couch and scoops Finn up; then he motions to the stairs, and we walk up to my room.

I crawl into bed, and Sawyer lays Finn gently down next to me. My son rolls into me instantly, and his warm little body and soft puffs of breath are a balm to my soul. I wrap my arms around him as Sawyer silently pulls the blanket up over us. But when I close my eyes, my mind swirls with nightmarish images of who might be out there, watching, planning their next move.

My eyes fly open. "Wait."

Sawyer stops, hand on the doorknob, and turns around.

"Don't go," I whisper. "Please."

He stands, uncertain, then silently walks around to the other side of the bed and eases onto it, sitting with his back against the headboard.

I let out a breath, close my eyes.

Only then do I sleep.

I'm deep in the darkness of sleep when I hear a bloodcurdling scream. I bolt awake in the inky-black night, blinking around my bedroom trying to orient myself to my surroundings. It's silent around me except for the whirring of the one working fan in the entire trailer, so the scream must have been part of a terrible nightmare. Then I hear a second scream and I gasp, stumbling out of bed. I clutch for my phone and click on the flashlight app.

"Mitch?" I whisper, but he's not here. Of course not—if he were here, I would've known it because he's only here when he wants one thing. I hear voices outside the bedroom door, shouts and murmurs, so I shrug into my hoodie and jeans and quietly open the door.

Down the dark hallway, I can see a lamp on in the living room, and my first thought is that it must be battery powered. Which is pretty sad and shows how long we've gone without electricity, because there's also a bleeding man sitting in a chair in the middle of the living room. I gasp, registering this gruesome sight. Rex steps into view, getting up in the man's face and saying something I can't hear.

Slowly, I creep out of the room and down the hallway, feet padding as softly as possible as I try to hear what they're saying. Rex hauls back and slugs the man, who cries out again—and his chair tips and he goes toppling to the floor. Lying there, his blood-soaked face comes into view, frightened eyes locking onto mine. "Help me," he cries frantically. "Please!"

I freeze as Rex whirls around, more rage in his face than I've ever seen.

Oh God. He's going to kill me. I'm more sure of it in this moment than I've ever been of anything in my life.

Out of the shadows bolts Mitch, running at me and shoving me back into the bedroom. I fall against the bed as he slams the door shut. "What the hell are you doing, Iris? You know you're not supposed to come out when we're working."

"But I heard screams . . . and that man." The full gravity of what I saw hits me with sickening force, and I look up at Mitch, wide eyed. "What are *you* doing?"

"None of your fucking business."

"But we got arrested last week," I say, panicking at the memory of Mitch shoving baggies in my purse when he knew he was being pulled over, one more trauma added to so many. "You said you would lay low for a while."

"Don't worry about it," he says through gritted teeth. "It's nothing you're smart enough to understand."

"Mitch—"

Without warning he raises his hand and strikes me across the mouth. The pain explodes through my face. It never hurts any less, no matter how many times he does it. He stares me down. "You always make me do this, don't you?" Then he grabs my phone, drops it on the floor, and smashes it under his boot. "Don't come out again."

He stalks out, and I crawl into bed, curl up as tightly as I can into myself, trying to drown out the screams. I remind myself that Mitch loves me. Tomorrow he'll apologize. Tomorrow will be different. It will be better.

It has to be.

CHAPTER SEVENTEEN

My sleep is a cavernous black hole, and when my eyes open, the sun is high in the sky and I'm alone in bed. Memories of last night flood back, and I bolt up into a sitting position. But before I can fully panic, my eyes land on a note propped up on the end table: *Come down for breakfast.* I smile as I push myself out of bed and make my way downstairs, the scents of bacon and coffee blending delectably as I walk into the kitchen.

Finn sits at the bar with his back to me as Sawyer stands in his usual spot at the stove. Warmth rushes over me again at the thought that they look so natural there. Sawyer turns to put fresh bacon on Finn's plate and sees me. "Hey, you're up."

Finn turns around with a grin. "You slept until *noon*, Mom."

"Whoa." I rub my eyes. "I think that means I need extra coffee today, right?"

Sawyer is already filling a cup, God bless him, and he sets it down on the bar. I scoot onto the stool next to Finn and plant a kiss on his head. We're silent, and it's almost as if nothing has happened. We eat and laugh like it's normal, until Finn announces he's going to jump on the trampoline. "No," I say quickly.

Sawyer raises his eyebrows, and Finn whines, "Why not? You always let me."

"Well, not today. Not until I can go out there with you." He glowers at me, and I sigh. "How about some extra tablet time instead?"

That brightens his spirits, and he races into the living room, where the tablet is charging.

I turn to Sawyer, and there's that concerned look again. For some reason it annoys me now, so I take a long slug of coffee. "What?" I say at last.

"How are you feeling?"

"I'm okay. Just rattled, and really wanting to know who has it out for me."

He frowns. "What exactly did the voice say last night?"

I shudder at the memory. "It said, 'You didn't save me, Iris. You ran away and left me behind.'"

"Whoa." Sawyer blows out a breath. "Do you have any idea who might say something like that?" At first I say nothing, but my face must give me away because his eyes widen. "Wait—*do* you?"

"Sort of." He furrows his brow, and I take a deep breath. "My ex. But . . . he's dead."

His eyes soften. "I'm sorry." He gently places his hand on mine. "I didn't know."

I shake my head, try to tell him there's no need to be sorry, but a wave of emotion hits me out of nowhere, terrible memories flooding back, and a sob escapes. Sawyer rushes around the bar to sit next to me, his arm around my shoulder. "You don't understand," I say, my voice breaking. "He wasn't . . . I'm not . . . It was the worst time of my life."

He turns toward me, brushing my hair back. "Do you want to talk about it?"

I don't, not at all. The only people in the world I've ever told about my painful past are the Gordons. I've known Sawyer only a few days, and I'm not sure I'm ready to share this part of me, the sadness and shame. But the way he's looking at me now, with so much concern—the way he's treated Finn with so much care and patience, the way he kisses me as if I'm the most cherished person in the world—he has to be for real.

So I take the chance.

I creep over to the kitchen doorway and peek into the living room, making sure that Finn is engrossed in a video game and out of earshot. When I sit back down, I tell my painful story. "When I moved here eight years ago, I was pregnant with Finn. A lot of people know that. But what they don't know is that I was running away. Finn's father . . . he wasn't good to me. I was scared all the time."

Sawyer's jaw tightens. "He hit you?"

I look down. "He did a lot of things. He was a terrible person, and he hung around a lot of bad people. One day there was a problem with a . . . deal that went wrong." I swallow back bile from my own phrasing. "There was an accident."

My eyes squeeze shut as I hear the sickening crunch, see the blood, so much blood, but not my own. I take a deep breath, try to force the images away, but tears leak from my eyes.

A warm hand gently wipes one away, and I open my eyes and stare into Sawyer's kind gaze. "If it's too hard to talk about it, you don't have to," he says gently.

I draw a quivering breath. "I just want you to know why I did what I did. When he died, it was my chance to escape. I . . . ran away."

Recognition fills his eyes. "And you think that's what the voice is talking about?"

I nod. "But I *know* Mitch is dead. I looked up the obituary online a few weeks later, just to be sure."

Sawyer nods slowly, a thoughtful look on his face. "You've been through a lot," he says finally. I wait, puzzled, as he continues his pensive gaze at a spot on the wall behind me. He takes a deep breath, and when his eyes meet mine, they're cautious. "Do you think it might be why you're hearing the voice?"

I stiffen, retracting my hand from his. "What do you mean?"

"I mean that grief and trauma can really mess with a person."

"You don't believe me," I say incredulously.

He holds up his hands in defense. "No, it's not that—God, I'm sorry; that came out all wrong." He takes a deep breath, his eyes pained. "Look, after I lost my wife, I used to hear her voice sometimes, too. When I first woke up in the morning, or when I'd come home from work, it was almost like I could hear her calling to me. The grief counselor told me that's totally normal. As the years went by, I realized that now I hear her voice whenever Natalie speaks. It's a gift, really."

Emotions swirl within me. "I'm very sorry about your wife," I say, fighting to keep my voice even, "but this isn't the same. I don't *want* to hear Mitch's voice. And the thought of Finn being like him . . ." My voice breaks, and I put a hand to my mouth. It's my nightmare that my sweet baby boy finds out about his terrible father—or worse, follows in his footsteps somehow.

"Hey," Sawyer says gently, "Finn is a great kid. He's going to be a great person because he's like *you*." He tentatively reaches for my hand again, and I let him. "I'm sorry, I shouldn't have said all that. I promise I'm on your side here. I'm only trying to help."

"I know," I say. "But the help I need right now is figuring out who that voice belongs to. You heard the police—they basically said they're not doing anything."

His brow furrows. "What do *you* plan to do?"

I sigh. "I don't know yet. I just know I want answers."

Suddenly Finn bounds back into the kitchen.

"Hey, buddy—were you listening to us talking?" I ask nervously.

He wrinkles his nose at the thought of listening to a boring grown-up conversation. "No." Then his eyes—and interest—shift to Sawyer. "You said we could go fishing today."

Sawyer chuckles. "I believe I said 'if your mom's okay with it.'"

I glance outside and notice the hanging baskets. "Don't we need to keep getting things ready for tomorrow's dinner?"

"We'll have time," Sawyer says, and when I turn back to them, they're both eyeing me expectantly—ganging up on me again, which is totally unfair. Plus, I really don't have room for more anxiety right now, and if Finn goes fishing, I'll be worried all day about him falling into the water and drowning. "I don't think I want him out in a boat."

"I was going to let him fish off the shore at Weber Lake." Sawyer smiles. "They stock it for the kids."

"Oh," I say, considering. "You know what? That sounds great."

Finn whoops with joy. "Are you gonna come, Mom?"

"It would be good to get some fresh air," Sawyer says. "Nat's coming, too."

My eyes darken. "Is Cole going?"

Sawyer's face matches mine. "No. He had a friend pick him up last night, so for all I know, he's already back in Minneapolis."

I smile in relief as I hear the creak of the mudroom door, and Natalie walks in.

"Hey, Nat, you ready for some fishing?" Sawyer asks brightly. "Finn's coming, too."

She looks down, saying nothing, and he presses on. "Remember you said you'd go if I agreed to add an extra half hour to your curfew?" Sawyer forces a smile. "Please?"

"Fine." She glances up, then quickly turns away, but not before I see her red eyes.

"Do you have a fishing rod for Finn?" I ask Sawyer.

"Yeah, there's a bunch in the garage."

"Would you mind getting that while I pack him some snacks?"

He walks out, and I pack up a travel cooler, my eyes flitting to Natalie scrolling on her phone at the table, her back to me. "How was work?" I ask.

"Same old bullshit."

I ignore the cursing, saying wryly, "Was it Brayden or Frank?"

There's a beat of silence, and she sets her phone down. "Fucking Brayden."

I cringe, walking over to the table to sit next to her. "I'm going to pretend you didn't say that. Mostly because I completely understand." She gives me the slightest of smiles. "So what happened?"

"The news editor wanted ideas for a feature series. I did so much research on the trafficking going on at local hotels." My eyes bulge from hearing her say it so casually, this terrible evil that I've witnessed in my past. But Natalie shrugs defiantly, and I admire her courage. "My friend's cousin almost got abducted last month. It was scary as hell. After that, I looked up a bunch of stuff online, and I printed it off before the meeting. When I went to the printer, Brayden was looking at one of the pages. Guess what he brought up right away at the meeting?"

"That *asshole*," I say before I catch myself, but maybe I would've said it anyway. Because sometimes there's no other word.

"I should just quit." She says it like it doesn't matter, but I see the hurt in her eyes. She really does care about this internship. And she's *good* at it.

"Please don't," I say softly. "Natalie, you are amazing at this job. Everyone there knows it, including Kallie"—the news editor—"and Mr. Gordon, too."

Her eyes flit to me, and for a moment she's a little girl soaking up praise, but then her scowl returns. "Yeah, a lot of good that does me if Brayden steals my ideas."

"Look, I'm no expert when it comes to careers, but from my little bit of experience, I can tell you that Brayden will be found out for what he is: a phony."

"What do you mean?"

"It was *your* idea, and *you've* done the research. He hasn't done anything. So when Kallie starts giving out assignments, that's your chance to say you had a similar idea, and then lay out your plan to execute it. Brayden won't know what hit him." I'm surprised at the venom in my voice, but I'm tired of men taking a woman's power away—whether it's stealing an idea at work or holding them under their thumbs at home.

Natalie looks at me, so young and vulnerable, like a version of my past self longing for a second chance. "You can do it," I say quietly.

She nods, sitting up straighter. "Okay."

"Okay, what?" Sawyer asks, walking back into the room.

"Nothing," Natalie says quickly, her eyes darting to me for confirmation. I smile and give a quick nod, and her shoulders sag in relief. Then she stands. "I'm, uh, going to go get ready."

As she leaves, I stand to finish packing the cooler. But when I turn, Sawyer is looking at me with a half smile on his face. "What?" I ask.

"I heard you two talking."

I shrug. "I don't know what you mean." Then I hesitate—if Natalie were *my* child, I wouldn't want someone keeping secrets about her from me. Especially someone I have a bit of a crush on—okay, a big crush on. I take a deep breath. "I don't mean to hide anything from you. I just want her to trust me. It's a work problem, but she plans to handle it on her own."

He nods. "You'll let me know if I need to have any words with anybody, right?"

My mouth twitches. "By *words*, I assume you mean *fisticuffs*?"

A deep, rumbling chuckle escapes him, and it warms me all over. "Do people actually say *fisticuffs* anymore?"

I shrug, laughing. "I'm not sure they ever did."

We smile at each other; then suddenly he reaches for my hand. "Hey, thank you," he says. "For talking to her, I mean."

The warmth spreads further, his hand strong and solid in mine. "Of course," I say. He gives my hand a quick squeeze, then releases it, and I turn to call to Finn in the living room: "Hey, buddy, make sure you go potty before you go!" I hear his little feet scamper toward the bathroom, and I add a hasty, "And wash your hands!"

Sawyer shoots me a quizzical look. "You're not coming?"

I bite my lip. Whatever Sawyer or the police think, the voice I've been hearing was not my imagination. And if they go fishing without me, it'll give me a chance to dig into whatever's going on. "I'm still kind of tired," I say. "I think I'll stay home, if you don't mind."

"Sure," he says, crossing his arms and eyeing me suspiciously. "But are you really tired, or are you staying so you can look for answers?"

Busted. I flash the best grin I can. "Both?"

His eyes twinkle and he leans in, kissing me softly, then pulls back to whisper, "Just don't do anything dangerous. Please?"

"I won't," I say, not sure I mean it.

CHAPTER EIGHTEEN

When they're gone, I'm alone in the house, alone with my thoughts, and that's never a good thing. For once, I'm not worried about Finn—he's 100 percent safe with Sawyer, and that makes me smile. My smile fades, though, as my thoughts return to last night.

To the voice.

Someone seems to know about my past. My mind swirls with every frightening possibility, from the ghost of Emma Miller to my ex somehow being alive to one of his vicious friends out for revenge. I shudder, gazing out at the golden prairie, as vast and endless as my fears.

But suddenly it occurs to me that someone else entirely could know about my past somehow. Yes, I've only ever told the Gordons what I went through in Minnesota with Mitch and his scary friends who constantly crashed at our place, showed up high or shot or needing to hide from the police. There's no way the Gordons told anyone intentionally—they would never do anything to hurt Finn or me. But accidents happen. Secrets slip out. Maybe Lowell hasn't been as careful as I thought.

Or maybe *I* haven't. I'm not exactly super skilled at stealth; I've just done a damn good job of being a loner—I have no family, I fled to an entirely new state without telling anyone, I changed my name, and I was lucky enough that my bosses/landlords went along with it all. I've also managed to avoid an online presence—no social media except for a bare-bones

Facebook account (username Iris J.; no profile picture) I begrudgingly created when Finn started preschool because his teacher encouraged me to join the local mom group—and Finn's media-release forms from school and youth sports never get signed. No, my son's image will *not* be appearing in your brochures or on your Facebook page, thank you very much.

Not a foolproof plan, but it's worked so far. At least I think it has.

It's time I find out for sure. With a sigh, I grab my phone and call Lowell, who answers on the third ring. "Ah, Iris. How are you? How are things at the lodge?"

"Fine," I say automatically, then sigh. "Well, not great, actually."

"Is something wrong? Is it Finn?"

"He's okay," I say quickly, sorry that I've worried him.

"Glad to hear it. Oh, and I'm sorry I forgot to mention a few things—like the dinner coming up tomorrow night. It doesn't have to be a huge event, just a nice meal for some potential buyers. Sawyer should be able to help out. I hope he's been taking care of things for you."

My mind flashes to our kisses, and my face reddens as if Lowell can read my thoughts. "Uh, yes, he's been taking care of a lot of things. I mean—the right amount of things." I take a breath, blow it out. "Anyway, I was actually calling about something else. You know that old box of toys you keep in the closet?"

"The toys?" He chuckles. "Sure, I remember those."

"Well, Finn found a walkie-talkie—only one, for some reason. So I guess, first of all, do you know where the other one is?"

He sucks in a breath through his teeth, as if thinking hard. "Boy, I really couldn't say . . . no one's played with those toys in years. Why do you ask?"

I swallow. "It's just that . . . well, I've been hearing things."

"Hearing what?"

I squeeze my eyes shut, go for broke. "A voice coming from the walkie-talkie at night, saying strange things to me."

"What? Iris, are you sure you're okay? Do I need to come home? I'm sure I can get a flight this evening—my niece says she'll drive me to the airport whenever I'm ready."

"No, no, don't worry about it," I say quickly. He sounds utterly flustered, and I feel bad for getting him worked up. "It took me by surprise, is all." I take a deep breath. I'm *definitely* not telling him about the police visit, at least for now, but I've come this far—I need to press on. "Look, some of the words I heard almost make it sound like someone knows about my past. You didn't . . . you and Ivan never told anyone, right? I mean, maybe accidentally, or—"

"Iris." He says it so firmly that I stop talking. When he continues, his voice is gentle. "Ivan never told a soul. I haven't, either, and I never will. You and Finn are always safe with us, dear."

My shoulders sag in relief. "I know," I say quietly. "I'm sorry for even asking. I just wasn't sure if something had slipped out, or if maybe someone was eavesdropping or something."

"Hmm," he says. "I admit I'm getting a little more forgetful these days." I cringe but keep listening. "I came in Monday morning, and my office door was open because I'd forgotten to lock it over the weekend. I don't keep valuables there, of course, but I do keep personnel files. And I only mention this because a file drawer was open—I remember because I banged my shin on the darn thing."

A small warning bell sounds in my mind, still too soft for me to get its full impact, but it sets me on alert. "What's in *my* personnel file?" I ask wearily. They'd kept everything off the books for me—maybe I was naive, but I thought it was enough.

"We were keeping it for—for when we . . ." He sighs. "For when we're both gone."

A pang of pain, but fear is pressing past it. "What's in my file, Lowell?"

"It's not in *your* file. It's in mine. It's my will, Iris. If I'm going to leave you everything, it needs to go to your name. But I'm also recommending a damn fine attorney that should help keep things quiet enough for you. The file has your real name, your Social Security number, and your last known address."

My head spins, love and fear combining. They've done so much to protect me, to protect Finn. "Wow, I don't know what to say . . . thank you . . ." I trail off, though, because God, what a fool I've been to think I can keep all this a secret.

He seems to sense this. "I'm sorry, Iris," Lowell says softly. "Do you really think someone might have found it?"

I force a deep, calming breath, though my hand shakes. "It's okay, it's not your fault. And I don't know. I . . . need to figure things out."

"I'll help you—I'll be home tomorrow night, okay? We'll figure it out together."

"Okay," I say, though I'm already mentally preparing my next step.

"And I'm sorry again about that walkie-talkie." He scoffs. "That's so odd. I can't believe it even works anymore."

"What do you mean?"

"I would think the batteries would be dead by now," he muses.

We hang up, and something cold settles inside me. Someone had to have changed the batteries. Someone might have dug into my file and Lowell's, looking for information.

It's right there, inside my brain, but I can't figure it out.

I pace the room, but whatever the thought is, it won't come. I walk through the main floor, and in the living room my eyes fall on the walkie-talkie. A burst of anger flares within me. *Damn you*, I think, glaring at this tiny little contraption. Damn you for taking the nighttime away from me, for stealing my darkness, my time of solace and peace, and replacing it with fear and sadness. Suddenly I can't look at it—I need for it to be gone. Part of me wants to walk outside and heave it into a cornfield, but I restrain myself.

In a flash of brilliance, I grab it, race up the stairs and directly into Lowell's office, take out the damn batteries, and place it on the desk with a thud.

"There," I say, nodding my head for good measure. I want it out of sight—even if I end up closing the office door, I want to know it's powerless and hidden away, where it can't hurt anyone, in theory at least.

I slide open drawers, looking for one that has space for the handheld radio, and when I open the drawer with the old photos, I flinch at the black-and-white faces. But there's plenty of room in this one, so I pull the drawer open all the way, preparing to place it inside. It sticks a little, like there's something in the back. I give it a strong pull, and it dislodges whatever was wedged in place—I look and it's an off-white file folder, now kinked in the corner where it was stuck. I hesitate, then take it out, folding it open.

Inside are more black-and-white photos, but these are pictures of a man and a boy—standing in front of the house, inside a church, out in the field. I peer closely and finally recognize that the man, though older, is the same as in the other photos—Jacob Miller. That must mean the boy is the baby, Reuben, though he looks about Natalie's age in these photos.

But where is Emma?

Her absence chills me for a reason I can't explain, my paranoia and exhaustion combining to create a spidery web of thoughts until I'm convinced something terrible happened to her—that she was a victim of her bleak surroundings, alone and cut off from civilization out on this endless wasteland of a prairie.

Did Emma also hear voices in the night? And if she couldn't handle it, how can I?

The deep buzz of my phone rattling on the desk startles me, but at least it stops my spiraling thoughts. I steady my breathing and pick it up, frowning in confusion. It's Lowell again. "Hello?"

"Iris, I remembered something."

He sounds excited, almost proud of himself, but I'm still rattled by my discovery, and I cut him off. "The photos in your office—where did they come from?"

"What?"

"I . . . I went into the office—I'm sorry, I hope that's okay—but I found these old photos of the original owners." I pause for a breath after my flurry of words. "Do you know anything about them?"

"Ah, that sounds familiar. Ivan collected a lot of antiques, as you know. I'd have to see the photos, but I do remember he was working on a research project a few years back. I think he was hoping to run some sort of historical series for the newspaper."

I swallow. "Do you know what happened to the mom? Did she go missing?"

I hear his sigh through the phone. "Oh, Iris, I'm not sure about that. But I do know that my Ivan was drawn to that sort of thing. He wanted to right wrongs. Always watching out for injustices, especially people who lived through trauma like he did."

My brow furrows. "What do you mean 'like he did'?"

He pauses, seeming to choose his words carefully. "It's a story for another time. Maybe we can talk about it when I get home?"

"Of course," I say quickly. Then: "I'm sorry for interrupting—what were you going to say?"

"Last Monday morning someone was sitting in my office, waiting to talk to me."

My eyes widen, back on full alert. "Who?"

There's a pause, and I hold my breath. "Brayden."

It's as if the room goes silent. As if all the air has been sucked out of this space—replaced by my own deep rage.

"I have to go," I say suddenly, ending the call. I grab the walkie-talkie out of the drawer and rush downstairs and out to my car.

As I pull out of the driveway, furious thoughts swirl through my mind.

Brayden, who is trying desperately to prove himself to Lowell. Brayden, who clearly hates me. Brayden, who would do anything to earn a ticket back to the big leagues in Minneapolis, no matter whom he has to step on.

Brayden is behind this.

CHAPTER NINETEEN

The ten-minute drive takes me only seven and a half minutes, and I spend the entire time gripping my white knuckles around the steering wheel, darting my eyes from the road to the walkie-talkie—which I tossed onto the passenger seat before squealing out of the driveway—and convincing myself that Brayden is absolutely 100 percent guilty.

My blood boils as I picture his smug smile, his condescending tone grating in my ears. I pull into the parking lot practically vibrating with fury, and I stride into the newsroom sucking in deep breaths so I don't go in guns blazing.

It doesn't work.

Something about the adrenaline and stress, the sleep deprivation and exhaustion from constantly being on edge, whips my severe anxiety into a frenzy. When I get like this, it's hard to calm down; usually, I'm able to spend time weeding my flowers, or shut myself in my room, with my comfort movie turned up loud to drown out my sobs.

But today I don't have my crutches. Today I stalk across the newsroom and slam the walkie-talkie onto Brayden's desk. He jumps, pushing back from his keyboard and glaring at me. "Iris, what the hell is this?"

"You tell me, Brayden. What the hell *is* this?"

He raises his eyebrows, an annoyed look on his face. "Uh, it's a radio. Anything else I can help you with?"

"Where's the other one?" I ask.

"What?"

"Where is it, Brayden?" My voice rises, and I realize that the rest of the newsroom staff members are watching us.

"How the hell should I know? Jesus, Iris, some of us have work to do."

"Bullshit!" I yell, and the sports reporter behind him abruptly stops typing, craning his neck to see what's up. Frank rolls his chair closer, making no effort to hide the fact that he's trying to get a better view of the show. I lean in closer to Brayden, speaking in a low but scathing voice: "I know you've been messing with me. I know you went through Mr. Gordon's files and you're trying to use my past against me."

Brayden blinks. "What the *hell* are you talking about, Iris?"

Something about the way he's looking at me—part horror, part fascination—cracks through my anxiety-fueled rage, and I pull back, suddenly unsure. The newsroom is now deathly silent, not even the click-clack of keyboards or the murmur of phone interviews in the background. All eyes—and ears—are on us.

I can feel my face reddening, and I struggle to salvage this train wreck. "Uh, I mean, I . . ."

Brayden seems to sense my weakness and pounces, like a predator smelling blood on its prey. "You seriously believe that I'm, like, searching through files and trying to find dirt on you for some reason? Like I'm threatened or something—by *you*, of all people?" His voice is slow and incredulous, and he breaks into a smile as he leans toward me. "Wow, Iris, I mean, everyone knows you're a paranoid weirdo, but I didn't realize you were a full-on delusional conspiracy theorist."

A soft chuckle erupts behind me, and I whip around, seeing two young copy editors quickly ducking their heads. Down the hall, Alice from advertising is peeking around the corner, probably trying to get the scoop on who's losing it in the latest round of newsroom drama.

Kallie, my news-editor friend, shoots me a confused, concerned look from behind her desk and mouths, "What are you doing?" I turn away, frozen in mortification and on display like a museum exhibit, flaws fully exposed.

Brayden gleefully continues: "Okay, there are so many layers to this; like, why would I even *care*? And why would I mess with Mr. Gordon's favorite—I mean, God, you're like the poor, sad little puppy he feels obligated to take care of." I wince, and Frank covers his mouth in faux shock, which seems to make Brayden's smug smile even bigger.

There's a beat where I'm at my low point, sunken into the ground, all eyes on me, everyone laughing. *Everyone knows you're a paranoid weirdo.*

Brayden goes in for the kill. "And I mean, Jesus, Iris, if I really *wanted* to get dirt on you, haven't you heard of Google? I thought even *you* were smart enough to realize anyone can find shit on the internet."

I squeeze my eyes shut. *Worthless.*

But along with my mom's voice, I hear Mitch's, too. *You're not smart enough.* It's something he would always say whenever I'd question him, whenever I'd have an opinion. He'd follow it up with only a slap if I was lucky, much more if I was not.

Something cracks within me, and my eyes fly open. *No more.*

Without thinking, I pick up Brayden's desk-side trash can and in one swift move, flip it over, dumping the contents onto his head. "There," I say calmly as what looks like the lid from a yogurt container slides down his shirt. "Now you're with the rest of the garbage."

I turn to go but catch Kallie's eye. "By the way, that trafficking-project idea? It was Natalie's. This asshole stole it." Her eyes widen, and I look back to see Brayden's face go pale.

Then I stride across the newsroom and out the door.

CHAPTER TWENTY

In my car, I stare at the steering wheel until it blurs in my vision. All the fight saps out of me, adrenaline oozing away as I think about all that Brayden said and what it means.

On some level I knew that nobody liked me—I even thrived on it. It meant I was sticking to my ideals, that I didn't care what anyone thought. I do what's right for me and Finn, and to hell with everyone else.

But the thing is, I *do* care. It's human nature. And it hurts like hell to find out you are generally disliked as a person. All of us ache to belong, to feel loved and accepted.

That will never happen for me here. Now I know I can never come back.

I drive, numb, nothing but city streets, the blur of cars, the red, yellow, green of stoplights. I cruise through town for what seems like hours but might only be minutes, nowhere to go, my head a jumbled mess. I pass bar after bar with nary a blink.

It's difficult to find a place to dull the pain when one has been sober for years.

Finally, I pull into the parking lot of the old Perkins. I trudge inside, and the hostess seats me quickly, a nice quiet booth in the back corner, and I order coffee and pie. The waitress—bleached blonde and probably incredibly pretty about fifteen years ago, now aging but trying to hide it, like most of us are—sets a steaming mug and heaping plate in front of me with a thin smile, then retreats.

I stare down at it, sniffing a hint of weak brew blending with chocolate cream. I don't plan on touching it, but I need a reason to stay. A reason to be left alone, to fade away.

I sit in silence, sipping the coffee amid muted restaurant chatter. My waitress tops it off. Still I sit, alone.

Finally, a presence, but it's not my waitress stopping to top off my coffee. "Hey, Iris. I thought that was you."

I look up into the smiling face of Jane—the kind woman from the literary luncheon. She slides into the booth across from me, setting her cane gently against the table.

"Oh." I blink, sitting up straight. "Hi."

She beams at me, her black hair shiny under the fluorescents. "What are you up to today? Where's Finn?"

I force a smile. "He's fishing. With Sawyer."

She raises her eyebrows, her smile even bigger somehow. "That's wonderful. So how's that going? You two seem to be hitting it off."

I smile, my mood instantly lifting at the mention of my budding relationship with Sawyer. "It's going well. Really well, actually. But, I mean, I've only known him a few days," I add quickly.

"Yeah, but it's different when you're our age, you know? Like, we're old enough to cut through all the bullshit. We know what we want, and when we've found it."

"That makes sense." I nod, my feelings now justified. *So it's totally normal that I'm completely falling for him already.* The sweet thought makes me reach for my fork, and taking a sugary bite of pie gives me the energy to speak more. "Do you know Sawyer pretty well?"

"Only through your typical parenting channels. My older son is in the same grade as Natalie. He's always seemed like a nice guy, and a good dad."

I smile, my insides warming at this confirmation. "I think so, too."

"Of course, dads get more credit, don't they?" Jane tosses a wry look across the room, where I assume her family is sitting, before turning to me again. "I can *guarantee* you that my husband is currently getting approving looks from old folks around the restaurant thinking, 'Wow, what a great dad for taking the kids out to eat by himself.' But a mom would get a disapproving, 'Why can't she keep those little brats quiet' type of look."

I nod in agreement. "And dads get believed more, too. I mean, I wouldn't know, but when I first suspected Finn had allergies, I had the hardest time convincing the pediatrician to refer us to an allergist. I was so upset that Ivan called for me, pretending to be Finn's dad from out of town."

"Let me guess—they referred him immediately?"

"Yes, because it was an authoritative dad calling and not a shrill, anxious mom."

Jane scoffs. "Men, am I right?"

I sigh. "Yep."

We both chuckle, and I'm relaxed now as we ease into conversation—from more parenting woes to gardening and everything in between. Jane is kind and easy to talk to. I talk more about Finn's food allergies, and a little more about how it's been going at the lodge.

"You thought it was a rattlesnake?" she says, though she can barely get the words out because she's laughing so hard.

I sigh, though I chuckle as well. "It was not my finest moment."

In turn, Jane tells me a little more about her life, how she moved to South Dakota from the Chicago area for college and then stayed after she met her husband. Now she works as executive director of the local domestic violence shelter.

"That's amazing," I say, in awe.

"Thanks," she says. "How about you? Where are you from?"

I shove a bite of pie into my mouth, giving myself time to prepare my abbreviated version of my past. "Well, I, uh, I moved here from Minnesota after my grandma passed away. I'd just gone through a breakup and wanted a fresh start. Little did I know I was pregnant with Finn. Luckily, I started working for the Gordons, and they were so supportive."

"Ivan sat on our board of directors for many years," Jane says softly. "He was a good man."

"Yes, he was," I acknowledge sadly.

"And I really admire you for being a single mom," she adds. "I'm sure that's not easy."

I smile, though I'm cringing inwardly, knowing the G-rated version of my past that I've told her paints me in a better light than I deserve. "Finn's my whole world," I tell her, because that is 100 percent the truth.

Jane tucks her hair behind her ear. "So, everything's okay, then? You looked a little sad when I first saw you sitting over here."

"I'm fine," I say automatically, then sigh—I really need to stop doing that. I set my fork down. Maybe I could try the truth for once. "Actually, I had a rough time at work today. Not the lodge—my full-time job, at least for now, is working as an administrative assistant at the newspaper."

Her brow furrows. "What do you mean 'for now'?"

I hesitate. The last thing I want to do is break Lowell's trust, but Jane is so kind, and it's been so long since I've had someone to talk to like this—the allure of friendship is too strong. "*Please* don't say anything, but I heard a rumor there might be layoffs. That's one of the main reasons I'm trying out this potential new job at the lodge."

"Oh no," she says sympathetically. "I won't say a word, but I'm very sorry to hear that."

"Thanks," I say softly.

"So, that's what has you down today?"

"Actually, there's more." I take a deep breath, unsure how much truth to let out. "I had an argument with one of the reporters. Like, a huge, loud argument that everyone overheard." I frown, the exchange still fresh, Brayden's scathing words flooding back with a vengeance. "God, he's just such a . . . a—"

"A dick?" Jane asks, one eyebrow raised. I nod, mouth twitching into a smile, and she shakes her head. "Well, I'm sorry you had to deal with that."

A rush of self-consciousness hits, and I take a deep breath. "Some of the things he said . . . well, they really hit home. I mean, I know what I'm like. I know I'm a lot to deal with. Not many people like me, and the fact that I can't let things go. But it's still hard to hear it coming from someone like him."

Jane frowns. "Iris, nobody's perfect. You might see only your flaws, but what I see is someone who is honest and caring." She shrugs. "If this Brayden guy or anyone else can't see that, then it's their loss."

Tears push at my eyes. "Thank you," I whisper.

"Maybe it would be a good thing to work at the lodge full-time," Jane says. "So you had a bit of a reptile issue—so what?" She waves her hand dismissively, and I laugh again. "Beyond that, how are things going overall? Are you enjoying it?"

"I really am. I was nervous for the event the other night, but it ended up being a lot of fun. Honestly, I could see that being something I could do permanently. And I think living out there would be a wonderful move for Finn and me. But . . ."

"But?"

I shove a chunk of pie in my mouth to buy some time again. Will she think I'm unhinged if I tell her about the voice? Jane waits, her kind eyes watching me, and I can't imagine her judging me. Here goes. "I've been hearing weird things at night."

Jane raises her eyebrows. "What kind of weird things?"

I take a slug of coffee before answering. "Like, sounds coming from this old walkie-talkie in the middle of the night."

"An old walkie-talkie?"

"It was in this box of old toys Finn found."

"Hmm . . . old house, a lot of old stuff . . . I feel like I would be pretty creeped out living there, too, especially alone with my child."

I nod vigorously. "I mean, it's a wonderful house in so many ways, but there's a definite creep factor to it." I tell her about the ancient photos and Emma Miller's sad, piercing gaze—and the fact that she was missing from later photos.

"Yikes." Jane shivers. "You sure that place isn't haunted?"

My shoulders sag. "I'm not sure of anything. I feel like I can't even trust myself, since I'm the only one hearing the noises." I look up into her sympathetic face and shake my head. "I'm sorry, I'm babbling. I know how I sound."

"You sound like someone who has a concern and is talking to a friend about it, that's all." *Friend.* Warmth spreads through me at her use of the word, and when Jane smiles at me, I smile back.

"So do you have any idea what to do about these noises?" she asks.

I sigh. "For now, I took out the batteries."

"Smart," she says. "Problem solved." Then her phone beeps and she glances down, then across the room. I follow her gaze and see a man wave sheepishly from a booth, where he sits with two kids eating their meals. She waves back and turns back to me. "I'm sorry—I want to hear more about this, but I'd better get back over there. Can we have coffee again? I mean, for real this time, not me barging into your booth."

We both laugh. "That sounds wonderful," I say, beaming.

"Maybe this weekend? Kids optional, though a playdate for Dante and Finn would be great." She cocks her head to the side. "Or drinks tonight, if you're up for it?"

"Coffee would be great because I don't drink, actually," I say awkwardly. "Plus, Sawyer has been watching Finn all day, so I really owe him big-time."

Jane winks, grinning mischievously. "Hmm, maybe you'll find a way to thank him."

I gasp, then giggle, blushing. "Let's not get ahead of ourselves."

When Jane walks away, I smile as I watch her go, feeling lighter. I pay for my coffee and pie and am reaching my car when my phone buzzes—a text from Sawyer. We're home. Where are you?

I type a response: Ran some errands. On my way!

The sun is dipping low as I drive back across the prairie. It's been a terrible day, by most accounts. I'm no closer to finding the source of the voice—if there truly *is* a voice—and yet I made a true friend, an ally, and somehow that makes everything more bearable.

CHAPTER

TWENTY-ONE

I pull into the driveway and park the car, then step out into a haze of twilight. I breathe in the scent of the open prairie, all fresh air and moist grass, frogs singing to me from the distance, then walk toward the house and climb the steps to the porch.

"Hey, Iris."

I jump, and Cole laughs as he leans forward out of the shadows of the porch. "What are you doing here?" I say.

There's a whoosh and a flash as he lights a cigarette, puffing it to life, illuminating his sly smile. "I'm beginning to think you don't want me around."

I'm still rattled from seeing him unexpectedly, so I take a breath, compose myself. "Sawyer said you left, and I didn't realize you were back. Are you staying longer this time?"

He smirks. "Haven't decided. And I don't think my brother needs to know where I am at all times." Something about his words doesn't sit right, and I don't know why. "But hey, I did run into a few old friends back in Minneapolis. Had some good chats. Very . . . enlightening."

There's a hint of menace in his voice, and I take a step back. Before I can say anything, the front door creaks open and Sawyer steps out, smiling at me. "You're home."

The way he says *home* warms my insides, and I beam at him. "How did Finn do?"

"Great." He scoffs. "Hell, the kid's a natural. He caught four."

I giggle, and Cole clears his throat. Sawyer glowers at him, and Cole flashes a brilliant smile. "So, you still got a place I can crash?"

"Yep," Sawyer says gruffly. "The garage is all yours."

Before Cole can respond, Sawyer takes my hand and ushers me inside. We step into the scent of warm, buttery popcorn and the sound of children's laughter. I peek into the living room, where Finn and Natalie are engaged in a lively match of some sort of video game. Finn cheers suddenly, and Natalie grins as they slap a high five.

I turn to Sawyer, melting, and his smile matches mine. "They had a lot of fun together today," he says.

"She's so patient with him," I say gratefully, sneaking another peek—and snapping a photo with my phone, in typical mom fashion—but careful not to disrupt their fun.

Sawyer motions for the kitchen, so we walk in and sit down side by side at the table. He turns to face me. "So, errands, huh?" he asks in mock suspicion.

I smile, wrinkling my nose. "Something like that." I fill him in on the phone call with Lowell and the confrontation at work.

Sawyer narrows his eyes. "I think I'd like to have a few words with this Brayden guy."

"That's sweet, but he's really not worth it. Plus, I actually think he's telling the truth—I don't think he's the one doing this."

"I don't care, he's still a piece of shit—isn't he the one Nat was talking about? And he shouldn't be talking to you like that." Sawyer looks into my eyes, searching. "You know you don't deserve to be treated that way, right?"

His words wash over me like cleansing rain, and I lean forward, place my hand on his prickly stubble, and plant a soft, tender kiss on his lips. He responds by scooting closer, placing both his hands on the sides of my face, and kissing me deeply.

"Mom, time for the movie!" Finn calls from the living room.

Sawyer and I pull apart, breathless. "Be right there," I call out.

We stand, and Sawyer grabs a large bowl of popcorn as well as a stack of smaller bowls. "You ready for a riveting viewing of *Transformers* something or other?"

I cringe. "Finn chose the movie, huh? Did Natalie get a say in it?"

"She'll be taking off soon. I'm letting her stay at her friend Maddie's house tonight." He sighs. "She said, and I quote, 'I hung out with you all day, Dad. Wasn't that enough?'"

"Oof," I say. "I realize I'm only a few years from Finn saying that, too."

"Until then, we'll be watching all the *Transformers* movies we can handle," he says, and my insides light up once again at his use of *we*.

After two bowls of popcorn and two hours of giant metal objects crashing into each other, Finn is curled up against me on the couch, sound asleep, as the credits roll. "He really got worn out today by all the fun," I say, smiling as I brush his hair back, kissing his warm forehead softly. I look over, and Sawyer is watching me from the recliner, and I can't read his expression. "What?" I ask, self-consciously.

"You're a really great mom."

More words I needed to hear, though I wave my hand dismissively. "I think the word you're looking for is *overprotective*."

"I meant what I said," he says softly.

For a moment we stare at each other, so much unspoken emotion between us. Then I break the silence. "Well, I should get him to his room."

"I got it," Sawyer says, standing. He walks over and gently lifts Finn off the couch, and I follow him upstairs. He lays Finn in bed, and I cover him up and plant a soft kiss on his forehead, then pull his bedroom door almost shut.

Back downstairs, Sawyer turns to me with a smile. "Want to sit outside with me?"

I nod and follow him out to the porch, where I gasp. He's plugged in the lights that we strung along the porch, and it makes a beautifully sparkling display. "Figured we could do a trial run," he says.

"I love it," I gush, and he looks pleased.

A blanket is draped over the swing. He motions for me to sit, and once I do, he gently drapes the blanket over my shoulders, then holds up a finger. "I'll be right back."

"Okay," I say, confused but happy as he walks into the house.

Soon he's back, carrying two steaming mugs. "I hope you like hot cocoa," he says, handing one to me.

I smile as I take it. "Of course I do. Thank you."

He eases down next to me, his arm automatically draping across the back of the swing, and I scoot toward him instinctively. We sit there—sipping our cocoa, admiring the lights and flowers, listening to the frogs singing their melodies, and watching the bright canopy of stars above us—for a long time. I'm content, the chill of the night air no match for Sawyer's solid warmth next to me. "I could sit out here forever," I murmur.

He chuckles. "Me too."

"I really like it out here. I mean, this lodge . . . I still don't know if I'm good at it, but I want to keep trying."

"I think you're doing great."

"Thanks to you," I say. "You're the one who should be running this place. You don't even need me." I laugh as I say it, but I also realize how true it is.

"No way," he says. "We make a great team."

"Well, that's definitely true." I nudge him gently with my elbow. "But really, why didn't Lowell ask you to take it over?"

Sawyer looks down. "He did."

"Oh, I'm sorry, I didn't mean—"

"No, it's fine," he says quickly. "Honestly, I was flattered, and I'd love to do it. I really love this place. But I can't afford to take any financial risks right now. I work just enough hours at the diner to get health insurance for Natalie and me. It was quite a hit financially moving back here, especially after all the . . . funeral costs."

I take his hand, give it a gentle squeeze. "If it's too hard to talk about this, you don't have to."

He smiles sadly, squeezes my hand back. "I just want to do the right thing for Natalie."

"You're a really great dad. You know that, right?"

He sighs. "I hope so. God, I love her so much." He sets his mug down and runs his hands through his hair. "She just doesn't talk to me like she used to. She doesn't talk to me much *at all* anymore. And sometimes I see her looking so sad, and I don't know what to do about it."

"Sounds like normal teenager stuff to me," I say gently. "She's a really great kid. You should be proud."

"I am." He beams, then turns to me, wrapping my hand in his. "You should be, too, you know. Finn is really smart. Maybe *he'll* be running this place someday."

I laugh, and he reaches up to brush my hair back from my face. "You are so beautiful," he whispers. "You know, it was hard to stay mad at you that first night because you were so cute and flustered."

"Oh, I had no trouble staying mad at you," I declare, and he chuckles. Then I bite my lip. "Even though it was *you* making me so flustered."

"Oh yeah?" he says, voice husky as he leans closer.

I light up from the inside all the way out as he plants soft kisses on my shoulder and up my neck before finding my mouth. Maybe it's his words or his kisses or the magic of the dark, starry sky, but I'm emboldened as I pull myself onto his lap and crush my mouth against his. He reacts instantly, gripping my hips and pulling me closer so I'm pressed against him, our bodies radiating heat, electric anticipation between us. Our kisses deepen, mouths exploring, and my head pitches back, his hungry mouth on my neck. He pulls back and I'm breathless, and when our eyes meet, an unspoken question hangs in the air. Longing courses through me, but I hesitate, breath hitching. "Maybe we should . . . I mean . . ." I trail off, unsure.

Sawyer brushes my hair back again, so gently. "We don't have to do anything you don't want to do," he says softly.

"I want to," I say quickly. I drop my gaze, the embarrassing truth pushing to the surface. It has been a long time—so very long. "I just . . . I don't want to disappoint you."

Sawyer lets out a breath, his arms tightening around me. "Iris," he says, but I don't look up. He puts a hand lightly below my chin, lifting it gently to meet his earnest, intense gaze. "You could *never* disappoint me."

I sag into him, and he leans forward until our foreheads gently touch. For a moment everything falls away, and it's nothing but the two of us. Then we stand and I take his hand as I lead him up the stairs, stopping only briefly to peek in on my sleeping son before continuing on to my bedroom.

I shut the door, lock it, and turn trembling to this man who has swept into my life out of nowhere, swept me up so completely. He comes to me immediately, takes me in his arms, and we're kissing again, grabbing at each other's clothing. I paw at the buttons of his shirt, my hands sliding down his strong chest. He takes off my shirt, hands exploring as we kiss passionately. Then he pulls back to look into my eyes. "Iris, I am completely falling for you."

A wave of happiness sweeps through me as he lifts me into his arms. I wrap my legs around him as he crosses the room and gently lowers me onto the bed, our deep kisses continuing. "Sawyer," I breathe, desire pulsing within me as he trails soft kisses down my neck, his hand slipping gently under my panties.

"Is this okay?" he whispers.

"Yes," I manage, puffing out quick breaths of anticipation. When he finds me, my back arches and I let out a low moan, sheets twisting in my grip as each motion takes me higher, climbing and rising before exploding with pure joy and light.

I'm breathless afterward, blissed out, and needing him more than ever. I reach for him, pulling his strong body onto mine, and our bodies arch and rock, all rhythm and flow and ecstasy, and I never want to let him go.

Afterward he holds me, and I love the way I fold so perfectly into him, the way my head snugs against his warm chest. I love having him here by my side.

I'm falling in love with *him*. The thought makes me smile as I drift off to sleep.

CHAPTER
TWENTY-TWO

I wake to soft kisses on my shoulder, Sawyer's strong arm wrapped around me. I smile before even opening my eyes. "Morning, beautiful," he murmurs in my ear, and I open my eyes and roll around to face him, wishing him a good morning with a deep kiss. He sighs, content. "I could *really* get used to this."

"Me too," I whisper.

Outside, sunlight is peeking over the horizon, and our eyes meet as if we both think of it at once. *Finn.*

"Finn should still be asleep," I say quickly.

"Is it okay if I'm in here when he wakes up?"

I bite my lip. He's too young to truly understand, yet finding a naked man in his mom's bed is *not* something that's ever happened before. I blush thinking about it. "Probably not."

"So you're telling me I need to sneak out the window, eh?"

I giggle. "Maybe just put your pants on before you leave the room?"

"Details," he says, leaning in to give me a soft kiss before slipping out of bed. I take great pleasure in watching him as he hikes up his jeans and slips his T-shirt back on. He catches me watching and winks.

"Okay, show's over. I'd love to stay and watch *you* get dressed, but I suppose I should jump in the shower before Finn wakes up."

He shuts the door softly behind him, and I step out of bed, chilled in the morning air. I quickly pull on a long nightshirt, then grab my robe and wrap myself in its warmth. I cinch it tight and then sneak down the hallway—popping my head silently into Finn's doorway to assure myself that he's asleep—before continuing down to the kitchen to make a pot of strong coffee.

Staring out at the lightening morning and letting my mind drift to last night, I am perfectly, blissfully at peace for what feels like the first time in forever.

At last, there was no voice last night.

It's because I removed the batteries from the radio, of course. But here in the light of day, part of me wonders if it would've disappeared anyway. The truth hurts, but it's a soft ache. Maybe the voice *was* a manifestation of my anxiety, the shame of my past rearing its ugly head. Or even if it *is* somehow real and someone is messing with me, perhaps it's more harmless than I imagined, and certainly something I can handle with Sawyer by my side.

I believe I can handle just about anything with Sawyer by my side.

The coffeepot pops and spits, announcing it's almost done brewing, and I pour myself a steaming cup, then take a careful sip before setting the mug back down with a contented sigh.

A freshly showered Sawyer walks into the kitchen and slips his arms around me from behind, leaning down to kiss the crook of my neck before nestling his head against mine. We fit so well, I'm so comfortable and serene, that the words come easily. "I was thinking . . . maybe tomorrow, when we're all done with this dinner tonight, we could go on a family date. Let the kids see us together?" I turn and gaze up at him. "Finn adores you."

Is it my imagination—it's only a moment—but I'm sure Sawyer's eyes flit sideways, a nervous swallow before he meets my gaze. I pull back—God, what was I thinking? He doesn't want this. He doesn't want *me*.

But before I can full on panic, he gently pulls me back toward him. "I would love that."

"Really?" I ask, vulnerable. "I don't mean to move too fast."

"No, that's not it," he says, eyes pained. "I don't know how to tell Natalie. I absolutely want to be honest with her. But she's been through so much, and she's barely talking to me as it is. I don't want to mess everything up." He sighs. "Maybe just let me talk to her on my own first?"

I reach up and gently touch his face. "Of course."

"Thank you," he says, taking my hand and kissing it softly. "But look, I meant what I said last night. I'm all in, Iris. I want nothing more than to date you—to take you on a *real* date, dinner and a movie, whatever you want."

I smile. I believe him. And even better, he punctuates it with a deep, lingering kiss.

"What's for breakfast?" Finn asks as he bounds into the kitchen. Sawyer and I pull apart faster than two human beings have ever moved in the history of the world.

"Uh, how about waffles, bud?" Sawyer says quickly, rushing to the cabinet and busying himself grabbing pans.

"I'm going up to take a shower," I say brightly, topping off my coffee cup and planting a kiss on top of Finn's thankfully oblivious head as I make a beeline for the stairs.

"Enjoy your shower," Sawyer calls out. When I look back, he winks, and I bite my lip, an extra bounce in my step as I go upstairs, certain all is well in the world and always will be.

As I take my shower, I hum absently, lost in happy thoughts from last night with Sawyer. I take my time getting ready, and when I come back downstairs afterward, I step into the kitchen and proceed to melt into a puddle of mama warmth—Finn is standing on a stool in front of the stove, Sawyer's hand protectively over his as he flips a pancake.

"Well, don't you two make a great team," I say, grinning.

Finn turns to me, beaming. "I'm making your breakfast, Mom!" He sounds so excited that I think my heart might possibly explode. "Sawyer's teaching me."

"That's great! I think I am the luckiest girl in the whole world," I declare, sliding onto a stool in front of the bar to wait for my feast.

Soon, they plop down a plate of misshapen pancakes in front of me, my son beaming with pride, and I make a big show of oohing and aahing before declaring it the very best breakfast I have ever laid eyes on. Finn prances around the kitchen with joy before losing interest approximately thirty seconds later and begging to be released to his screens. "Fine," I say, "but brush your teeth first."

He groans but skips off to the bathroom to pay his screen-time tax. I settle into my pancakes, which are actually quite good with the pure maple syrup Sawyer slides across the bar to me. We sit, content, for a few minutes; then his phone buzzes. "Hello, Lowell," Sawyer says. He's smiling at first, but it quickly fades. "No, it's fine—yes, that'll work." He listens, scrambles for a pen, and writes something down on the kitchen notepad. I'm antsy now, waiting, so I check on Finn, then come back and load up the dishwasher as I listen to Sawyer's clipped answers.

At last he ends the call, and I turn to him expectantly. "Well?"

He rubs his face. "Lowell is coming back on the afternoon flight from Minneapolis."

"That's good," I say, trying to be positive. "I mean, that he's flying—I'm glad he's not driving five hours alone. Plus, we'll still have enough time to prepare for the dinner."

Sawyer nods, but worry is etched on his features. "He wouldn't tell me who any of the potential buyers are. Says we'll talk about everything when he gets here. All I know is there are three of them."

I narrow my eyes. "So is this an open house–type event, where everyone comes and goes?"

Sawyer grimaces. "We're all going to sit down to one big dinner. He thinks it will make the place seem more appealing if we sort of pit them against each other, so to speak." He shakes his head. "Does this feel like a bad idea to you?"

I sigh. "Yes, but I'm not sure there's anything we can say at this point to change his mind."

Sawyer runs his hands through his hair. "You're right. I'm sorry; this has me more rattled than I expected. It all feels wrong somehow." We stand in fretful silence—I can tell he has more to say, that he's searching for the words. "It . . . reminds me of the last big dinner I had to put on at the restaurant I worked for in Minneapolis. Some big shot showed up at the last minute with a lot of demands, and I had to cancel plans at home. I . . . shut my phone off." He squeezes his eyes shut. "It was the night my wife died."

I clasp my hand to my mouth. For a moment I don't know what to say, what to do. I have so many questions, but all that can wait—I want to be there for him like he's been there for me. Slowly, I walk toward him and place my hand on his back. When he opens his eyes, I wrap my arms around him, and he folds his arms around me. "I'm so sorry," I whisper.

Sawyer leans back to look at me. "I know the two things aren't related, but it's like I just can't shake this bad feeling about tonight."

"I understand," I say meaningfully. "And I'm here."

"Thank you." He takes a deep breath. "I'm okay. Everything will go fine tonight."

"It will. We'll get through it together."

"Together." He smiles. "I like the sound of that."

CHAPTER TWENTY-THREE

The rest of the morning passes in a flurry of activity. Inside, I scrub the floors, press the thick green tablecloth, and set out the fancy, hand-embroidered place mats while Sawyer cleans the kitchen, chops vegetables, and prepares the salmon for tonight's dinner.

Around midmorning, Sawyer makes a supply run to town. It takes him longer than expected, and when he returns, he seems distracted.

"Everything okay?" I ask.

He forces a smile. "Yeah, sorry that took so long. I stopped at home to make sure Natalie was back from Maddie's. We only argued a little, so I'm calling it a win."

He chuckles, so I join him, and we launch back into work mode before I can ask more about it.

When we break for lunch, Finn almost catches Sawyer and me sneaking a kiss in the pantry. Flustered, I quickly announce that Finn can eat his lunch in front of the TV, which distracts him *and* leads him to declare me the Best Mom in the Universe.

In the afternoon, I coax Finn off his screens with the promise of a run through the sprinkler—only after he helps water the flowers. He grumbles but gets his trunks and swim shirt on and makes a quick round through the flower garden, showering them gleefully with the hose attachment, and is done just as I finish sweeping the deck. I attach the sprinkler to the hose, set it out in the yard, and smile as I listen to his giggles as he runs back and forth through the water. Then I eye the hanging baskets—too high for Finn to reach, so I scoot a patio chair over and climb up to douse them with a watering can.

Behind me, the screen door opens, and I hear Sawyer's boots clomp toward me across the deck. "Don't fall and hurt that beautiful body, now," he says, wrapping his arms around me.

I turn and smile, and I see keys dangling in his hand. "Where are you going?"

He sighs. "Back to town. I forgot to get lemon for the sauce. Do we need anything else?"

I shake my head. "I don't think so. Hurry back, though."

It's a slower process than I anticipated, dragging the chair to each of the six hanging baskets to water. I have one left when I realize it's been well over the allotted fifteen minutes of sun-exposure time, and Finn did not put any sunscreen on. "Time to go in," I call to him.

"Mo-*om*," he whines. "I'm not done."

"Three-minute warning, mister." An idea strikes. "Besides, we still need to make your special allergy-friendly brownies. And maybe have some lemonade?"

From the deck, I can see his eyes light up. He turns, determined, for one last dash through the water, then makes a beeline for the front door. "Make sure you change out of your wet—" The screen door slams behind him, and I sigh. "Clothes."

I finish up the last flower basket, and as I'm stepping off the chair, Natalie pulls into the driveway in her old Honda Civic. She steps out of the car but hangs back, so I call out, "Hey, we're about to get some brownies in the oven, if you're hungry!"

She nods but doesn't smile, doesn't even look at me fully. Then Sawyer's truck comes rumbling down the county road, dirt spraying behind him, and soon he's pulled to a stop in the driveway. "You're here," he says brightly when he hops out. "How about you come help me in the kitchen?"

"Whatever," Natalie says, but she follows him inside, passing me without even looking in my direction. The sting surprises me—I guess I was feeling a little closer after our talk yesterday, when we bonded over our mutual hatred of Brayden.

I gasp. Brayden. Maybe Natalie stopped at the office today or talked to someone from work about our argument—and learned how I made a total fool of myself. Dammit. I'm going to have to talk to her about it at some point, but now is not the time.

Finn bursts through the door, still in his swim trunks, wet hair askew. "Mom, Sawyer wants to know where the centerpiece is!"

"Oh shit." The word slips out before I can help it, and Finn claps his hands to his mouth, giggling. "I mean shoot!" I say quickly, but the damage is done.

"Mom! You *swore!*" He's looking at me with a mixture of judgment and awe.

"I'm sorry." I usher him toward the door. "Now *you* need to go change, young man."

"But why did you say the *s* word?"

"Because Mommy completely forgot about clipping some roses."

"From Rosie?"

My brow furrows. "When did you name our rosebush?"

"Yesterday." He beams. "Natalie helped me think of it. I told her how much you love it."

I smile, and Sawyer pokes his head out. "Did he ask you about the centerpiece?"

"Mom forgot," Finn announces. "*And* she said a swear word."

"Snitch," I say dryly, then turn to Sawyer. "I'm sorry, now *I'm* going to have to run to town. Can he stay here?"

"Of course." Finn skips inside, and Sawyer grins at me. "You don't have to ask. He and I are buds."

I love it, but it stings, too—I wish I could say the same for Natalie and me. But all I can do is keep trying. "Thank you," I say. "I'll be back as soon as I can."

I try to shake off any lingering worries as I set off to get some flowers from my home in town. But as I drive, the sky clouds over as if matching my thoughts, and a familiar ache settles within me—an ominous, expectant tingle of dread.

Like something is about to go terribly wrong.

It's probably echoes of Sawyer's bad feeling, the stress of the day, anxiety over the dinner. And yet it stays with me as I park in front of my small gray house, intensifies as I walk around the side and my rosebush comes into view.

I see a small group of petals first, crushed red and smashed into the grass.

At first my mind tries to make sense of it, to fill in the blanks— maybe it was a pesky squirrel, or a freak windstorm. But as I walk closer, dread bursts within me—petals are splayed everywhere, a sad red explosion. Green leaves ripped, stems bent.

My rosebush is destroyed.

I whimper, sinking to my knees. The grass is littered with tender fallen petals, and I reach a shaking hand out to touch them, then crawl across the chunky dirt to the mangled bush.

Along the way I see the worst part of all: footprints in the mud.

This was no accident.

This means someone does have it out for me.

And it means the voice must be real.

Rural Minnesota
Eight years ago

The air is thick and hazy, and it's hot, so hot. There are too many people. We only go out at night, and we only go to parties at other trailers like ours, small and cramped, with faces I don't know, people who scare me.

I swig the scorching liquid Mitch handed me before he disappeared into the crowd, telling myself I'm only drinking it to stay cool. But it also cuts the fear, dulls the edges, so I take another gulp, then another, until the faces around me are even more blurred. Until I feel like I can fade even farther into the background.

He's punishing me. I told him I didn't want to come, that these parties scare me, the way the men look at me, the things he talks about, the jobs he takes. But Mitch doesn't take no for an answer, especially in front of Rex. He not only made me go, but he walked away from me the moment we arrived, thrust a drink into my hand and then slipped into the crowd, claiming he and Rex had business to attend to.

"Got a light?"

I blink, force my eyes to focus on the face before me. He's blond and scruffy, with piercing eyes and a face too young for a party like this. "What did you say?" I ask. Someone turned up the music. It's so hot in here that my cheeks feel like they might catch fire.

He smirks, looking me up and down as if realizing I've been drinking too much. "You here alone?"

"No, I'm with my boyfriend." But it occurs to me I could be alone now. Mitch could've left for the gas station—the back parking lot is his favorite place to make deals. Though if he were going there, he probably would punish me more by making me go with him, knowing I hate it.

The man chuckles. "Whatever you say. If you decide you need any company, let me know." He reaches out and trails a finger down my arm and I shiver, lurching back.

But it's too late. Through the crowd, I suddenly see Mitch's face from the hallway, shocked and angry, Rex right behind him.

"Just leave me alone," I say through gritted teeth, shoving past the surprised stranger and walking toward Mitch, but I stumble, crashing into a coffee table and causing everyone nearby to turn in surprise.

Pain shoots through my shin, and I lean down to grab it, but Mitch has reached me and grabs my wrist hard, yanking me back upright. "You're making a fucking scene."

"I'm sorry." I say it automatically because it's what I always say.

He says nothing, just drags me through the crowd toward the door. Outside it's blessedly cool, but the air offers no solace from the oppression I'm facing. Mitch whirls to face me, tightening his grip on my wrist until I whimper. "You didn't look sorry when that son of a bitch had his hands on you."

"I didn't know what was happening. I was looking for *you*."

"Didn't look too hard, did you? Did you like it when he touched you? Huh?"

"No, Mitch, please," I say, tears falling.

I hear the door open behind me, and then Rex steps around next to Mitch. He says nothing, only stands silently, watching, and somehow Mitch's anger is more emboldened. He clenches his fist, and I brace for the blow like I'm used to, but it doesn't come. Instead, he reaches in his pocket, and I hear the soft click, see the glint of his pocket knife. My eyes widen.

"You need to remember that you're *mine*. Forever."

One quick motion: searing pain, hot and sharp, and I cry out. Mitch releases me, and I crumple to the ground, clutching my bleeding arm in shock.

For a moment it's as if the whole world is silent except for the deafening ringing in my ears, my thoughts racing. *He cut me. He loves me. He cut me. He loves me.*

"Goddamn it!" Mitch cries, kicking the door in anger. "Iris, look what you made me do."

"Calm the fuck down and go get a towel," Rex commands.

Mitch runs into the house as blood continues to seep through the fingers of my clamped hand. Panic rises up in my throat. I need to get out of here. I need help. I need to *go*.

When Mitch returns, Rex grabs the towel from him and sends Mitch to the car. He hands the towel to me. "Take it," he says, and I do, wrapping the towel around my arm.

I look up at him, offering the faintest "Thank you."

He says nothing at first, just stares at me, his face chillingly unreadable. Then he crouches down in front of me. "I don't give a shit about you. But he wants you around, so you gotta stay or it's gonna fuck up my business. That means you're not going anywhere." I shudder as he leans closer, his eyes darkening. "So just remember, there's nowhere you can run that's far enough, little girl. Nowhere we wouldn't find you."

He walks away, and I sit in the darkness, stunned, more alone than I have ever been.

CHAPTER
TWENTY-FOUR

I lie on the ground with my fallen petals, tears falling as if they will never end. This was the bush Ivan and I picked out together, planted together, all those years ago. Every year when the flowers bloom, they're a reminder of him. Now everything's gone.

I have no idea how much time passes; nor do I care. When my phone buzzes, at first I ignore it. But it persists, and finally I answer. "Hello?" My voice is hoarse from crying.

"Iris?" Sawyer asks cautiously.

I try to answer, but a sob comes out.

"What's wrong?" Sawyer cries, sounding alarmed. "Where are you?"

"My house," I say.

"I'll be there as soon as I can."

I push myself into a sitting position, wrapping my arms around my knees protectively. Soon I hear an engine stop, a car door slam, hurried footsteps rushing across the lawn. Sawyer drops to his knees in front of me. "Iris." His voice is as gentle as his hands, cupping my face. "Are you okay? What happened?"

Tears brim in my lids, but inside I'm hollow. "My rosebush. Someone destroyed it. Someone was here."

"Who? Are you hurt?" I look up, and his worried eyes are scanning the yard.

"I'm fine," I say. "Whoever did it was already gone when I got here."

My voice breaks on the last word, and he folds me into his embrace. "I'm so sorry," he murmurs, smoothing my hair.

"But who would do this?"

"I don't know. Do you want me to call the police?" I grimace, and he shakes his head. "No, of course not, sorry. We'll figure it out. Okay?"

"Okay." Then my eyes widen. "Where's Finn?"

"He's okay. He's with Natalie."

I nod, relieved, then let out a breath. "I'm sorry we won't have a centerpiece."

"Don't worry about that." He helps me to my feet, and I lean shakily against him. "We don't have to go through with the dinner at all. I can call Lowell and cancel."

"No," I say quickly. "This could be his only chance to sell the lodge and keep it going. We have to do this."

He frowns. "Are you sure?"

"No," I say honestly. "But I can't let him down."

Sawyer smiles sadly, then sighs. "Okay. We'll get through tonight; then we'll figure this out together. I promise."

Back at the lodge, I do my best to shove the scene of floral carnage out of my mind. Then Finn, in his innocence, smiles and says, "Did you get some flowers from Rosie?"

I falter, but Sawyer saves the day. "Nah, we decided we didn't need a centerpiece after all." Finn shrugs, appeased by this explanation.

I nod my thanks to Sawyer. "Where's Natalie?"

"Upstairs getting a movie going on the laptop, I think," he says, grinning at Finn, who cheers in excitement.

"Okay, buddy," I say, attempting to morph back into assertive-mom mode. "You need to head upstairs to stay with Natalie now. This is a big dinner tonight, so we need you guys to stay up there, and we'll bring up supper later."

Finn's eyes brighten. "Natalie said Sawyer is making chicken nuggets."

"You got it, bud," Sawyer assures him.

Finn races upstairs, and Sawyer and I look at each other, one shared wire of nervous energy frayed and crackling between us. "Almost time," I say wearily.

He nods; then his phone buzzes, and he looks down. "Lowell landed. He should be here soon."

Suddenly I'm not sure we've done enough to prepare. "God, I just want to know who these potential buyers are," I say anxiously. Before Sawyer can respond, the doorbell rings. We stare at each other for a moment, frozen, then leap into action. "I'll get it," I say.

"I'll get the drinks and hors d'oeuvres ready," he says, rushing to the kitchen.

Taking a deep breath, I march toward the door, plastering what I hope is a warm smile on my face. I open the door, and for a moment, my smile fades, but I quickly paste it back into place. "Uh, hello," I say weakly.

Sherri—the queen bee of the Literary Ladies' Luncheon—pushes past me, shrugging out of her shiny silver cardigan to reveal an even sparklier dress. "Okay, who does a girl have to sleep with to get a drink around here?"

I wince, remembering her crush on Sawyer. "I'm sorry, but what are you doing here?"

"I'm here for dinner," she says crisply.

I suck in a breath, realization slapping me in the face.

Sherri breaks into a wicked grin. "That's right, Iris. I might buy this place."

CHAPTER TWENTY-FIVE

Sawyer walks into the dining room, a charcuterie tray in one hand and a stack of small plates in the other. Then he sees Sherri sitting at the table and stops dead in his tracks, eyes flicking between her and me.

"Well, hello there, stranger. Haven't seen you in a while," Sherri purrs.

"She's our first potential buyer," I say with all the false enthusiasm I can muster.

Sawyer sets the tray of meats and cheeses down stiffly, and Sherri eyes him, her face positively glowing at his confusion and discomfort. An odd sense of déjà vu washes over me, and I compare myself to her, noting all the ways my plain, frumpy self falls short against her polished poise.

Then when Sherri's not looking, Sawyer looks at me and widens his eyes, quick but horrified, and it's a reminder we're on the same team—that he wants *me*. I stand up straight. "Let me help you with that," I say, placing a hand gently on his back as I take some of the plates from him and set them out.

"Thanks." He flashes me a warm smile.

Sherri's face turns cold. She crosses her arms, shrewd eyes taking us in as the realization hits her. "You have *got* to be kidding me," she mutters.

I take a deep breath and turn to Sherri with a cheerful, "Can we get you anything to drink?"

"Yes, please, God, anything with alcohol," she says.

We both scramble into the kitchen and stare at each other, the same look of desperate disbelief in our eyes. "Well, we're screwed," Sawyer grumbles.

"She's not *that* bad," I offer.

"You're not the one who shot her down. She called me a bastard before she stormed out."

My eyes bulge. "You never told me that."

"I wasn't exactly proud of it."

Just then the doorbell rings again, and hope sparks within me. I smile at Sawyer, then march back through the dining room.

"Where's my drink?" Sherri asks with a huff, but I point toward the entryway.

When I get there, I fling open the front door and smile widely.

"That big smile all for me, sweetheart? Lucky me." I cringe as Dave Donnelly—the guest from my very first day on the job—stands in the doorway, eyeing me the same way he did that first morning.

"You must be here for dinner," I manage to say through my shock. "Come in."

I walk back into the dining room and shoot a defeated look at Sawyer, whose brows furrow in confusion until he sees the man who walks in behind me.

Sherri immediately turns on the charm, sidling up to Dave. "I'm Sherri Simpson, and *you* must be my competition."

He leers at her. "Dave Donnelly. And I'm happy to have such a beautiful competitor."

She giggles, and I stand next to Sawyer, biting back nausea as we watch this increasingly terrible scene play out before our eyes.

Dave sits at the table, looking up at me. "You got a drink for me back there, sweetheart?"

Sawyer's jaw tightens, and I say quickly, "We'll bring out some wine." I pull him along with me toward the kitchen.

"Remember, little lady, I like it sweet," Dave calls after us with a lecherous grin.

A look of pure hatred flashes across Sawyer's face, but I steer him through the kitchen door, shutting it softly behind us. Sawyer runs his hands through his hair. "I'm gonna wring his neck." He gestures to the door. "I mean, that asshole? Lowell wants to sell to *that* asshole?"

I frown. "I don't understand it, either. There's no way I could work here if he were the owner. I don't want him around Finn."

"I don't want him around *you*," Sawyer says.

"Okay," I say slowly. "So . . . that means right now we're Team Sherri? The lesser of two evils?"

Sawyer shudders. "I never thought I'd say that, but yes."

I reach for his hand. "We can still hang our hopes on the third person, right?"

"Right," he says.

We stand in silence for a moment, and for some reason the ominous feeling is back, like we're missing something.

"Hey! Drinks?" Dave's voice shouts from the dining room, followed by a high-pitched giggle from Sherri, and I grimace.

Sawyer glowers but sets to work placing the glasses on a tray while I grab a wine bottle and corkscrew. We walk back in, and they're both still seated at the table, Sherri leaning in close to Dave, and his arm draped across the back of her chair.

"Finally. This is quite a place here. I got a hot girl on my arm and another one pouring my drink," Dave says.

Sawyer sets down the tray of glasses with a thud, and I see the flash of rage in his eyes, but once again the doorbell rings.

"I'll get it," I blurt out, lacing my hand through Sawyer's and dragging him toward the door. I place my hands on both sides of his face. "Breathe," I command. "This might be our saving grace right here, okay?"

He pushes out a long breath. "Okay. But can I punch that guy? Please?"

A smile twitches at my lips. "Once Lowell signs a contract with this third buyer, you can do whatever you want."

Sawyer plants a quick kiss on my lips; then we turn hand in hand and open the door.

Lowell is on the other side, smiling at us. "Ah, this is quite a welcome home!"

There's another man standing next to him, and as I turn to look at him, my smile falters. The man is tall and confident, dressed professionally in a suit, young face clean shaven, blond hair slicked back. He's not dressed like I've seen him before, and yet I recognize him.

Sawyer does, too. Of course he does—it's his brother, after all.

CHAPTER TWENTY-SIX

"Cole?" Sawyer says incredulously.

"Please." Cole holds up a hand. "To keep things professional, I'd prefer Mr. Jones."

"Mr. Jones," Sawyer growls, "you're wearing my suit."

Cole holds out his hands, as if putting himself on display. "I think we can all agree it looks better on me."

Poor Sawyer looks like the veins in his neck might burst, so I step forward. "Please, come in." I usher them inside, then shut the door. "Mr. Jones, if you would please join the other investors in the dining room, we have some hors d'oeuvres and wine."

He nods, looking impressed. "Thank you, Iris. I appreciate your professionalism."

He walks into the dining room, and Sawyer stares after him, then turns to Mr. Gordon. "Lowell, with all due respect—what in the hell is going on here?"

Lowell chuckles. "He asked me not to tell you. He approached me about it, said he'd overheard you talking about this dinner. I liked his gumption, so I thought, why not?"

Sawyer rubs his neck. "Sir, I'm afraid he might be scamming you. He . . . he doesn't have any money, doesn't have a job—not a legal one, anyway."

"He's actually working with a partner—he's here representing a Minnesota firm. I think you'll want to hear him out, Sawyer."

A Minnesota firm. Something about the words makes my insides twist, the ominous feeling pulsing within me as I think back to my odd exchange with Cole.

Lowell claps Sawyer on the back. "Give him a chance. Your brother might surprise you."

Lowell walks into the dining room, and Sawyer's shoulders sag. "That's exactly what I'm afraid of."

The buyers mingle quite well together. I have to hand it to Cole—he's a charmer. Within minutes he has both Sherri and Dave eating out of the palm of his hand. He seems to have a knack for recognizing what a person needs to hear. For Sherri, he's an attentive gentleman, complimenting her looks but respectfully. For Dave, he's an eager learner, asking questions and soliciting opinions from the more seasoned businessman.

All three of them are talking and laughing with Lowell as if they're having a great time. I head to the kitchen to get another bottle of wine and find Sawyer standing at the oven—partly because it's his job but also because I'm pretty sure he's hiding out in here.

"Things are going surprisingly well out there," I say, grabbing a bottle of chardonnay. Sawyer grunts but doesn't turn, so I set the bottle back down and walk over, wrapping my arms around him from behind. "You okay?"

He sighs, then sets down a ladle and turns to face me. "I don't know what my brother's game is."

"Whatever it is, he's playing it very well."

He scoffs. "It's what he does. I'm just afraid someone will get hurt from Cole's games."

Worry washes over me. "Who do you think this partner is? This Minnesota firm?"

"No idea," he says. I bite my lip, and his brow furrows. "Do *you* have an idea?" he asks.

"No. I mean, I don't know." I swallow. "Your brother said something strange to me the other day."

"What did he say?"

The kitchen door swings open, and Lowell pops his head in. "Ah, there's that bottle of wine." He walks over and grabs it. "Smells wonderful in here, Sawyer. Will dinner be ready soon?"

"Absolutely." Sawyer turns back to his duties again as Lowell saunters back into the dining room.

"I'd better get back in there and help him with that corkscrew," I say.

"Wait, but you were going to tell me—"

I cut him off with a wave of my hand. "I'll tell you later."

"Are you sure?"

"It's fine." But the pit in my gut is here to stay, I realize as I walk back into the dining room.

Dinner goes more smoothly than I expect. Sawyer and I are able to discreetly hold hands under the table, and I latch on to him like a life raft. Afterward, we scurry around picking up plates and silverware.

Lowell stands. "Let's give Iris and Sawyer a big round of applause for this fantastic event. I couldn't have asked for better employees, for better *friends*." Sparse clapping breaks out, though none of the potential buyers seem able to meet our eyes. "Now, as they grab the dessert and coffee, I'd like for each of you to present me with your plans—tell me about your ideas for this place. This lodge has been important to me for many years—it's been my home, in fact—and I want to make sure I leave it in good hands. Let's all retire to the porch, which I understand has been decorated quite beautifully, shall we?"

Everyone stands, but Cole speaks up: "If I may, my partner has put together a video presentation for this evening, and I'd like to stream it to the big-screen TV in the living room."

Sherri and Dave exchange a frown, but Lowell nods his approval. "Ah, impressive. Absolutely. By all means, let's head in there first."

Everyone moves to the living room, Lowell easing into a recliner, Sherri and Dave settling into the sofa. Sawyer and I linger in the doorway as Cole stands up front. "Ladies and gentlemen, as you know, my name is Cole Jones, but I am here on behalf of Rex Enterprises, whose headquarters is located near Independence, Minnesota."

I freeze, a chill sweeping through my body. *Rex Enterprises?*

"Independence?" Sherri says, giggling, tipsy from the wine. "Where is that?"

"West of Minneapolis. Rural Hennepin County." Cole's eyes flick to mine only briefly, but long enough to send a ripple of fear through me. "Let's get started." He taps at his phone, and it begins streaming to the large smart TV mounted on the wall behind him. But instead of a sleek marketing video, it's a photo slideshow with no sound.

The first picture is beautiful—all green trees and blue skies. It could be anywhere, but it looks familiar—I'm guessing it's a wooded area near Independence. Near where I used to live, all those years ago. I grip the bottom of my shirt, twisting it in my hand nervously.

"This is rural Hennepin County, Minnesota," Cole begins. "It's the headquarters of Rex Enterprises. Now, Rex never thought he'd have an interest in a hunting lodge way out in South Dakota. But when I told him some of the more . . . intimate details of the way this place is run, he became very interested." I'm sure that Cole's eyes are on me now, and alarm bells sound within me, but his smile is sickeningly sweet, and he shifts his gaze away from me as if everything is perfectly normal.

He taps his phone, and the picture changes to a front view of the lodge. "I showed him pictures of the grounds, the facility, and also the employees." He taps it again, and it switches to a picture of Sawyer and me hanging flowers on the porch. Sawyer leans forward in surprise, and coldness seeps into me. I didn't know Cole took that picture. "This photo, in particular, really interested Rex," Cole says.

"You keep saying Rex like it's a person," Lowell says, brow furrowed in confusion. "I thought it was a business."

"It's both. Rex Enterprises is run by a friend of mine." Cole's eyes shift to me, his smile gone. "Rex McNeil."

My breath leaves me; my legs threaten to give out.

No.

Rex McNeil. Mitch's best friend. His terrible, violent best friend.

He saw my picture. He knows where I am.

The room spins, and I sink to the floor. Sawyer crouches down, eyes wide in concern. "Are you okay?"

I shake my head, unable to speak. *I'm just afraid someone will get hurt from Cole's games,* Sawyer said.

It's clear now that someone is me.

"Let's continue, shall we?" Cole says. He taps his phone again, and the photo switches to a scene I never thought I'd see again—a dilapidated trailer house perched precariously out in the middle of the woods, garbage strewn out front.

My old home.

"This is where Rex used to live—actually, it belonged to a friend. Mitchell Wheeler."

Memories flood me, sights and sounds—terrible screams, sometimes my own, when Mitch came home drunk: sometimes an associate of theirs whom they needed answers from, who didn't pay their debt, who didn't provide a clean enough product. I bury my face in my hands like I used to back then, trying to drown it out, make it all go away, make my life different somehow.

"Iris, what's wrong?" Sawyer says it louder, and the others crane their necks to see.

But Cole keeps going, relentless. He taps the phone again, and an even worse scene fills the screen—nighttime, a dark highway lined by trees, two vehicles mangled together.

I whimper, and Sawyer gasps. "What the hell is this, Cole?" he says, anger and pain in his voice.

I look up at him, surprised by his reaction, but before I can say anything, Sherri speaks: "What kind of a photo is that? What does any of this have to do with buying the lodge?"

Dave leans forward. "Let's see how this plays out," he says, clearly interested.

"All in good time," Cole says. "Now, this tragic scene may look familiar to a few of you here tonight." His eyes flash around the room, looking at everyone but seeming to linger on me. "But there's one person in particular who was at this scene the night this photo was taken. This is the person my friend Rex is interested in—and it's why he wants to buy this lodge."

Cole's eyes don't leave mine now; there's no question where this is headed. My hands shake, bile rising in my throat as he taps his phone one more time. I'm expecting it; still, I flinch when I see the disheveled hair; pale, gaunt face; eyes puffy from crying and dazed from booze, or worse.

It's a terrifying, humiliating thing, staring into your own face—a face from the past, from when you were a completely different person. A different person in a terrible situation, lost and scared and alone. I don't even remember when this particular mug shot was taken—was it the time Mitch sent me in to steal cigarettes from the gas station? The time he shoved drugs into my purse when we got pulled over? I have no idea.

All I know is that it was taken long before the night of the crash— the last night of that life. The last night of that version of me, when I fled through the protective cover of darkness. When I escaped.

I stare into my own face, my vision blurring as tears fill my eyes.

"This, my friends, is Evelyn Iris Johannson." Cole stares at me, eyes hard. "You, of course, know her by a different name."

I squeeze my eyes shut, but it doesn't stop the pain.

"Iris Jenkins."

CHAPTER
TWENTY-SEVEN

I wait for the uproar, but instead it's deathly quiet. That's almost worse. I open my eyes, and everyone is staring at me—on the TV screen, then right in front of them—in some degree of shock and disgust. Even Sawyer has backed away from me, looking stunned, confused, as if he doesn't know me at all, and the pain is striking.

"That's enough." Lowell grabs the remote control from the side table, and the TV screen turns black. "Get out."

"I wasn't finished," Cole says. "Rex has a legitimate proposal. He wants to buy this place."

"I said get out." Lowell stands, trembling with rage.

"I don't understand—Iris is a criminal?" Sherri's voice squeaks, part terror and part awe, as if she's already writing the gossipy post to her parents' group on Facebook. "You have a felon working here?"

Dave leans forward, chuckling. "Yeah, I kind of want to see the rest of that video. I mean, don't get me wrong, I'm a man who can handle having a psycho bitch working for me—I've got plenty of them already—but I want to know exactly what kind of psycho bitch I'm dealing with, you know?"

Sawyer leaps to life, lunging at Dave and leveling him with a punch across the jaw. Sherri screams, and Dave falls back against the couch. I push myself to my feet and grab Sawyer's arm before he can deal another blow. When he turns and looks at me, the rage in his eyes turns to pain, and he pulls his arm away.

"Iris," he says, defeated. "What were you doing there—in that photo?"

I wince. "I don't remember what I did, but it was a police mug shot. I was a different person back then. I'm—"

"No," he says, cutting me off, his voice bitter. "The . . . car accident. You were there? Iris, why were you there?"

His eyes brim with tears, and I shake my head in confusion at his question, at the emotion behind it. "I told you about the accident . . . it was a long time ago."

"I know exactly how long ago it was," he says, and the anguish in his voice pierces my soul.

I reach for him, but he pulls away. "Sawyer, please," I whisper, tears in my eyes.

Cole steps between us, arms crossed. "There's a lot you don't know about her, Sawyer." He turns to me. "And there are people looking for you."

Lowell stalks over and grabs Cole more forcefully than I've ever seen him grab anyone. "That is enough. You get the hell out of my house before I call the police."

"I've already done that," Sherri says angrily, gesturing at Dave's groaning, possibly concussed form on the couch.

"Lowell, take it easy," Sawyer says, arms up defensively as he tries to calm the old man.

"I will not take it easy. This young man thinks he can come in here and hurt Iris this way? This is still my house. And I will not tolerate him hurting my Iris in my house."

Unexpected warmth spreads through me, but briefly, as Lowell continues shoving Cole toward the door. In a moment of panic, I grab Cole's arm. "Wait—does Rex really know I'm here? Is he coming for me?" My voice breaks.

Cole's eyes shift left and right, and I thrust myself in front of his gaze. "Answer me," I demand.

He meets my eyes at last with a defiant glare. "He knows enough. But maybe we can make a deal, and I can help you out."

I huff out an incredulous breath, shaking my head. "You think this is about money? This isn't some game. He will kill me."

Sawyer reaches for me, but it's too late. I pull away. "I need to get Finn." My voice rises; I'm spiraling into panic. "We need to leave. *Now*." Without another word, another thought, I race upstairs. "Finn, we're going!" I yell as I pass his bedroom, but I rush first into my room, grabbing my go bag for the second time in a week. Then I race back to Finn's room and push my way inside. "Natalie, I'm sorry, but Finn and I have to—" I stop, look around the room.

It's empty.

"Finn?" I peek inside his blanket fort, where the laptop is still playing an animated film, but they're not there. "Natalie?" I poke my head in the closet, under the bed, panic rising within me.

They have to be somewhere. They *have* to be.

"Kids!" I race down the hall, opening every door—the office, bathroom, closet.

But they're nowhere.

"Sawyer!" I scream as I race down the stairs. "Where are the kids?"

He turns to me, all traces of apprehension gone—nothing else matters now. "They're not upstairs?" I shake my head, and together we race around the main floor, checking every room—the first-floor guest rooms that haven't been used since we arrived, even down into the basement, where there's nothing but a furnace room and storage. Sawyer tries Natalie's phone, texting and calling again and again.

Nothing.

"Oh God oh God oh God," I whimper, pacing the floor of the kitchen when we come back up to the main floor. "This can't be happening."

"We'll find them," Sawyer says, though his voice doesn't have his usual confidence, and it scares the hell out of me.

Lowell comes in, pulling Cole along with him. "Did you find the children?"

Sawyer shakes his head, and my eyes latch on to Cole, who is guiltily looking down at the floor. Suddenly a flash of fury so intense hits me that it takes away my breath, takes away all reason and thought except that this bastard took my baby. The knife is in my hand, and I'm across the room before I even realize it, shoving him against the wall, wielding the shiny blade. "You son of a bitch," I snarl. "Where is he? What did you do?"

Tears stream down my face, but I can see the panic in his eyes. For a split second I think I'm going to do it, but then Sawyer grabs my arm firmly, pulling the knife from my hand. "Iris, I'm sorry, I don't want to hurt you, but you don't want to do this."

"He took my baby," I sob.

"No," Cole says, eyes wide, face pale. "I never—I would never hurt them." His eyes flit to his brother. "Sawyer, come on? I love Nat, you know that. She's my little buddy. She helped me with the pictures. I would never hurt her."

His words barely register before the kitchen door opens again, and in walks Sherri, her finger pointing accusingly at Sawyer. "It was him—*he* punched out Mr. Donnelly—oh!" Her hand flies to her mouth when she sees Sawyer holding the knife. A police officer rushes past her, brandishing his gun. "Drop it!" he yells. It's Officer Barnes.

"No," I say quickly, but he ignores me, gun pointed firmly at Sawyer, who slowly lowers the knife, then keeps his hands raised in the air.

"What the hell is going on in here?" I bristle when I hear Officer Watson's voice from the doorway. He walks across the kitchen, taking out his cuffs and snapping them onto Sawyer's wrists.

"Please," I say, eyes searching both officers' faces. "Sawyer didn't do anything. This is all a mistake. Our kids are missing!"

"What?" Barnes asks, his eyes going wide.

Watson scoffs. "Nice try. You would seriously make up a kidnapping just to throw us off?"

"I'm not making it up—my son is gone; Sawyer's daughter is gone!"

"Jesus, lady. This is a new kind of low, and I've been on the force for years." Watson shakes his head in contempt. "You are one sick bitch."

Sawyer lunges at him, which Watson deflects easily because of the handcuffs, knocking Sawyer to the ground. "Get this guy into the squad car!" Watson bellows, and Barnes complies.

"No!" I cry, but Barnes continues pushing Sawyer out the door. I turn to Watson. "Please, this isn't about me—this is about our kids."

"Dammit, we got people needing medical attention here," he yells. "The EMTs are loading up the guy your boyfriend knocked out."

"I've got a black eye," Cole pipes up. Watson looks at him, and Cole motions to Lowell. "This old dude assaulted me."

"Fine, we'll get you checked out, too."

"Liar!" I scream, but then my attention shifts to Lowell, whose face is contorted not in rage anymore but in pain. "Lowell!" I rush to him as he clutches his chest. "He needs help!"

"Christ, it's a goddamn circus in here," Watson mutters, but he steps out of the kitchen and calls for the EMTs.

In a flurry of activity, Lowell is loaded onto a stretcher, and he, Dave, and Cole are all whisked away in ambulances. Barnes has already driven Sawyer away in one squad car, and Watson is ushering a freaked-out Sherri into the passenger side of his squad car to take her home.

"Wait!" I call out.

Watson cringes, but he walks back over to me. "What?"

Pride is no longer a concern for me—nothing matters right now but Finn. "Please," I beg. "I know what you think of me. I know I've overreacted before, a lot. But I'm not making this up. My son and Sawyer's daughter are *missing*."

For a moment I think I catch a glint of empathy in his eye, or maybe it's the reflection of the ambulance lights driving away. Watson sighs. "How long they been gone?"

"I don't know. They were supposed to be upstairs watching a movie . . . maybe an hour or two, I guess?"

"Could they be outside somewhere? Out playing, or for a walk?"

I shake my head. "They wouldn't just go for a walk this late in the evening."

"Ages?"

"Finn is seven," I say, voice breaking. "Natalie is sixteen."

He narrows his eyes. "Wait, she got a driver's license?"

"Well, yes, but her car is parked right there."

"Could she have taken another vehicle? Or maybe had a friend pick her up? Did you try her cell phone?"

"No. I mean yes."

He sighs. "Which is it, lady?"

"*No* about leaving in another vehicle or with a friend. She was babysitting, and she's very responsible. *Yes* about trying her cell phone—Sawyer called and texted her a bunch of times, and she didn't answer."

"Because she's a teenager." He shakes his head. "Trust me, even the responsible ones screw up sometimes. The kids are out there having fun somewhere. They'll turn up."

"No, you don't understand."

"Don't understand what?"

I brace myself. "Someone . . . might be after me. I need to make sure Finn is safe."

Watson stares at me for a moment, then shakes his head with a disgusted chuckle. "Wow. It's like you just can't help yourself, can you?"

"Please, you have to believe me," I say, but more tears stream down my face because I know there's no way he will.

"Tell you what. I'm gonna take this nice lady here home; we're gonna get your boyfriend processed and locked up for the night, because I'm sure someone like you ain't got bail money. I'm gonna make sure all the people who needed medical attention after spending time in the house *you* are responsible for are okay. *Then* I will send the rookie back to take your bullshit statement about people out to get you and your allegedly missing kids or whatever. Sound good?"

I don't answer, just sink down onto the porch steps. He shakes his head again, then walks away. He stops, turns back for one more jab. "You know, maybe you can spend this time to yourself thinking about all the people you hurt with your lies and false reports. All the lives you're making worse just by being you."

He drives away and I'm alone now, alone in the darkness.

CHAPTER

TWENTY-EIGHT

Darkness. For so long I've kept it on my side, like a prisoner who's fallen for her captor. Finding reasons to embrace it, revere it. Pretending that if I stare into the abyss, I can control it instead of it controlling me.

Tonight I know it was all a mirage.

Because now there is nothing but darkness, relentless and pulsing.

I didn't fear it enough, the darkness. If I would've worried more, prayed harder, it wouldn't have taken Finn from me. But I failed, and he's gone.

Oh God, he's gone.

Somehow I drag myself on hands and knees into the house, collapse on the carpeted floor of the living room. But it's as if it's happening to someone else. Because I am here now in this endless darkness, this upside-down nightmare world. I cannot be in the real world because the real world cannot function without Finn.

I cannot function without him.

He is the stars in the sky, the tinkle of laughter, the sprinkle of rain. He is in everything, every scent, every sound. The smell of his soft hair, the light snoring breath when he sleeps. The feel of his little life kicking and rolling within me. He saved me from darkness.

Now, though, the darkness creeps into me, eating me up, threatening to consume me.

It has come for me, come to claim its own. And I am ready to let it.

South Dakota
Seven and a half years ago

Tiny squawks wake me in the night—not quite the newborn grunts anymore from my growing, pudgy two-month-old. I roll over and smile. So tired, but so happy.

"Are you hungry again?" I coo at Finn, then I sniff. "Ooh, nope—time for a diaper change."

I wiggle his little feet gently and make funny faces at him as I get him fresh and clean, then sit in the rocking chair and try to nurse him, but he's fussy, not hungry.

So I stand and walk around the bedroom of our cozy little apartment, rocking him as I walk—sometimes a little movement is all he needs. "Tomorrow we are going to the zoo with Papa Ivan and Papa Lowell," I say in a singsong voice, my face extra expressive. I thank God once again that I met the Gordons, that they've been so kind to us.

I close my eyes briefly, picture their faces when I met them that day, like angels walking into my life. *It's okay, sweetie, you're safe,* Ivan had said. *Everything is going to be okay now.*

He was right. Things are more than okay. They are perfect.

I open my eyes now and look down at the love of my life in my arms, soft tufts of dark hair and big blue eyes staring back at me in wonder. "How about a song?" I ask with a grin, then start to sing. "You are my sunshine, my only sunshine, you make me happy when skies are gray . . ."

Finn coos. I stop singing. He stops cooing.

My grin widens. "Finnegan Charles—are you singing back to me, my love?"

And so I continue the song, dipping and rocking him to the music as he coos back at me, staring up at me with so much love and trust, and I am overwhelmed. My heart is bursting, overflowing with happiness.

Everything, he is everything. And it was all worth it, every last bit of pain.

I'm okay, Grandma. I'm not alone.

He is heaven on earth. I want to freeze time. Instead, I snuggle him closer, savor it, do my best to feel grateful, pray it can somehow last forever.

CHAPTER TWENTY-NINE

The thing about darkness is that it destroys you, but it doesn't. It hollows you out and leaves you to rot. And this is what I am now: a shell of myself, yes, but still forced to exist, sobbing, spiraling—*he's gone my God he's gone my baby's gone*—flooded with a tidal wave of pain, lost in oppressive despair until I black out.

When I come to, I'm weeping, but also humming a soft, gentle song I sang to my baby. *You are my sunshine, my only sunshine, you make me happy when skies are gray . . .*

I can't say the words, only form the sounds, each note a knife in my heart. Then I remember when I first heard it. My grandma would sing to me when she'd braid my hair, a soothing nightly ritual that began when she and I both needed it most—when I was five years old and found out I'd be living with her permanently.

One night as Grandma sang and braided my hair, she gently told me that Mom was not coming back, for good. I wasn't that sad at first—Grandma was my normal; Mom was never around. But Grandma was crying, and that made *me* cry. So Grandma wiped her own tears and mine and said something I'll never forget: *Sometimes when we can't see light anywhere, we need to make it for ourselves. We need to reach deep within and find that light, and carry it for those who can't. Can you do that, my little Evvie Iris?*

My shoulders tremble now, as if shaking me into action. The fear and pain are constants, but still I stand. I *have* to.

Finn needs me. He needs me to carry the light.

He needs me to find him. And I will.

CHAPTER THIRTY

Alert now, determined, I look at the clock on the living room wall. It's been almost an hour since the party ended in chaos, since everyone was carried away in squad cars and ambulances. The sun is long gone, and I pace the floor of the dark living room, thoughts swimming and swirling in my brain as I try to make sense of this.

After the slideshow tonight, Cole all but confessed to making a deal with the devil. *Is* Rex here already? Has he been behind this all along in some sort of sick revenge plot—the trampled rosebush, the voice I've been hearing, over and over?

Wait. I haven't heard it, not for two nights now, because I took the damn batteries out. Is this now a kidnapping in retaliation for being ignored?

I scramble to my large mom-purse, then dig deep and find the walkie-talkie buried at the bottom, where I threw it after leaving the newsroom the other day. I race to the kitchen and paw through the junk drawer until I find batteries, clicking them into place. Trembling, I turn on the radio and press the side button. "Hello?" I say timidly. Then more loudly, "Hello? Is anyone there?"

I wait, holding my breath as long as I can, then push it out with a frustrated "Answer me!"

At last, it crackles to life. *"Hello, Iris."* I shudder at the voice, so calm and childlike. *"I've been waiting for you."*

I draw in a ragged breath, pulse pounding in terror. "Rex?" I spit the word out, feel like I might vomit.

"Guess again."

I let out a shuddering breath, then grip the radio tighter in my shaky hand. "Cole?"

"Please. Like he could pull this off."

I wince at the taunting tone and rack my brain—but in the end it doesn't matter who it is; it only matters *where* Finn is.

"Where is Finn?" I ask softly.

There's a pause. Then the voice is softer. *"He's here."*

My knees buckle—in relief, but also in this real-life confirmation that my son was indeed kidnapped. "Oh, please. Please don't hurt him," I say desperately, voice breaking. "He's just a little boy. He must be so scared."

"He's fine. He's not hurt."

"Please." I start to cry softly. "None of this is his fault."

"None of what?" There's a challenge in the voice, like this question is important.

But before I can process it, another thought strikes me, and I gasp. "Where is Natalie? Is she there, too?"

The voice scoffs—an odd, tinny sound with the creepy, childlike voice changer. *"You don't care about her."*

"What? Of course I do." Cold terror seeps into me. "Did you hurt her?"

"It doesn't matter."

Oh God, no. Everything changes in that moment. "You'd better not touch her." My voice drips like poison through the walkie-talkie.

"Oh yeah? And what are you going to do about it?"

I grip the phone tightly, all my fear morphing into a primal rage. "I swear to God and everything on this earth that if you touch one hair on their heads, I will hunt you down, and you will wish you had never been born." I don't know where it comes from—the phrasing, the venom—but it's real, a mama bear unleashed, ready to tear out the throats of anyone who comes near her cubs.

Silence. But no—I hear breathing, heavy, and—scared? "Did you hear what I said?" I ask. "If you hurt them, I will hurt *you*."

The pause lasts longer; I think maybe I've lost them for real, but then, the voice speaks.

"You have to find us first."

CHAPTER
THIRTY-ONE

Oh God, what have I done?

I stare down at the handheld walkie-talkie, ready to cry, ready to scream, ready to throw the goddamn thing across the room, watch it smash to pieces.

But I can't—Finn needs me. Natalie does, too. I pray I didn't screw up absolutely everything as I race upstairs to grab a sweater, realizing I left it in the office. When I reach for it, my eyes fall to the drawer that didn't close all the way. I peek in, glimpse one of the newer photos without Emma. *Where did you go, Emma?*

A surge of pain. *Where did you go, Finn and Natalie?*

I press through the sadness, back down the stairs, grabbing my purse and my keys and striding toward the door. But when I yank it open, I stand there. Where am I going? The police don't believe me. Sawyer's in jail—and I'm not sure how he feels about me anymore after those pictures. Lowell is in the hospital.

I'm all alone.

There's no one who can help me, no one at all.

I stand there on the porch looking out into the same darkness I see every single night, and it looks back at the same me. The me who overreacts. Who doesn't trust anyone. Who is paranoid, jumps to conclusions, and is extremely overprotective. This is who I am, and I'm ready to swallow my pride and turn my flaws into powers. I will bug the shit out of everyone in this whole damn town if it means gathering help to find the kids.

I call 911 on my way down the porch steps. I hear the way the dispatcher's voice changes when I say my name, but dammit, she takes my report. And as soon as I hang up, I call the police chief—yes, I have her cell phone number; no, don't ask me how I got it. (I might have happened upon the reporters' "for emergency use only" source contact list—and I'd say this definitely qualifies as an emergency.) Of course, the chief doesn't answer, but you'd better believe I leave a rambling voice mail about missing children and a potential drug dealer and human trafficker on his way from the scary Twin Cities, which I happen to know a fair amount of country folk around here consider to be the Upper Midwest's epicenter of sin and evil.

Then I dial a number I have memorized—the newsroom. A woman answers. "Kallie!" I yell.

"Iris?"

"What time is it? Shit, did you guys already go to press?"

"No, but we're close. What's going on?"

"Finn's missing." God, I can't say it without my voice cracking.

"What? Iris, I'm so sorry."

"Natalie is, too."

"Our *intern*, Natalie? Holy shit."

"I need your help. I need to get the word out. Can you print something?"

There's a pause. "In the newspaper? Iris, I would need it to come from authorities."

"It's my child, Kallie."

She sighs. "What does Mr. Gordon say?"

"He's in the hospital." She gasps, and I sigh. It's been a hell of a night. "Look, could you at least post something on the newspaper's Facebook page? Even if you say it's an unsubstantiated claim, and even if you have to delete it in the morning, I just need it out there. I need people looking for them. *Please*."

There's a pause, and I add, "Look, Kallie, I know I don't understand journalistic integrity and standards—"

"Fuck that."

"What?" I say in surprise, then realize I can hear her typing. "Kallie?"

"Frankly, they don't pay me enough to worry about that shit as it is, and we're all probably going to be laid off in a month anyway. I'm posting it. My cousin is an admin for the local Rummage Sale Facebook page, so I'll have her post it there, too. And I'll also call my brother— he's a tribal police officer. I'll ask if they can get the word out. If there's anything else I can do, let me know."

A wave of emotion rocks me. "Thank you," I whisper.

I end the call and get in my car; then I click into Facebook on my phone. Kallie's comment gave me an idea, and I make my first-ever post in the local mom group I joined a few years ago when Finn started preschool. MISSING KIDS!!! PLEASE SHARE!!! Yes, I use all caps and way too many exclamation marks—that's the point. Let them make fun of me or share it ironically; at least it'll spread the word. I upload the picture I snapped of Finn and Natalie playing video games that day and hit "Post." I look at the picture, their happy faces, and almost break down, but I shake it away, open a new text to Jane. I need help—can't find Finn and Natalie! On my way over.

Her response buzzes, and I glance down at it—OMG!! Yes, get over here and I'll help you look! Then I drive away, down the county road, gravel flying. Within minutes, I pass Sawyer's house, and I slam on the brakes.

There's a light on inside.

I wrench the steering wheel and press down on the gas pedal. It never occurred to me to look here because I haven't actually *been* to Sawyer's house before, even though he lives right next door. Which goes to show that—despite the fact that I have fallen madly in love with him and it feels like we've known each other forever—we have *actually* only known each other for a few days.

I roll to a stop in front of his house and step out of the car, my entire body tingling in fear and anticipation as I stride across the dark yard toward the house. The stars and moon are bright above, a dazzling display illuminating my path yet keeping me hidden as the wind blows its melancholy song through the prairie grass.

I reach the front door and freeze. The light is coming from an upstairs window, but I realize I have no plan as to how to get up there undetected—if, in fact, the kids are inside with a kidnapper. A wave of nausea hits, but I force it down. If it's Rex or one of his thugs, they are likely armed and extremely dangerous.

But I can't stop now. I won't. My baby needs me—and so does Natalie.

My hand trembles as I reach for the knob, giving it a soft twist. The door creaks slightly as I press it open, and I curse under my breath, inch it a little bit more, enough to slip through. Inside, I blink, willing my eyes to adjust to the darkness. It's a small entryway leading into the living room. I crouch down, stalking stealthily forward, eyes sweeping the room. But it's no use—all I can make out are dark, amorphous blobs, which I assume are pieces of furniture. If somebody is hiding in here, I'm totally screwed, and yet I keep going because I have to. My eyes land on the coffee table—an empty glass tumbler calls to me. I reach for it, holding this potential weapon out in front of me.

The staircase is at the edge of the living room, and I place a careful foot on the first step, slowly easing my weight onto it, thanking God when it doesn't creak. One by one, I make my way up the staircase, painstakingly slow, praying with each step that I don't cause any creaks. I glance at the photos on the wall. Most are of Natalie at various ages, but one is an old family photo—a much younger Sawyer holding a chubby toddler in one arm, the other arm wrapped around a beautiful young woman with long, strawberry-blonde hair. They're both beaming, so happy, oblivious to future pain, and a pang of sadness hits me. But I shake it away and press forward up the stairs.

As I near the landing, a soft, filmy light starts to illuminate my way. Whichever room has a light on, the door must be open, and yet I don't hear any sounds—no voices or other noises signaling that people are up here.

Finally at the top, I look both ways down the hall until I see the light coming out of an open doorway. I walk slowly toward it, raising the glass in front of me, ready to strike if needed. I stop outside the door and peek my head around the edge. It's a bedroom. My eyes sweep the space quickly—bed, dresser, closet—but it looks empty. I step in cautiously, first looking behind the open door, then crouching down to peer underneath the bed, tugging up on the navy-blue comforter to get a better look. Nothing but dust bunnies. Then I stand and bite back a gasp.

The closet door is ajar.

A wave of fear—both past and present, from terrible old memories and the horrifying reality I'm facing now. But I have to do it. I *have* to. I take trembling steps toward the closet, shoving down the pain from years ago, and yet terrified that I'm walking right into a trap set by the kidnapper. As I reach the closet door, I can't stand it anymore—I whip it open, reach inside for the light switch. Nothing. My shoulders sag in relief, and I let out a breath.

Then I scan every corner—this must be Sawyer's room, I think, as I shove aside hangers of men's shirts and pants. But it's a small, cramped closet, so there's really nowhere someone could be hiding in here. On the floor, though, I notice a shoebox with its lid askew, so I crouch down to pick it up. Inside I see a jewelry box, photographs, and old news clippings. The ominous feeling pulses within me, either instinct or anxiety, but I have a feeling it's right for once—something is about to shift, something important is about to be revealed.

I slink to the floor and take out the top photograph, turn around the shiny silver frame, and see the smiling face of the woman with strawberry-blonde hair from the hallway photo, holding an adorable little girl, around preschool age, who has pigtails the same color as her mama's. I smile sadly at this picture of Natalie and her mom. But then my thoughts drift to the old photos of the Millers in my office drawer—*the mother was there, but then she was gone*—and the deep ache inside me intensifies.

I set down the photo carefully and then pick up a news clipping. Sure enough, it's an obituary, the same smiling face looking up at me, but in black and white on newsprint. I read the words: Samantha Catherine (Brewster) Jones, age 31, died in a motor vehicle accident on August 3rd, 2014, in rural Hennepin County, Minnesota.

I drop the paper, hand flying to my mouth.

Why were you there?

Sawyer asked me that after Cole's photo slideshow, so shocked and pained. He recognized the devastating scene of the picture because one of the vehicles belonged to him.

Oh God, no.

Sawyer's wife died in the crash that killed Mitch.

CHAPTER THIRTY-TWO

I set down the box with shaky hands. Samantha Jones lost her life on the day I got my second chance. Guilt and shame pummel me. I was so grateful for the accident afterward—it was terrifying when it happened, but it provided a fresh start, an escape. It never occurred to me to worry about what happened to the other driver, and I feel so selfish now thinking of it. Back then, I was just trying to survive. I was running for my life.

My hand flies to my mouth. I feel sick with terrible thoughts of Sawyer blaming me, of the past few days being nothing but a mirage.

But I take a deep breath, force myself to focus, for the kids. The connection must be the key, and the answer is there on the tip of my brain, fighting to push through the surface, thorny and painful as it may be. I need to know more about what happened that night after I fled.

Suddenly, Brayden's grating voice sticks in my mind: *Haven't you heard of Google? I thought even you were smart enough to realize anyone can just find shit on the internet.*

Dammit, the little jerk was right. I take out my phone—ignore the six worried texts from Jane, for now—and type in the date and the names "Mitchell Wheeler" and "Samantha Jones." At first, I only get their obituaries. I think for a moment, then add "car accident" and "Hennepin County, Minnesota" to the search. Finally, after scrolling and scrolling, I find a link to a news story.

The headline reads: Two die in two-vehicle wreck. I click into the story, scroll down, scanning the information—One vehicle was driven by Samantha Jones and one vehicle was driven by Mitchell Wheeler; both drivers were later pronounced dead at Sacred Heart Hospital in Independence, Minnesota.

Then suddenly, in the middle of the story, I find words that stop me cold: A passenger in Jones's vehicle—a child, age eight—was taken by ambulance to the hospital and is now listed in stable condition. This newspaper does not release names of accident victims if they are minors.

But I don't need them to tell me.

An eight-year-old child in Samantha's vehicle. *Her* child.

Natalie.

CHAPTER THIRTY-THREE

My mind spins, playing back the many events of the past few days. Natalie is the best researcher on our newspaper staff. She looked through Mr. Gordon's files, figured out who I am.

Something Cole said—*she helped me with the pictures.*

And something the voice said: *You didn't save me, Iris. You ran away and left me behind.*

My hand flies to my mouth.

Natalie was in the vehicle that night. She saw her mom die. She saw me run. In her little-girl mind, I left her behind.

And now she has Finn—and if she helped Cole gather pictures and information, Rex or one of his henchmen could find them both.

Guilt and shame and fear and sadness rage within me, an agonizing mixture, and my blood boils with the need to find them, to hold them each tight, ease the pain.

To right this wrong, somehow.

I push myself up and race back downstairs, out to my car. Shit. *Think.* In a desperate effort, I call Natalie's cell. It goes straight to voice mail. Of course. My finger hovers over the text function, but this is way too heavy for a text. Then a flash of realization hits.

The walkie-talkie.

I dig through my purse, hand trembling, and bring the two-way radio up to my face. I say a silent prayer, then press the button. "Natalie?" I say softly.

I wait. Nothing. "Natalie?" I say it louder, more firmly.

Still nothing but silence. Somewhere within, a part of me is angry—furious—that she would do this. This terrifying, elaborate scheme. Endangering Finn. The deception, the cruelty.

But that's nothing compared to the fear, the deep grief, as I think about how hard that night was for me, and imagine how much worse it would be for an eight-year-old child.

After all, what finally got me to escape, to run through the darkness for my life, was my own child, growing within my body that night. In saving us, I left another woman's child alone, left her there, watching her mom die.

A sob escapes, but I keep the button pressed. "Natalie, I know . . . I know everything. And I am so, so sorry. I didn't . . . I had no idea. I never would've left you. Please just tell me where you are so I can make this right."

I let the tears fall, not even wiping them away. I let myself cry, let myself hope against hope that she heard me—that she listened, that she believed me. That there is still a chance at redemption.

An eternity passes; then, the radio crackles to life. *"Mom?"*

My shattered heart stitches itself back together at the sound of his little voice. "Finn?" I cry. "Where are you? Are you okay?"

"I'm fine, Mom. We're in the tree fort! Did we fool you?"

I press a trembling hand against my mouth, bite down onto the soft flesh to hold back my emotion, to make sure this is real. He is really okay. "Oh boy, you sure did. I'm going to come out there, okay?"

"Okay. Bye, Mom."

I gasp, not wanting to let him go, but I need to trust now. I need to believe. I drive back down the gravel road to the lodge. When I pull into the driveway, I position the car's headlights so they point across the dark prairie to the grove of trees. Then I get out and I run, straight into the darkness, stumbling, falling, time and again, but not stopping. Never stopping.

When I reach the trees, I click on my phone's flashlight, shining it along the path flanked by thick branches until it opens up and I see the tree fort. "Finn," I whisper loudly, then slip my phone in my pocket and climb, slow and steady, to the top. When I pull myself onto the ledge, I breathe a sigh of relief, then crawl toward the door. Inside, I let out a sob. Finn looks up. "Oh, hi, Mom," he says casually, as if nothing is wrong in the world, and for some reason it makes me laugh, and when I laugh, he laughs, and then I crawl up to him and wrap him in my arms, kissing his little head, his little cheeks, over and over again until he whines, "Mo-*om*."

I lean back, assessing him. He's perched on what looks like a miniature throne of blankets, with two more wrapped around him, even though the summer night is pleasant, a backpack full of applesauce and juice boxes—all safe for him to consume—next to him. His eyes are glued on his screen, as usual, and he is perfectly content. I reach out to smooth his hair, assuring myself once again that he is real, he is okay. Then I send quick texts to Kallie and Jane.

Jane texts back within seconds. Thank God! Anything I can do to help?

Could you call First Memorial and check on Lowell Gordon? Ambulance took him earlier—I'll explain later.

OMG yes, will do. She adds a praying-hands emoji at the end, and I set my phone down, then turn back to my son. "Where's Natalie?"
He shrugs. "I don't know."

I glance out the window of the fort, into the darkness. "Is . . . anyone else out here with you guys?"

Finn looks at me like I've sprouted a new head. "No."

Thank God. "Good," I say. "Okay, time to go home."

"But I just started a movie," he whines, holding up his tablet. "I have *Minions* downloaded on here."

"You can watch it in the lodge," I say as I frantically gather up the items around him. Then I hear a sound—creaking on the ladder leading up to the fort. I gasp, rush to the door, and look down, where I see Natalie climbing up.

She looks up, and even in the darkness I can see the pain and anger in her eyes. "You," she says.

"Wait." I glance back at Finn. "Please, not in front of him. I'll come down."

She stares at me, stone faced, then slowly retreats. I call back brightly to Finn, "Fine, you can watch the movie—put your earbuds back in." He whoops and replaces them, settling back down with his tablet and a smile, and I slowly make my way down the ladder.

At the bottom, I turn to face Natalie, but her head is down, arms wrapped protectively around herself. For a moment it's silent, nothing but the darkness and the soft wind whistling through the trees. "Natalie?" I say softly, leaning toward her.

Then she looks up, her eyes on fire. "You took everything from me."

The fury of her words and the force of her pain push me back. "I'm so sorry."

"So sorry that you just have to take my dad, too, huh?"

"No, I'm not taking him, Natalie."

"That's not what he told me. He said he wants to start a relationship with you and he wants to know that I'm 'okay with it.'" She scoffs. "Like it matters what I want. He already took my mom's picture off his dresser." I wince internally, thinking back to the photo I found earlier tonight. "I went into his room to get a charger, and the picture was gone. I found it in his fucking closet. Like he wants to forget her."

Oh God. "Natalie, I—"

She glares at me. "He had to know what you did. You looked at us; then you just *left*. And she died. And I was all by myself." Her voice breaks, and she crumples. I walk to her, and she tries to push me away, but I wrap my arms around her until she stops fighting, until she lets the tears fall. "I hate you for that," she says through her tears.

"I know."

"I fucking *hate* you."

"I understand."

"Stop that. Stop being *nice*," she cries.

I say nothing, just sit with her in the darkness. Finally, she looks up at last, and for the first time I notice she has Sawyer's eyes, now heavy with sadness. "Why did you leave me?"

Grief shatters me, and I place a gentle hand on her face. "I swear that I didn't know you were there. And now, knowing what happened to your mom that night, and knowing that I left you in that car, all alone . . . it's devastating beyond words. You don't have to forgive me, but I want you to know how sorry I am. If I could go back and take it back, I would get you out of there and take you someplace safe. I would *never* leave you behind."

She sags against me, and I listen to the hitch of her breath as she quietly cries. We sit together for a long time. When at last her crying slows, she draws a shuddering breath and looks over at me. "I didn't mean for all this to happen. I would never hurt Finn. *Never.*"

"I know, honey."

"I swear I was only going to mess with you and leave it at that."

I grimace. "The walkie-talkie?"

She looks down. "I found it out here in my old box of toys when I was showing Finn around the other day, so I put new batteries in it, and the one in the lodge. I was just trying to scare you. I'm sorry." She darts her eyes up at me. "And I'm sorry we wrecked your flowers."

"We?" I ask; then it dawns on me. "Cole."

She looks down guiltily. "He's been helping me look up information and come up with ideas ever since I figured out who you were." I bite my lip—I want to ask exactly what Cole has done and whom he has contacted, but I want to let her talk. She rubs her face. "God, I didn't even want the newsroom internship at first, but Dad and Mr. Gordon were excited about it, so I said I'd go in for an interview, and the first face I saw when I walked into the newsroom was yours."

A chill runs through me, and now I wrap my arms around my own knees as she starts talking again. "You looked so familiar, but different." I nod, picturing the gaunt face of my mug shot from Cole's slideshow. "I told myself I was imagining things, but then I started researching. I already knew the name of the driver that night, Mitchell Wheeler, and then I saw that he'd been arrested with a woman named Evelyn Iris Johannson. Then I went through Mr. Gordon's files and found the truth about you. But you had no idea who I was. So I wanted to make you remember. To hurt like I hurt." She winces and glances up at the tree house, where Finn is happily oblivious with his headphones and movie. "But I really would *never* hurt him. And the more I got to know you, the more confused I got about hurting you, too." She squeezes her eyes shut. For a moment we're silent; then her soft voice asks, "Do you hate me?"

"No," I say quickly. "I could never, ever hate you, Natalie. It took a lot of courage to tell me this. Thank you for sharing all that with me." I take a deep breath. "If it's okay, I would like to share something with you, too. I don't expect you to feel sorry for me, or anything like that—I would never expect *anything* from you—but I'm really hoping you can someday decide that *you* don't hate *me*. Is it okay if I tell you my story?"

She nods, and I say a quick prayer, take a deep breath.

And then tell her my story.

If I squint my eyes, I can pretend I'm somewhere else, in some other place, some other life. The thick trees outside the trailer window congeal into a uniform green blob, and I imagine it's an enchanted forest of magical creatures, waiting for me to come claim my throne as the rightful queen. There's a king there, too, waiting for me. He is strong, handsome—and kind. Above all, he is kind.

Behind me, the bed squeaks as Mitch rolls over in a smelly, hungover heap.

"Go grab me a beer." He smacks my backside, and I wince but say nothing as I step away from the window and toward the door. I will be quiet as long as I have to be. I have learned to be quiet ever since that night at the party, after Rex's warning. I have learned to escape in my mind to my make-believe place.

Besides, things are different now. My hand goes to my belly. Maybe Mitch will be different, after I tell him. Maybe we can still be a happy family. There's a pain in my chest as I think it, but I smile it away, like Grandma used to say when I skinned my knee. *Smile it away, Evvie, and it won't hurt anymore.*

I walk down the hall, swatting at the flies as I go. Somebody left a window open all night, but the flies are a small price to pay because otherwise it would be suffocatingly hot in here without electricity. I reach the kitchen and gag at the thick scent of ripe garbage and ashy cigarette butts. No open window ever gets rid of the stench in here, and now with my heightened sense of smell, it's almost unbearable. I pinch my nose and swipe a beer bottle—wet from the already-melting ice they picked up at the convenience store—out of the fridge with my other hand. When I turn around, Rex is standing right behind me. With a yelp I step away, back against the fridge. "I . . . I didn't hear you come in," I say.

A slow grin spreads across his face—he does this on purpose now, and I hate it, but I've learned that showing any fear around here only makes things worse. "Did your old man tell you about our new plan?" he asks in his low, gravelly voice.

I frown. "What new plan?"

"A way for you to help with a new gig."

"Mitch said I was staying here from now on," I say meekly. My cheek burns where Mitch struck me the first time I brought it up, but ever since the party, I haven't gone anywhere—which is lonely and dark but better than being a part of the drug deals and break-ins.

Rex snarls, rubbing his shaved head. "This is different." He leans in, and I hold my breath against the waft of body odor and booze. "We need a sweet little thing to lure in some more sweet little things, and you know you need to play nice from now on, right?"

A wave of nausea hits, and I mumble "Mitch is waiting" and slip past him, hurrying back to the bedroom, unsure what he's talking about but hoping I can smile this pain away, too.

August 3, 2014, 5:38 p.m.
Rural Hennepin County, Minnesota

When Mitch goes out with Rex—and whoever else is part of their crew on any given day, I've stopped asking for names—I am alone in the trailer. But it doesn't bother me anymore to be away from Mitch, no more than it bothers me to be with him. There's pain to both; there's fear. When I'm with him, there's no pattern to it. I can't always predict what will set him off or when.

But when it's just me, I know the pattern. I know that approximately twenty-seven minutes after they leave, the silence will be too much. I won't be able to push out the doubts, the grief of wondering what Grandma would think of me now. So after twenty-seven minutes, I know I need to do something. I used to clean, but it got too gross. Plus, Mitch got real mad the time I found his secret stash of drugs because then everybody else knew he had it.

Then I'd go outside and take a walk around the yard, or down the driveway. But then it got too littered with trash—the time I tripped and cut my leg on a broken bottle, Mitch didn't like me getting blood everywhere. Plus, it's summer and the mosquitoes are terrible, and Mitch stopped letting me carry any cash, and he always forgets bug spray when he drives to the convenience store down the highway.

That's when I really started getting lost in my imagination. Grandma always said I had a good one. I would play my "squint and pretend I'm somewhere else" game or even act out little performances. In high school, I read a play once, *Romeo and Juliet*. Back then I wasn't sure if I was supposed to think it was sad or romantic, but now I've decided it must be romantic—it *has* to be because they were in love, and that means no matter what happens to me now, no matter how much pain and fear I go through, it's okay as long as Mitch loves me.

Now, though, I also spend the time talking to my baby. I haven't said it out loud, not yet. But I'm going to have a *baby*. I've only been sure for a few weeks, and I had to do a lot of lying to find out. I told Mitch I had my period, which grosses him out, so he not only let me go along to the convenience store, but he had me go in by myself. I savored it—the working lights, the air-conditioning. I almost felt bad for stealing the pregnancy test. It wasn't the first thing I'd stolen, but it was the first time I'd *chosen* to do it, not something Mitch put me up to.

It almost made me feel good, but then I felt bad, and anyway I sneaked it into the bathroom, and now I know.

I already love him. I'm not sure the baby is a boy, but I have a feeling. "Daddy will love you, too, I just know it," I coo at him now. But there's that pain again, that fear. It's getting to where I almost can't smile it away. And I wonder . . . my eyes drift to the window, longing.

Then suddenly I hear a sound—a muted thud, followed by another. I freeze, listening. It came from somewhere else inside the trailer. There it is again—I push up from the bed and walk to the bedroom door, then walk slowly down the hall until I hear it again. I gasp—it's coming from Rex's room. I have never been in there, nor do I ever wish to be. And yet I have to know; for some reason, I have to find out where this noise is coming from.

The door is ajar and I push it open, gagging at the musty smell of dirty laundry, unwashed sheets, and man sweat. Clothes are strewn about the floor, along with beer bottles and empty pizza boxes. I scan the room, listening, and finally—there it is again, *thump, thump, thump,* coming from the closet. Slowly, I creep forward, dread and fear that go beyond this moment, that somehow feel as though they encompass my whole life, pulling me forward. I place a trembling hand on the knob and open the door—and scream.

Inside is a young woman, obviously drugged, bound and gagged, crumpled against the back corner, terror in her eyes. She blinks when she sees me, then immediately starts trying to talk frantically, her words muffled by the gag.

"Okay, okay, shh," I say, raising my hands and looking at the bedroom door. I know they won't be back for hours, and yet fear of retribution is a constant companion now. I drop to my knees before her and reach around and try to remove her gag, but it's no use. Rex has tied it tight with some complicated knot I have never seen before. "Wait here," I say.

Her panicked, muffled cries follow me through the trailer as I race to the kitchen and grab the largest knife I can find, and when I return, she whimpers fearfully. "No, no, I'm going to use this to cut you free," I explain, dropping down again and setting to work. "It's okay, trust me."

I take a deep, steadying breath and set to work sawing the knife at the thick cloth gag. It takes almost a full minute, but the girl is still, and I get it free. "Thank you," she slurs as it falls to the floor, tears streaming down her face.

I say nothing, only glance at the door again and then set my sights on the rope that binds her hands. That one is quicker—I'm more confident, now that I'm not cutting near her face—and soon her hands are free. I'm starting to tire, and she softly says, "Here," then takes it from me and lazily cuts at her own ankle binds.

I lean back in relief. "Who . . . who are you? How did you get here?"

"Someone grabbed me," she says, her voice sounding drunk. She shakes her head. "I stopped for one drink after work. He must've drugged my drink. Then I woke up here."

My eyes widen. "How long have you been here?"

She slowly shakes her head. "I don't know. But I'm getting the hell out of here." She looks up at me, eyes wide and hopeful. "Do you have a phone?"

I shake my head sadly. Mitch broke my phone months ago. "Sorry, no."

"That's okay," she says, looking determined as she finally cuts through her ankle binds. "I'll just run for it." She looks around, squinting. "Where *are* we?"

"A trailer out in the woods, west of Minneapolis." The words come out before I can even think about it, so automatic. It's what Mitch told me when I moved out here with him. *Why rent your own place when we can use that money to live together?* Soon, though, I was making no money at all because he made me quit my job. He didn't want me out of his sight—unless he had somewhere to go; then I was expected to stay here and wait for him. The pain inside me expands, threatening to burst.

The young woman nods. "I'll walk to a gas station or a fucking Walmart or something."

"The gas station is five miles up the road—" I hesitate. "But . . . they go there a lot."

She nods grimly. "Are you stuck here, too?"

"No," I say, too quickly. "I live here. With . . . with my boyfriend."

Her face softens with understanding, almost pity, and she reaches for my hand. "You can come with me if you want."

"I need to be here when Mitch comes home," I say softly, blinking away tears that surprise me.

She says nothing, only stands shakily, holding up the knife, wrists glistening red with blood from the abrasions caused by being tied up in the closet. "Can I keep this?" I nod, and then she says, "How do I get out of here?"

I beckon her forward, holding my breath as I peek outside the bedroom. Nobody. I breathe again, then lead her down the hall to the front door. I step outside first, eyes sweeping the premises, then finally motion her outside. "Go down the driveway," I say, pointing. "Then take a left. The gas station is to the right, but they always go that way. To the left, there's an exit to the interstate after about eight miles or so. It'll take a little longer, but I think it's safer."

Without warning she wraps me in a sloppy hug. It's been so long since I've been embraced in such a tender, innocent way, and beyond the twinge of blood, she smells of warm jasmine and hope, and I sink into her, hugging her back. "What's your name?" she asks softly.

I draw a shaky breath. "Evelyn. But I've always liked my middle name better. You can call me Iris."

She smiles. "Well, Iris, I'm Finley. But you can call me Finn." She squeezes my hand. "Thank you for saving me. Promise me, someday, you'll save yourself, too?"

She doesn't wait for my answer before she wobbles off down the driveway. I watch her run away until I can't see her anymore, and then I stand silently in the darkness, alone.

August 3, 2014, 10:49 p.m.
Rural Hennepin County, Minnesota

I'm back in the bedroom, sitting on the bed, jittery but determined, when Mitch, Rex, and a bunch of guys I see nearly every day but who remain nameless burst through the door, loud and drunk and high and rowdy. Apparently tonight wasn't a work job, or if it was supposed to be, they're too drunk to realize it. Perfect.

A few minutes go by before Mitch stumbles into the room, beer in hand. "You ready for this, baby?" he slurs, grabbing his crotch with his free hand.

I ignore his crudeness, asking calmly, "Where's Rex?"

"Fuckin' passed out on his bed. Why?"

Good. I closed his closet door again, so there should be no immediate trace of suspicion, but the fact that he's passed out buys me more time. "He said something earlier about me being part of jobs again," I say. "I thought you said I didn't have to do that anymore?"

"Yeah, but these are different jobs, so this is different." He slides up beside me, and I have to hold my breath so the pungent smell of whiskey emanating from his pores doesn't cause me to vomit.

I lean away. "What do you need me to do?"

"Just, you know, be nice."

"He said something about young women . . . ?"

"Goddamn it, Iris." Mitch has morphed into anger at his typical lightning speed, but still I flinch when he throws his beer bottle against the wall, smashing it to pieces. "I have told you not to ask me questions. Haven't I told you? You're too fucking stupid to understand."

Something breaks inside me then. And even though it's painful—so painful there's no way I would ever be able to smile it away—it's freeing, too, and I realize that my someday is today. I take a deep breath. "I need to go to the store."

Mitch is still on his tirade, oblivious to any response that is not directly in line with his own words. "You're gonna have to make it up to me now," he says.

I straighten my shoulders. "*Mitch*, I said, I need to go to the store."

"What?" He frowns, blinking, processing. "Why?"

"My period, Mitch," I say, glancing pointedly at him. "I need more supplies."

"Already?" He scrunches up his face, but my gamble that he's too drunk to do any math has paid off. "Shit. Fine."

"I'll be back before you know it," I say brightly, pushing off the bed.

Mitch grabs my wrist, and I wince. "I'm driving you."

"But you're drunk," I say, a seed of panic planting within me.

"You don't fuckin' tell me when I'm too drunk to drive, woman." With that he drags me out of the room, through the trailer house, and out the front door.

I trip down the steps and go down to one knee, crying out in pain. "Mitch, please, you can drive—just let go of my arm so I can walk."

He does, though he mumbles about me always bitching at him nonetheless. I ignore him and get in the car, waiting as he slides in, drops his keys twice, swears loudly—because it's always someone else's fault—and then finally gets the car started. This is okay, I think. As long as we leave, this is okay. He's drunk enough that I can trick him into coming into the store for more beer, and then I'll sneak out, take the car, and drive away.

He puts the car in drive, but suddenly someone's at the window, pounding for Mitch to open it. "Jesus Christ," Mitch says, but he rolls the window down, and it's one of the nameless men, stoned but serious. "What the hell do you want?" Mitch growls.

"Dude, she's gone."

"What? Who?"

"The first . . . uh, package. The one that we were supposed to deliver tomorrow. I looked in Rex's closet, and it's empty."

Mitch slams his hand against the steering wheel and swears loudly.

My hands shake, but I fight to play the part. "What's he talking about, Mitch? Who's gone?"

He doesn't even look at me, instead barking at the nameless man, "Well, get your asses out there and find her, then. I'll keep an eye out while I drive down to the store. We'll meet up down there, in the parking lot—she won't get far."

With that we take off, and I focus on the road ahead, illuminated by the headlights. As we drive away, my hands twist together nervously on my lap, small doubts forming. Mitch and the trailer are all I've known since Grandma died—I've never been on my own. I have nothing, no money, nowhere to go. Mitch is far from perfect, but in his twisted way, he loves me. Maybe he would love our baby, too. I stare into the silent night, thinking.

Come to think of it, it's too silent. The car swerves then, and I whip my head over just as Mitch's head droops—he's falling asleep at the wheel. "Mitch!" I cry, and his head jerks up, the car swerving back and righting itself.

"Goddamn it, woman, don't you yell at me!" he snarls. I brace for a smack, but he's apparently not there yet. "Biggest fucking job of our life, and she fucking gets away," he mutters. Then he stops, sitting up straight.

He turns to look at me, his eyes swimmy but trained directly on mine. "You were there."

"What?" I ask.

He blinks, rubs his face as if to clear his thoughts, his eyes darting to the road and then back to me. "You were fucking there, Iris. Did you see her leave?"

My heart hammers in my chest. "Did I see who?"

"Don't you—" He raises his hand but stops midair, and I flinch. Evidently satisfied, he turns back to the road. "Don't try to trick me, Iris. I am smarter than you'll ever be. You are nothing. You hear me? Nothing without me. Now tell me, did you *see* her?"

I say nothing, just glance out the windshield, around the car, anywhere but at him, and suddenly my eyes catch a glint of silver in the ashtray. I peer more closely and gasp—it's a glittering silver chain, pooled among the pennies and lint.

My Grandma's necklace.

I grab it, hold it up to him. "Where did you get this? Were you going to sell it?"

For one moment I see a flicker of recognition, then a cold sneer. And it's like a dam bursts inside me, the painful truth pouring forth. Mitch knows how important the necklace is to me; he just doesn't care. He has *never* cared, all this time. This false utopia I've been desperately hoping to get back to never actually existed.

He never loved me.

And he will never, ever meet my baby.

"Don't fucking change the subject," Mitch slurs, glancing at the road again and then back at me. "Dammit, Iris, tell me."

I say nothing, but I don't look away. I refuse to.

Mitch is seething with rage, confused that for once I'm not cowering. "Tell me!"

"I helped her."

"What?" Mitch splutters.

I look him straight in the eye. "I helped her leave, and *I'm* leaving, too."

The car goes silent, and I savor the split second of shock on Mitch's face, this disbelief that I could've done something, anything, against his wishes. He raises his hand, and this time I don't flinch—and he sees it at last, this change in me, this ending between us. The power in that moment will get me through whatever happens next. No matter what he does, I'm leaving with my baby and never looking back.

Today is my someday.

But suddenly the world shifts. There's the blare of a horn, the flash of oncoming lights, the loudest crash I've ever heard pounding in my ears, reverberating throughout my entire being.

And then there is nothing but darkness.

August 3, 2014, 11:11 p.m.
Rural Hennepin County, Minnesota

My eyes open slowly, everything muted, the world turned on its side. I brush hair out of my face, and pain radiates through my arm, and that's not hair, it's blood, so much blood. There's a gash on my head—Mitch hit me again. No, something worse. I push through the fog in my brain and try to make out shapes in the darkness around me. There's a breeze blowing. Am I outside? No—it's air through a shattered window.

I gasp. A car accident. My hands go to my stomach instinctively, but there's no way to tell. I'm okay, though. I'm awake, alert. My arm hurts, my head is bleeding, but I'm here. I'm *alive*. And so is my baby— he is okay, he *has* to be.

I turn toward the driver's seat, and oh God—Mitch is slumped forward, rammed into the steering wheel, the dashboard, everything crunched together, so crushed and compact, the metallic smell of blood on the air, and I whimper, reach out, wincing at the pain in my arm. "Mitch?" I shake him, but he's limp, not breathing.

He's gone.

There's pain somehow, but mostly release, the heaviest weight lifted.

With a shaking hand I reach for my seat belt, and miraculously, it unlatches. My door won't open, but I shrug out of my hoodie and wrap it around my hand, turning my head away as I punch out the rest of the glass in the window. I heave myself up and out the window, getting a small rip in my shirt but nothing else.

Outside in the dark, the night air is cool, but I barely notice, adrenaline coursing through my veins. I survey the mangled scene—the front of our car has nearly merged with the front of the other vehicle, though its back half is intact, like some macabre piece of modern art. I turn and retch into the ditch behind me and then wipe my mouth, set my shoulders.

Mitch is gone, but I am not yet free. If his friends find me, they will kill me—especially Rex, I think, shuddering violently. I can't let that happen. I need to find a way to keep my baby safe.

One last look at the mangled scene before me, one last glance at my past, and then I turn away and I run.

We're less than a mile from the store, but I know that's where the others are going. So I do another unexpected thing—I run back the way we came, back to the trailer house, nothing but me and the night, feet scraping along the pavement, stars shining brightly in the sky.

And my baby. All this is to protect my baby. I have to get away, to give him a better life than this. A home and a family. Safety and warmth and love.

Headlights in the distance, and I dip down into the ditch until they pass. Then I think I best stay there, slinking along through tall grass and muck with the ticks and the shadows.

I stay here in the darkness because it hides me. Because it saves me.

Around me, a forest of stately pine trees lines the road, the wind carrying the fragrant scent of their needles, carrying me forward as I pray for my baby. For myself. For Finley. For anyone who needs to escape to a better life.

At last I reach our driveway, my feet scuffing cautiously along the gravel until I reach our yard. As I suspected, it's dark and the vehicles are gone—everyone is out looking for Finley, as Mitch commanded.

Then I squint at the side of the trailer house. Also as I thought—Rex's truck is still here, since he's passed out inside. I creep up and ease the door open, gasping as the inside light comes on, then scramble in and quickly shut the door so the light goes off. *He could wake up at any moment,* I remind myself, terrified. I pull down the sun visor, and keys fall to my lap. With shaking hands, I put them in the ignition, and the truck rumbles to life.

At any moment I expect Rex's snarling, evil face to appear against the door, for him to lock me in his closet and trap me in the most terrible life imaginable. But I put the truck in drive and slam down on the pedal. I turn left, driving the eight miles to the interstate, then west away from the city, away from this state, away from this life.

I don't look back. I keep going forward, to freedom.

CHAPTER

THIRTY-FOUR

There's a lot about that night, about my life, that I don't say out loud to Natalie. A lot I will *never* say out loud. Like how it all began with my mom's cruel dismissal—that I was worthless. It was seared into my psyche, starting me on the path to always feeling "less than" throughout my entire life.

What followed were years of taunting in elementary school—for my crooked teeth my grandma couldn't afford to fix, the ripped clothes she couldn't afford to replace. *Low class* is what my ex–best friend called me in middle school. In high school, the word was *pitiful*—that one came from the perky teacher's pet responsible for doling out hall passes when I had to pick up my weekend Salvation Army snack bag in the principal's office. I even overheard a high school social studies teacher telling a colleague I was *forgettable*.

None of that matters, not really. Screw them, right? That's the mentality strong women are supposed to have. It's what I would tell anyone else in this situation. And yet those words fed my inner monologue from a very young age. The ones that always told me it made sense that I was treated badly because I wasn't as good as everyone else. I was worthless. Forgettable.

It's what set the stage for the woman I became. The lonely young woman working double shifts at the twenty-four-hour diner to try to pay for her grandma's funeral, crying herself to sleep every night and wondering at age twenty-seven when life would begin.

When someone, anyone, would care about me ever again.

So when Mitchell Wheeler walked into my life—drunk and ornery and craving french fries at three a.m. one Saturday night—I was the perfect target. He put me through hell but left me with the only piece of heaven I've ever seen, the only person I'd live and die for. And for that, I can never fully hate Mitch. It's why I gave Finn his middle name. Because as much as I hate that I will someday need to tell my son about his terrible father, the fact is, the worst time of my life gave me Finn.

And my son's first name—that one I chose to honor the bravest person I ever met, the person who saved my life and my child's by reminding me I was *worth* saving. I don't know where she is now, but I hope she's free and happy and safe; someday, I hope I can thank her.

But none of that is where I start with Natalie. I blow out a long breath and tell her my tale from that fateful night. "The driver of the other car—Mitch Wheeler—he was my boyfriend. He was not good to me. I should never have been with him, but you're old enough to understand things, I think. To understand that sometimes people—women, especially—get trapped. Things start okay with a man. He showers you with compliments and tells you how much he loves you, so you ignore the warning signs. The way he yells at you over nothing. The way he grabs your arm too hard when you're in a fight, and then eventually shoves you down; then pretty soon he's slapping and punching you, forcing you to do things you don't want to do." I stop, eyes darting to Natalie. "Do you understand?"

She nods. "Yeah."

"Has that ever happened to you?"

Her eyes widen. "No. I haven't had a boyfriend before."

"Good," I say, relieved. "One day you will choose to date someone—if you want to, I mean. So I just want you to know your worth, okay?"

"Okay," she says softly.

I continue. "That's how it was with Mitch and me. It was bad, and then it was worse. But by then I had moved in with him, I was committing crimes with him—which I'm not proud of—and I had no money of my own and nowhere to go. No way to escape."

"So what happened?" Natalie whispers.

I smile. "Finn happened. I found out I was pregnant with him. Something inside me snapped into place, and I knew I *had* to get us out of there—I had to get us away from Mitch so he could never, *ever* hurt my baby. I just didn't know how."

I squeeze my eyes shut as I prepare to recall the haunting memory. "That night, Mitch was drunk, but he insisted on driving. We argued, and when he reached over to hit me, he took his eyes off the road exactly when we met the other car—your car," I say softly. "He swerved into the other lane, and we hit head-on. I blacked out for a while, and when I came to, I was okay, but Mitch . . . he was dead. And as terrible as it sounds, I realized that was my chance to escape." I swallow, remembering the chill of the night air on my face as I stepped out of the car, the smell of burned rubber and gasoline in the air. "I think I remember looking at the other car, but I didn't really *see* it, or think about who might be inside it. And I'm so sorry about that. I only knew that I had to get away. So I ran."

Natalie's face is in her hands. I wait, and finally she looks up, tears in her eyes. "Ran where?" she asks softly.

"Back to our house. I took a truck that was parked in our driveway, and then I just drove all night. I made it across state lines into South Dakota, but as the sun was coming up, I was *so* tired, so I pulled into this big truck stop. That's where I ran into Lowell and Ivan Gordon." I smile. "They were like angels on earth, rescuing me and taking me in."

We're silent for a moment, and I gather my emotions from telling a story I've only ever told once in my life—to the Gordons. "Thank you for listening, Natalie," I say softly. "Like I said, I don't expect you to feel sorry for me or forgive me. I hope, someday, you won't hate me, but I understand that's a lot to ask. And I know that it's only words, but I want to say again that I am so, so sorry."

Silence, complete and devastating. The prairie wind picking up, rustling through the trees in this dark night. Then Natalie's shoulders slump forward, trembling again with her silent tears. I place a hand on her back, not wanting to invade her space after we've both shared such intimate tales of our personal pain. I give her time, let her cry, say a prayer. At last, Natalie looks up, swipes at her eyes. "I don't hate you," she says softly.

I let out a breath, say a prayer of thanks, and blink away my own tears. "That's all I can hope for," I say. It's something, I tell myself. It's a start.

I hope against hope that, somehow, it's a new beginning.

CHAPTER THIRTY-FIVE

Together, Natalie and I gather up Finn and all the supplies from the tree fort and slowly make our way across the field to the house. Inside, I get Finn settled on the couch and turn to Natalie, serious. It's time to know for sure what we're dealing with. "I have a question, and I need you to tell me the truth—no judgment, but I have to know if we're in danger."

She nods, eyes wide.

"Did anyone *actually* contact Rex McNeil? Cole led me to believe he did, and if that's true, we could be in trouble."

"No, we never did," Natalie says, eyes pained. "I found information on him, and I'm the one who told Cole about it."

"Are you *sure* Cole didn't?" I press.

She shakes her head. "He said he met Rex before, a long time ago or something, and he knows what he's like, so he wanted to make sure he could really get money from you before he got someone like Rex involved." She drops her eyes. "I'm sorry."

I nod grimly, relief flooding me. "It's okay. That's good to know."

My phone rings then, and I look down. "Hello?" I say, confused, as I answer.

"Iris Jenkins?" a woman's voice, crisp and commanding, asks.

"Yes?" I ask nervously.

"This is Chief Virginia Nader. I got your voice mail about missing children, and then proceeded to get several more calls from concerned residents who've seen some Facebook posts. I was actually off duty, but when I came into the station, they knew nothing about this. Did you report it?"

"I'm sorry. I tried when the officer was here. He said he would come back later to take my report. But it's okay," I add quickly. "The kids were found safe."

"I'm glad to hear that," she says. "What happened?"

My eyes make contact with Natalie, who looks apprehensive. "A misunderstanding," I say. "They went for a walk in the woods and got turned around. Thank God for cell phones. I'm very sorry for the trouble."

"No trouble. We're here to help." She clears her throat. "By the way, which officer responded?"

I swallow. "Officer Watson."

There's a pause, muffled voices in the background. "Got it," she says, her voice harder. "Thanks for letting me know. I'll be following up with him."

"But Officer Barnes is great," I add.

"Noted," the chief says, a smile in her voice. "Is there anything else you need help with tonight, Ms. Jenkins?"

Sawyer. I glance at Natalie, who's now sitting on the couch watching Finn's movie with him. I step a little farther away from them. "Actually, uh, a friend of mine had a little trouble tonight and was . . . well, he was arrested. I was wondering if he's okay?" I ask nervously.

"Who are you looking for?"

"Sawyer Jones," I say softly.

There's a pause. "Looks like he posted bail already."

"Oh," I say, surprised. "Can you tell me who bailed him out?"

"Sure, it's public record. The name listed is Cole Jones."

I suck in a breath. "Okay, thank you so much for your help, Chief Nader." I end the call, mulling this over. Cole bailed out Sawyer. I'm grateful that Sawyer won't spend the night in jail, yet I still don't trust Cole at all. I need to call Sawyer, but first I should try to get Finn to sleep.

I walk over to the couch but see that he has already nodded off—in fact, both of them have, Finn curled up against Natalie, and her head resting on his. A rush of emotion hits me—they are both so young and innocent. Suddenly none of the pain and fear of today matters at all because they are safe at home.

Home.

Is it still possible? I hope so. I swipe at my eyes as I reach for the blanket on the edge of the couch and gently cover them up. Sawyer and I have so much to talk about, though truly, he and Natalie need to talk first. My feelings for him haven't changed, but I don't know if he still feels the same. I don't know if we can still find a way forward, together.

Not wanting to wake the kids, I step into the kitchen as I call Sawyer—and immediately let out a shocked cry. Sitting there at the kitchen table, one hand against his bruised face and the other holding a bottle of some sort of liquor, is Dave Donnelly. "Ah, there you are, sweetheart."

His smile is menacing, and I take a cautious step back, as if he's a wild animal that could pounce at any moment. He very well could be. "What are you doing here?"

He shakes his head, ignoring my question. "You really fucked up tonight, Iris. Are you going to make it up to me, or what?"

Alarm bells ring in my head, and I wonder if I'm fast enough to run to the kids, rouse them enough to somehow get them out the door and into the car before he catches up to us. There's no way—and then I see the glint of a knife, lying sharp and ready on the countertop in front of him. Oh God.

I muster my strength, pray my voice doesn't shake. "You need to leave."

"Why? This place is mine now, or it's gonna be as soon as that senile old man signs the paperwork."

I take another step toward the door, but he notices. "Uh-uh, sweetheart." His hand drops to the knife, hovering above it. "You come sit down over here by me."

Everything within me screams at me not to comply, but my terrified brain can't think of an alternative. I walk toward him slowly, easing down into the seat across the table from him. "Good girl," he says, and I feel sick. He takes a long swig of the liquor, then sets the bottle back down on the table with a thud. "Actually, you were quite the bad little girl, weren't you?" I drop my gaze, and he chuckles. "Ah, don't worry, drug charges and theft are kiddie play, really. But I'm glad that Cole clued me in to your past, because what it *does* tell me is that you don't want that secret getting out, so you'll be a nice, compliant employee in my business ventures."

I force myself to meet his gaze. "What are you going to do?"

He grins and it's sickening. "What I've been trying to tell you ever since we met. I'm expanding my operations into the Dakotas. I provide hospitality and entertainment for hunters, businessmen, the occasional traveling politician. Make sure they have companionship during their stay—beautiful, attentive companionship, day or night."

A wave of nausea rocks me as I realize what he means. "You're despicable."

He frowns. "Now, that's not very nice. And I happen to treat my girls very well, as long as they stay in line. But that's what you'd be helping me with—you would be their manager."

My eyes widen. "Never."

He stands and walks slowly around the table, crouching down before me so his face is inches from mine, knife glinting in his hand. "Seems to me you don't have much of a choice, do you? Face it, Iris: you're a loser with a shady past and a bad reputation for lying. Nobody would believe a word that comes out of that pretty little mouth of yours." He raises the knife, and I tremble in fear as he glides the flat side against my face.

I squeeze my eyes shut, hot tears pressing behind my lids. But as much as they're tears of fear, they're also tears of fury—because I didn't come this far to let another cruel, evil man cage me. Never again.

Dave lowers the blade, and I seize this moment—now or never. I shove him back, and he falls to the floor; then I leap up from the table, ready to run for the doorway. But he latches onto my leg with one hand, and I scream as I go crashing down to the floor. He climbs on top of me, and I scream again as he smacks my face. "You stupid bitch. You're gonna pay for that."

His hand wraps around my throat—I can't breathe—and I thrash in panic, kicking and clawing at him, but he won't let go. Then behind him, movement, and my eyes bulge. Oh God—it's Natalie, holding a large pan, stalking slowly forward. *No,* I want to scream, *run, take Finn and get out—save yourselves!*

But she lunges forward and smacks down hard on his head with the pan. He yowls in pain and rolls off me, and Natalie tries to help me to my feet. But Dave growls like an animal and swipes at Natalie's legs, knocking her over. I crawl up, placing myself protectively between them. Behind me, Natalie cowers, and in front of me, Dave stands wielding the knife like a maniac, ready to strike.

"Please," I plead. "Just let her go. I'll do whatever you want."

"It's too late for that," he growls.

Suddenly, the sound of the front door, footsteps, and the kitchen door swings open. I whimper in relief.

Sawyer. He surveys the scene in shock, and Cole walks in right behind him. "What the fuck?"

"Hey, now, fellas, you're just in time." Dave holds up his hands, chuckling nervously. "They . . . they were trying to attack me. This crazy bitch wanted my money—you know what she's like."

Sawyer looks at us, at my own frightened face and then at Natalie, still curled up on the floor behind me, terrified. Then his gaze lands on Dave again, and his eyes go black. "You son of a bitch."

He lunges at Dave, Cole close behind him, and they knock him to the ground, the knife clattering as it hits the floor. I help Natalie to her feet, and when I turn back, Sawyer has his hands wrapped around Dave's neck. It's sweet poetic justice to hear him cough and sputter for breath, yet his daughter is also watching. "Sawyer," I call, my voice breaking. He looks up, face softening as he relaxes his grip. Then he turns to his brother. "Don't let him go."

"Yes, sir," Cole says, delivering a swift kick to Dave's side and then sitting down heavily on top of him.

For a moment, Sawyer stares at us and we stare at him, as if we're all in shock. Then Natalie whimpers, her face crumbling. "Daddy," she says, and Sawyer rushes to her, wrapping her in his arms.

"Are you okay?" he asks, pulling back to search her face. Then he wraps her up in his arms again, kissing her head.

His worried eyes turn to me, and he reaches out a hand to gently stroke my face. I squeeze my eyes shut, trying to hold back my own tears—then my eyes fly open. "Finn."

"He's still asleep on the couch," Sawyer says. "I saw him; then I heard the commotion and came in and saw that . . . that animal, and I . . . I lost it. I'm sorry." He kisses Natalie's head again, and she burrows deeper into his chest.

"I'll call the chief," I say.

"Cole already did—he saw Dave's car parked out back as we drove up."

"Thank God you guys got here . . ." My voice breaks, and I can't finish the sentence.

Natalie holds out her arm to welcome me into their embrace, and it's the sweetest gesture I have ever seen. I hesitate, my eyes darting to Sawyer, unsure of his feelings, but he wraps an arm around me, pulling me in, and I close my eyes, exactly where I'm meant to be in this moment.

CHAPTER THIRTY-SIX

It's nearly one in the morning when the blinking glow of police lights appears through the windows. I'm rushing into the living room to sit down by Finn, hoping to avoid having a freaked-out little boy, just as Chief Nader herself bursts through the front door.

"Ms. Jenkins," she says. Her gun is drawn, her face taut, and I motion her toward the kitchen with one hand, my other rubbing the back of my son, now shifting on the couch. The chief proceeds to the kitchen, followed quickly by Officer Barnes and members of the South Dakota Highway Patrol.

Within minutes, they return, two of the highway patrolmen escorting a handcuffed Dave, disheveled and beaten, toward the door. I glare at him, but he doesn't look up as they usher him outside. The chief comes back into the living room, then walks over to me and sits down on a chair. "Are you okay?" she asks softly.

I nod. "Thanks to Sawyer and Cole."

"I took their statements. I also took Natalie's. Sounds like you were pretty brave in there, trying to protect her from that monster."

I shake my head. "She was the brave one. She saved me."

"Well, you don't have to worry about that asshole anymore. Turns out David Roderick Donnelly has prior charges in a number of states, including an outstanding warrant in Oklahoma. They're coming to get him tomorrow, and there's no way he'll be getting out of jail anytime soon."

I shudder, nodding in relief, and she clears her throat. "Ms. Jenkins—Iris—I want to say I'm sorry for the way Officer Watson has treated you. I shouldn't have let that shit go on."

It feels good to hear it, but it's the least of my concerns. "Thank you, but it's fine, really."

"No, it's not. Things will be different now. I promise."

As the chief walks away, I ponder her words. Some things I do in fact want to be different. But others I want to desperately cling to.

The kitchen door opens, and Sawyer walks out, his arm still around a shaken Natalie, with Cole close behind them. I ease off the couch, where Finn is miraculously still asleep, and walk over quickly. "You're not leaving, are you?"

Sawyer shakes his head. "We're all a little rattled, so we were thinking maybe we should all stay together tonight, if that's okay."

Relief washes over me—I didn't realize how much I don't want Finn and me to be alone right now. "I agree. I can get Finn's sleeping bag and move him to the floor."

"I can sleep on the floor with him, if you want," Natalie says softly. I beam at her. "That's a great idea."

We retrieve the sleeping bags and get the kids settled; then Sawyer, Cole, and I stand in tense silence. Finally, a stone-faced Sawyer looks at Cole. "Thank you for your help in there," he says stiffly. "I'll transfer you the bail money tomorrow."

"I don't want your money, man," Cole says.

"I don't care what you want. You need to leave."

Even I wince at Sawyer's harsh tone. "That's it?" Cole says. "We're just not gonna talk about it? Just like with Sam eight years ago, huh?"

"Don't you dare talk about that," Sawyer says slowly.

"Why not? She was on her way to pick me up, Sawyer. *Me*." Tears stream down his face. "I'd rather have you yell and scream at me and even kick my ass—it wouldn't hurt any more than it does every single day knowing it was my fault."

"You're so hurt, huh? That's why you drag my daughter into your shitty life of crime? That's why you terrorize the woman I lo—" He stops, and so does my heart. Sawyer squeezes his eyes shut. "Just get out, Cole."

Cole's shoulders sag in defeat. He turns to me. "I'm sorry, Iris. I really fucked everything up."

I take a deep breath. "Did you really know Rex?"

"He was my dealer years ago, but I swear I didn't know about any of that shit he was doing—the *trafficking*." Cole spits out the word like it's poison on his lips. "But I didn't call him. I really am sorry. I should've known you were a victim in all this, too."

I nod. Cole takes one last look at Sawyer, who continues to stand expressionless and unwavering. Then he walks silently out the door.

Just then my phone buzzes—Jane. Sorry for the late text, but Mr. Gordon is stable. They think it was a heart attack and are going to keep him a few days for testing.

"Lowell is stable," I say to Sawyer as I text Jane back with a thank-you.

"Thank God," he says.

I nod. "I'll go see him in the morning."

We stare at each other then, suddenly awkward, so much to talk about, but so much exhaustion and emotion from this terrible night.

Sawyer lets out a breath. "I need some air. Want to join me on the porch?"

"I'd like that."

Outside in the darkness, the stars are breathtaking. We sit side by side but apart on the porch swing, so much unspoken between us. I shiver in the chilly night air.

"Are you cold?" Sawyer asks.

"I'm fine," I say.

"I can hear your teeth chattering."

"I'm giving you space," I explain.

He sighs. "Come here." He opens his arms, and I lean into him, letting out a warm, grateful breath. We're silent for a long time, content. For a moment, I almost drift off, lulled by his heartbeat and the sound of a soft night breeze whispering through the trees. But visions of tonight's events startle me awake. "Are you okay?" he asks softly.

I don't answer at first, an aching dread creeping back as I wake up fully. I take a deep breath—I don't want to know, but I have to. "Do you hate me?" I whisper.

"What?" He twists his body so he's looking at me while still holding me. "Why would you think that?"

Tears fall before I can stop them. "Because I feel like you should. You said it. I was there that night." I squeeze my eyes shut at the painful memory of the way he looked at me earlier, the way he pulled away—so sad, so betrayed.

"You weren't driving," he says softly. "It was still an accident."

"But I was there. And I *left*. I had no idea—it didn't even occur to me to check on the other car. I had to escape, for me and for Finn." I'm rambling, tears streaming down.

Sawyer shushes me, his hand stroking my hair. "I know, Iris. It wasn't your fault."

Hearing him say the words is a balm to my soul, and I savor it, the way I savor being this close to him, my head against his warm chest.

But the guilt remains. And I realize I'm savoring all this because it might be the last time. I pull back, let out a long breath. "I don't want to push you into anything too quickly."

His brow furrows. "What do you mean?"

"You told me you were all in. But I just wonder, after tonight . . . if you still want to be with me. Or if you still *should* be with me, I guess.

Natalie and I had a really great talk. She is an amazing person. But she's also in a lot of pain. She needs you."

We're silent for a long time, watching the stars, listening to the sound of a gentle wind through the trees lining the house. Finally, Sawyer sighs. "This morning I felt like I had my life figured out for the first time in a long time. Now, nothing makes sense. My feelings for you haven't changed, but you're right—we moved way too fast. I need to focus on Natalie first. She's my number one priority."

"Okay," I say.

He smiles sadly. "Can we just sit out here a little longer, though?"

I smile back. "Sure."

He slips his hand into mine, and I hold it, happy he can't see my silent tears in the dark. We're doing the right thing—it's what we have to do.

But it's still shattering my heart into a million pieces.

CHAPTER
THIRTY-SEVEN

I wake late that morning, neck aching from a night in the living room recliner. Sunlight filters through the window, and the muted sounds of a *Mario Kart* video game trail from across the room. "Good morning, Mom," Finn calls from the couch. "You slept late."

I grumble, looking around the room. "Where is everybody?"

"They had to go home. Sawyer said to tell you there's breakfast leftovers in the fridge."

I didn't get to say goodbye. I sigh. It's probably better this way.

"They'll be back tomorrow, right, Mom?"

I look up and Finn is watching me, picking up on my emotional cues more shrewdly than I expected. I smile brightly. "Actually, I think we're going to close the lodge for a few weeks."

"What?" he whines. "Why?"

"Consider it our summer vacation. We can spend time together, go to the park a lot . . ."

"Play video games?" he asks brightly.

"Sure, bud." I laugh, stretching. "Now, Mom's going to drink a lot of coffee, then what do you think about having a playdate with your friend Dante?"

His eyes widen. "From school? Yeah!"

I smile, hoping it works for Jane. I don't want to bring Finn with me to the hospital to see Lowell. Not only because it might scare him to see him there, but also because we have a lot of adult stuff to talk about. I've gotten so used to relying on Sawyer and Natalie these past few days, and it hurts again to think about them. I march into the kitchen and say a silent prayer that there's a full pot of coffee made, then realize Sawyer probably made it for me before he left.

Dammit, I need to stop this wallowing—we made the right decision. It'll get easier; the wound will scar over and hurt less. I need to give it time. For now, I pour an enormous cup of coffee, then slug it back to wash away the still-fresh pain.

I drop Finn off at Jane's, where I hand her his EpiPen bag and give her a quick allergy rundown—and also apologize profusely for taking advantage of her, promising I'll explain everything soon.

She waves her hand dismissively. "That's what friends are for, Iris."

Friends. My smile lasts the entire drive into town. I walk into the lobby of First Memorial Hospital and ask for Lowell's room at the information desk, then ride the elevator to the third floor and walk down the long white hallway to his room.

The door is ajar, but I knock softly anyway. "Come in," I hear him call out, and I smile in relief—he sounds like himself. Indeed, as I enter, I see him sitting up in his bed, hospital robe on, eating an ample bowl of Jell-O. I'm so relieved I start to cry.

"Ah, Iris," he says, setting his bowl down onto the table next to his bed. "I'm fine now, don't you worry."

I sit down in the chair next to his bed and reach out to squeeze his hand. "I'd hug you, but I don't want to mess up any of your monitors," I say.

He laughs. "Yeah, I can't wait to get these off. Hopefully they won't send me home on them."

"What did the doctor say?"

He sighs. "Heart attack. But a mild one. I'll need to take it easy, get on some medicine, and follow up with the cardiologist. But I'm still kicking." He beams; then his smile fades. "Are you okay?"

I take a deep breath and launch into the night's events, spilling out every last detail of the story I can. "That rat," he says through clenched teeth when I tell him about Dave.

"Now, don't get worked up," I warn. "He's going to prison, and we won't have to worry about him anymore."

"Still would've liked to knock his block off."

"I'd say Sawyer and Cole took care of that," I reply, which makes him smile.

"Well, I hope things settle down now, and you and Sawyer can get better acquainted."

There's a twinkle in his eye, and I narrow my eyes. "Was that your plan all along?"

"No, no," he says, chuckling. "I mean, I *did* think you two would hit it off, so it was more of a bonus, I guess."

I shake my head. "Well, we're actually taking a break for a while now."

"Why?"

"He and Natalie need to figure some things out. Plus, I . . . I feel bad. Like it was all my fault somehow."

Lowell leans in. "Iris, when are you going to see what you're worth, huh?"

Tears prick at my eyelids again, and I wipe them away. "It's for the best, okay? Besides, we have more pressing matters. Like, what are you going to do about the lodge?"

"I'm going to do what I should've done right away: give it to you."

I blink. "What? I can't afford it."

"You can if we sell your house in town."

"But that's *your* money. You bought the house for me. I haven't paid it off yet."

He waves his hand. "Ah, we let you make payments because we knew it was important to you. That house was yours the minute we bought it. And the lodge is yours. I'm sorry about all of this hoopla—I thought it would be a good way for you to see if you truly wanted it, but I'm afraid my forgetfulness kind of turned things into a big mess."

I squeeze his hand. "It's okay, Lowell. But I can't just take the lodge from you. How will you afford your own living expenses?"

"Eh, we can figure out how to split the profits, don't worry. But trust me, I'm doing fine."

I narrow my eyes. "But what about all your medical bills? From . . . Ivan's treatment?" He shoots me a questioning look, and I wince an apology. "In your office—I'm sorry, I didn't mean to snoop. But I found them, and it was so much money."

Lowell smirks. "Our insurance company finally came through—only because of my brilliant niece. She got them to cover what they owed—she's the damn-good lawyer I mentioned to you on the phone, by the way."

I shake my head, so relieved for him and yet still unconvinced. "That's great, but . . . I still can't let you do this for me. You've already done so much."

"Iris, I want to. Hell, I *need* to. I promised Ivan." He sighs. "Look, I should've told you this earlier, too, but we didn't have it easy. We kept our relationship a secret for a long time. It was only the last ten years or so before he died that we truly felt comfortable being ourselves. But I would've done it sooner—I would've shouted from the rooftops at the very beginning, but Ivan was scared. I always had the support of my family. He didn't. He . . . went through some terrible times before we met. The moment he saw you that day, scared and alone in that truck stop, he saw himself in you. You're both survivors. And he knew he would do anything to protect you. He loved you with his whole heart, like a daughter. I do, too."

I'm sobbing now, and I get up and gently wrap him in a hug. "Now," he continues, "my plans are made. My brother has informed me I am moving into this swanky retirement community he found for us north of the Twin Cities—which I expect you and Finn to come and visit regularly—and I have more than enough money to do that. So the lodge is yours, Iris. The only question I have is: What do *you* want?"

I blink. "What do *I* want?"

He nods. "Yes. It has to be your decision. Don't say yes because you think *I* want you to or because you feel obligated. Only say yes if it's what *you* want for you and for Finn."

I look out the window at the bright-blue sky, thinking.

What do I want?

For so long, I never had the luxury to ask myself that question. I was too focused on surviving from one day to the next. Then, too focused on hiding, on keeping myself and my son safe. But I don't have to be that woman in the dark anymore. Now, for the first time in so long, I can truly let myself think about the possibility of my own hopes and dreams—of thriving, not only surviving.

And what I want more than anything in this world is a home for Finn and me, and work that makes me happy and fulfilled. I want to feel secure and strong enough that I can pay it forward and help others feel that way, too. The truth is, the lodge is the perfect place for that. It doesn't need to be a place for overnight guests anymore—after last night's events, only the outer house will be used as lodging—but I might have an idea for the lodge itself that would be perfect and would honor Ivan at the same time.

"So, Iris, what do you say?"

I smile. "I say yes."

CHAPTER THIRTY-EIGHT

We close the lodge for almost two months, and I'm careful not to see Sawyer that whole time. I'm too busy to, anyway. Finn and I are packing up to move into the lodge for good, and we're also helping Lowell decide what he wants to take with him from the lodge to his new home at the retirement community with his brother—what should stay and what will go to storage.

The August day when Lowell is set to leave is hot and humid, and I have a fan whirring at us as we're going through paperwork in his office. I glance at the left drawer and suddenly remember the photos—the mystery of Emma Miller.

"Oh, Lowell," I say, opening the drawer and picking up a few of the delicate black-and-white photographs, "these are the pictures I was talking about. What do you know about these?"

He squints at them, and then recognition floods his face. "Ah, now I remember, the Millers. Yes, Ivan found those years ago when we were remodeling the upstairs."

"What do you know about this family?"

"They were the home's original owners, when it was first built. Ivan was working on that project for a while, I think. It was the same time the newspaper was running the pioneer series, focusing on the hardships of the region's early settlers."

I swallow. "So did the mother go missing?"

Lowell raises his eyebrows. "Uh, not that I know of. Actually, in the end, Ivan didn't think the Millers' story fit with the theme of settlers' hardships, so we gave most of the photographs to the county museum—these were the ones they didn't want."

"Wait—there's a display at the museum?"

He nods. "Some went to the exhibit on early pioneer families. But a few were used in a women's suffrage exhibit as well. Apparently when Emma was older, she was one of the leaders of the local women's suffrage movement."

My eyes widen, and I hold up the photos. "So that's why she wasn't in these photos—she was out rallying for women's suffrage?"

He shrugs. "I think so. You should go see the exhibit—she's the little old gray-haired lady in all the pictures. Looks like a real spitfire."

I smile as I pull out the original photo I found, Emma's stoic eyes now seeming to stare back as if challenging me. "I think I might frame this one for over the fireplace. What do you think?"

"That's up to you, my dear." He smiles. "The place is yours now."

Yes, it is, I think, smiling as I survey the room. *It's my home.*

The sun is high overhead when it's time for me to drive Lowell to the airport. Finn is clingy and tearful, and I'm the same way on the inside. I'm glad that Jane has offered to take Finn and Dante on rides at the county fair today—I'll meet them later, but for now it'll be a nice distraction for him, and for me.

But as we step out onto the porch, I hear voices coming from the side of the house.

"Sawyer!" Finn calls, running down the steps and around to the flower garden. "Natalie!"

My insides leap, but I tamp down the unexpected joy as I walk down the steps after Finn. There they are in the flower garden, Sawyer with a shovel in hand and Natalie holding a plant. As I walk up, I realize it's a rosebush, small and thorny with tiny buds not yet ready to bloom.

"What are you doing here?" I ask, hoping my voice is neutral. Seeing his handsome face after almost two months sends me spinning. I've missed him—both of them—so much.

Sawyer smiles but looks to Natalie, raising his eyebrows. "Um, we wanted to plant this," she says, tucking a lock of hair behind her ear shyly. "It's kind of an apology, but also a housewarming gift since we're going to be neighbors for real now."

I beam, emotions tugging within. "Thank you, Natalie. That is so thoughtful, and I love it."

"Mom, can we call it Rosie 2.0?" Finn asks excitedly.

We all laugh. "We sure can, buddy," I say.

"We also wanted to say goodbye to Lowell, of course," Sawyer says, reaching out to shake his hand. "Thank you for everything."

Lowell pulls him into a hug, and Natalie joins in. "Thank you both. It's been such a pleasure living next to you." They step apart, and he places a hand on my shoulder. "But I think you'll find your new boss is even better than your old one. She'll do great."

My eyes widen—I didn't want Sawyer to find out this way, and I haven't even thought about how to continue working together once the lodge reopens. But the look in his eyes is one of pride, and I match his smile. "That's great, Iris," he says. "I'm really happy for you."

"Thank you," I say softly. "I've been meaning to tell you—I'm planning on reopening next week. Does that work for you?"

He nods. "Whatever you want."

"I'm going to do some things a little differently. No more guests in the main house." Sawyer nods firmly in agreement, and I continue: "They'll stay in the outer barn, which will be perfect for hunters. But the house will be an events space only. Jane and I have an idea of a really special event—a retreat of sorts—that I'm hoping will work out."

"That sounds amazing," Sawyer says.

Before his praise can wash fully over me, a red crossover pulls into the driveway and honks. "Oh, there's Jane now," I say quickly.

Finn's eyes brighten. "Dante!" He turns to Natalie. "I get to go on rides at the fair!"

"Sweet," she says, fist-bumping him.

Jane steps out and raises her eyebrows suggestively at the sight of Sawyer, and I shoot her a look as I wave, hoping no one else notices. "Finn, go grab your EpiPen backpack."

I turn back, and Sawyer is eyeing me. "You're not going with him?" he asks, clearly impressed.

"I'm meeting them after I drop off Lowell at the airport." I shrug. "Baby steps, right?"

He laughs. "Right." Then he clears his throat. "So, uh, we'll just get this planted and be on our way, then."

"Okay," I say.

We both stand for a moment; then I finally force myself to turn away, and it takes all I have to leave him standing there. Even as I'm driving Lowell to the airport, I wonder when—or if—it will ever get easier to walk away from him.

CHAPTER
THIRTY-NINE

"Wait, wait, wait," Jane says, setting down her lemonade. "You are seriously telling me the man shows up at your house planting a brand-new freaking rosebush *just for you*, and you tell him, 'Okay, bye'?"

I groan, leaning my head onto my hands on the picnic table. Around us are the sights and smells of the county fair, all deep-fried goodness and children screaming from sky-high rides. We made sure to find a shaded spot under one of the many tentlike canopies so that Jane can stay cool in the afternoon sun, and now we're enjoying a glass of lemonade as the boys are on the Tilt-A-Whirl—within our view, of course. "I know, I know," I say. "But what was I supposed to do?"

She sighs. "You were *supposed* to drag him up to your bedroom and show him how you feel about him. *That's* what you were supposed to do."

I cross my arms, smirking. "Seriously?"

Jane laughs. "Okay, *I'm kidding*, of course. But why not call him already and tell him how you feel? You two are both adults. Hasn't it been long enough?"

I sigh, thinking of all he and Natalie have been through, and my connection to it. "I don't think I get to decide that. I need him to make the first move."

"Again, you wouldn't call the whole rosebush thing today a first move?"

"No." I grimace. "Okay, maybe? I don't know—it's so complicated because it involves his daughter, too. He needs to do what's best for her."

Jane lets out a long breath. "And *you* need to stop punishing yourself for your past."

I meet her kind gaze. Jane and I have been inseparable the last few weeks, texting and calling, taking the kids to the park or going for coffee on our own. I've told her everything about my past—it's funny how it's getting easier to do that, like every time I tell it, I'm taking away a little more of the power my past has held over me all these years. I sigh now. "You're right. I'll think about it."

"Good. Now let's work on scheduling that strategy meeting for the idea we came up with for the lodge."

I beam. All I had to do was mention my seed of an idea—providing a space at the lodge for survivors to heal—and Jane, the director of the local domestic violence shelter, has helped me make it bloom and flourish. "Yes, I was thinking right after Labor Day, if we want the retreat to be held in November."

Jane nods. "Good idea."

"I also thought of a possible name for the event: the Ivan Gordon Survivors' Empowerment Retreat."

Jane places a hand on her heart. "I love it, Iris." Then she reaches across to squeeze my hand. "He would be so proud of you."

"Thank you," I whisper.

Her eyes shift over my shoulder, then widen. "Uh-oh, Super Bitch Barbie alert."

I glance over my shoulder and see Sherri Simpson standing by the Ferris wheel, glammed up in that county-fair way—jeans and a sequined tank top with a glitzy cowboy hat and boots. I sigh. "I'm really not looking forward to hosting the Literary Ladies' Luncheon anymore."

"I didn't tell you?" Jane says brightly. "She stepped down from the book club. Says it would be 'too stressful to go back' after the trauma she experienced at the lodge. Don't worry; everybody knows she's just embarrassed that she threw herself at Sawyer and he turned her down."

I laugh, then cock my head. "Wait, so does that mean there's an opening in the group?"

"I told you, you're already in."

"No, I was thinking I might ask someone." Kallie Horn believed me when I needed her the most—plus, she's the only part of the newsroom I actually miss. "Would that be okay?"

Jane smiles. "Absolutely! The more the merrier."

I smile as Finn and Dante run up. "Mom, can we go on the Sizzler again?" Finn asks.

"Again?" I sigh, turning to Jane. "I'm fine with it if you are."

"Are you kidding? Let's wear these boys out—they're staying at my house tonight, so I want them to fall asleep the minute we get home."

We laugh together as the sun shines down on a beautiful day, a beautiful friendship.

CHAPTER FORTY

The sun is dipping low as I drive across the prairie toward home. I smile to myself. I still love that I can now call Windy Acres home. As I pull to a stop at the house, though, I automatically glance back where Finn should be, and the empty seat sets off a twinge of worry. Maybe I shouldn't have let him spend the night at Dante's. He could have an allergic reaction, and I wouldn't be there to help him.

But I take a deep breath. He's safe with Jane. She will definitely call me if anything goes wrong. Maybe I'll text her later, anyway. Baby steps.

I step out of the car and stretch, let the breeze push my hair off my neck. Sighing, I walk up onto the porch and ease into the swing. Then I sit, rocking, listening to the wind and the frogs. I close my eyes, reach for the silver chain around my neck—my grandma's necklace, which I finally feel ready to wear again—and I soak in this feeling. It's part contentment, knowing my son is safe and happy, and part pride, knowing I have conquered the darkness. That I can sit here with it, on my own, and be okay.

Knowing that after the darkness comes the light.

Headlights illuminate the driveway, and I open my eyes as a truck door shuts. Footsteps.

"Hey there," Sawyer calls out, and the sound of his deep voice spreads warmth throughout me.

He's wearing a suit coat with his jeans, and he looks so handsome that I can't help but smile. "Hey yourself."

He climbs the steps and holds out a bouquet of roses. "For me?" I ask.

"Of course."

"Thank you." I take them, inhale their fragrant scent.

He looks around, concern in his eyes. "Where's Finn?"

I let out a breath. "First-ever sleepover, at Dante's."

"Wow," Sawyer says. "Those baby steps are really speeding up."

I chuckle. "Yeah. I'm pretty nervous, but I know he'll be fine."

He stands awkwardly for a moment, so I gesture to the swing. "Sit with me?"

He eases down, and I set the flowers carefully on the table next to the swing. For a moment we rock silently, mixed emotions swirling through me. I take a deep breath. "What's Natalie up to tonight?" I say at last.

"She's at a friend's house, too. First time I've let her go since . . . well, since everything happened."

"How is she doing?" I ask quietly.

"Good. Her therapist says so, too. I've, uh . . . I've been to a few sessions myself." He smiles. "Our goal is to try to move a bit more toward normal."

"That's great." I don't know what else to say. I want to know what normal looks like for him, whether I can ever be a part of it, but I want to let him lead the conversation. "I'm glad things are going well."

He nods. "Yeah, the therapist even got me to talk to Cole. Well, email, at least. It's the best I could do." He smiles, and I smile back. "It's actually gone pretty well. Natalie and I might go visit him for Thanksgiving. Or he might come here. I don't know; it's all a big maybe, but it's a step, anyway."

"That's really great," I say, and I mean it. "I'm happy for you."

"And you and Finn are good?"

"Yeah, we are. He really misses you guys. I mean, we both do." I squeeze my eyes shut. "Sorry—I wasn't going to say that," I say quickly.

"I miss you, too," he says softly.

"You do?"

Sawyer turns to look at me fully, eyes intense. "Iris, I've thought about you every second of every day since I left that morning."

Warmth floods me, and my soul heals. I know now that I'm okay without him—that I can take care of Finn, thrive, and lead a full life on my own. But I also know that life is better with Sawyer—that I *want* to be with him, forever, if he wants me. "Me too," I whisper, voice breaking. "But I want to do the right thing for Natalie."

He smiles wryly. "Well, she *is* the one who told me to quit moping and get my butt over here and tell you how I feel."

"Really?" I swallow. "Can we make this work, Sawyer?"

Sawyer takes my hand in his, bringing it to his lips to kiss it. "All I know is that I can't spend one more minute without you in my life. I'm in love with you, Iris. And I'd love to be with you, if you'll still have me."

A sob escapes me, and I throw my arms around his neck. "I love you, too."

He kisses me tenderly, then pulls back to gaze into my eyes. "I've missed you so much."

I smile, holding him tight. "You're home now."

He takes me in his arms, and we hold each other as if we will never let go, as if we could stay out here like this forever, the two of us under the starlit sky, together at last.

EPILOGUE

Four months later
Christmas Eve

The night is dark and quiet, and I embrace it. We've made peace, the darkness and I. All of us contain a delicate balance, after all—darkness and light blending together in an intricate, beautiful tapestry. But I don't need to hide inside the darkness anymore. I know that now.

On this dark night, snow falls light and fluffy, and I watch the slow, meandering descent of the fat flakes from my perch on the porch swing. It's forgivingly mild out tonight, and I'm wrapped up tightly in a blanket, warmed by the mug of cocoa in my hands and the twinkling red-and-green Christmas lights, perfectly happy as I wait for Sawyer to get home.

Home. I sigh, content.

Soon enough, headlights illuminate the yard as Sawyer's truck rolls to a stop in the driveway. I hear the thud of his truck door, footsteps crunching across the snow. "How was the diner?" I call as he approaches.

"Hey, good, not too busy on Christmas Eve—but what are you doing out here?" He bounds up the porch steps and slides down next to me, wrapping me in his arms. "Aren't you cold?"

"It's not too bad," I say. "I was actually getting kind of warm in the kitchen after we made the popcorn."

"Ooh, did you save me some?"

"Of course. We're waiting for you—I told the kids we couldn't watch Christmas movies without you."

"Well, let's go in and get started, then, shall we?"

"Hold on," I say. "I have a question for you."

He looks at me strangely. "You do?"

I take a deep breath. "I know we're taking things slowly, but I was thinking logistically—would it just be easier if you and Natalie moved in here? I mean, especially over the winter, with all the early-morning events we have planned. Maybe after your New Year's father-daughter trip to New York with Natalie, we can talk about you moving in."

His mouth twitches, and he clears his throat.

"What?" I ask.

"I love you, but could we maybe just wait until we open gifts? Then I promise we can talk about whatever you want." I narrow my eyes at him, and he grins. "Please?"

I sigh. "Okay, *fine*—the kids are waiting for us anyway."

A relieved-looking Sawyer helps me to my feet and leads me inside.

"Finally!" Finn calls out from the couch, though he looks pretty cozy leaned up against Natalie, especially since they're wearing their matching reindeer pajamas—a gift sent from Lowell, who's excited to spend the holidays with his brother at the retirement community.

Lowell is living his best life now and has checked on the newspaper only once or twice since the new owners took over—which, thankfully, has resulted in only minimal layoffs thus far. Kallie has kept me informed, and so has Natalie, who decided she liked it enough after all to keep interning there throughout the school year. She and I have been getting coffee once a week, just the two of us, as a way to slowly keep getting to know each other better.

Natalie has also helped me close the final door on my past, using her research skills for good and tracking down what truly happened to Rex McNeil. He was convicted of multiple charges—among them, kidnapping and attempted murder—and sent to prison in Stillwater, Minnesota, five years ago. He died there two years later. Learning of his death was like the final link in a chain breaking, like I could finally lay that sad chapter of my life to rest for good.

Now, sitting in the lodge, I smile as I think about this new chapter of my life. We have quite the cozy Christmas scene in here—the living room is all decked out for the holidays, with a huge tree and lights and the whole nine yards. My favorite is the garland draped along the fireplace mantel, but even more special are the pictures that adorn it.

Our memory shelf, we've decided to call it. On it sit framed pictures of all the unforgettable people we love, and a memory book—a journal in which to write our unforgettable memories whenever we think of the loved ones we've lost. Along with this journal, there's the framed photo of Samantha and Natalie, a picture of Ivan and Lowell when they first moved into the lodge years ago, and a picture of Jane and me at the inaugural Ivan Gordon Survivors' Empowerment Retreat this past fall.

The retreat was an even bigger success than we could've imagined, raising funds for the shelter, garnering media coverage—and, most important, making a difference in survivors' lives. Jane and I are already excitedly preparing for next year's retreat, and I've started thinking about more events we can host at the lodge that can help people who need it most.

Also on our memory shelf, there's even a picture of the Millers—including Emma, of course. Her stoic eyes don't bother me anymore. She has the eyes of a woman who's been through hell and come out the other side—a woman who knows there's beauty to be found in the darkness and the light.

A woman like me.

Behind me, Sawyer claps his hands. "Okay, let's get this movie night started," he declares.

Natalie holds up her phone. "Uncle Cole says Merry Christmas, by the way."

I smile. Cole has been working on making amends—he visited over Thanksgiving, and he and Sawyer had a long talk. They still have a ways to go, but he's trying, at least.

"He says he also wants more movie recommendations?" Natalie says to me, a confused look on her face.

I smile—Cole is trying to make an honest living for the first time in his life, which means he can't afford streaming services and has been relying on old DVDs for entertainment. I lent him a few of mine, including my copy of *Nights of Cabiria*, because for some reason, I haven't needed Cabiria's company at night as often anymore. "I'm glad he likes my taste in movies. I'll find him some more."

"And tell him Merry Christmas," Sawyer says gruffly. I squeeze his hand.

"Can we start the movie now?" Finn asks. Then he looks at Sawyer and says, "Sit by me, Dad."

My eyes widen—we haven't talked about this—but I see Natalie's smile, see the grin spread across Sawyer's face. He winks at me, and I melt, bursting with pure joy. My baby got his wish. "You got it, buddy," Sawyer says, joining Finn on the couch. Then he leans down and whispers in Finn's ear. They fist-bump each other, and Sawyer clears his throat, asking loudly, "Uh, Mom, can you plug in the Christmas tree lights, please?" Finn giggles.

I shoot him a confused look but walk over to plug in the tree. When I lean down, I notice a small gift by the wall that wasn't there before—a tiny square box wrapped in red paper. I pick it up, turning around. "What's this one?"

Sawyer is no longer on the couch. He's on the floor, down on one knee. "I had a whole thing planned for tomorrow, so keep that in mind," he says, grinning. "But you started asking questions about moving in together, so I thought I'd improvise."

Finn is jumping on the couch excitedly. Natalie is recording with her phone.

I am in shock. "This is okay?" I ask Natalie, and she nods, laughing. I look at Finn, who is already chanting, "Say yes, say yes, say yes!"

Trembling, I open the small package—it's a jewelry box, and I gasp when I open it and see the shining diamond ring inside. I look down at Sawyer, who is looking at me with so much love it takes my breath away. "Iris, I love you so much. Every day I love you even more than the day before. And I'd love to keep loving you more, every day for the rest of our lives. Would you do me the honor of being my wife and Natalie's stepmom?"

Tears are falling freely from my eyes. "Yes," I cry. "Absolutely, one hundred percent, yes."

He gently slides the ring on my finger, then stands, kissing me softly and wrapping me in his arms. "I love you," he whispers.

"I love you, too. So much."

Sawyer pulls back, grinning wide. "Come here, you two."

Natalie and Finn race over and join in our embrace. They are my life, my world, my family. With them, I am home. There will always be darkness, but there will always be light, too, as long as we are together.

AUTHOR'S NOTE

Around the world, one in three women will experience physical or sexual violence by an intimate partner or sexual violence from a nonpartner in her lifetime, according to World Health Organization estimates. In the United States, intimate-partner violence affects millions of Americans, according to the Centers for Disease Control and Prevention. If you or someone you love needs help, please contact the National Domestic Violence Hotline at 1-800-799-7233 (and TTY 1-800-787-3224) or visit www.thehotline.org.

ACKNOWLEDGMENTS

I'm blessed with a supportive, loving family—and writing this book has made me even more grateful for that. Thank you to my parents, Bill and Elaine Grossell, for giving me the gift of knowing that they will always love me and will always be there for me, no matter what. Thank you, also, to the best sisters anyone could ask for: Erika Grossell, Eva Moore, and Elana Evans, and their families.

To my husband and children, Ted, Isabelle, Jack, and Ernie Dickey: thank you for being not only my family but also my home, my heart, my everything. To Alisa Kocian, Meghan Kutz, and Kari Nurminen: thank you for being my first readers and my best friends.

To my amazing agent, Sharon Pelletier: thank you for your continued belief in my stories and your caring, supportive guidance in my writing career. To my wonderful editor, Danielle Marshall: thank you for believing in Iris's story and in my ability to tell it, and for helping me truly make it shine.

To everyone at Lake Union and the entire publishing team who had a hand in making this book, thank you so much: Nicole, Bill, Jill, Kellie, and the production team; Gabe and the author-relations team; Tim Green and Faceout Studio for another gorgeous book cover; and Christine Williams for another fabulous job narrating my book.

To my longtime critique partner, Gretchen Mayer: thank you so much for all you do; I don't know what I'd do without you! Thank you to the kind and supportive authors who have shared their blurbs, wisdom, and guidance: Suzy Krause, Megan Collins, Kristin Wright, Elle Marr, Meredith O'Brien, and Kimmery Martin. To my APub debut friends—Mansi Shah, Eden Appiah-Kubi, Paulette Kennedy, Sara Confino, Kate Myles, and Jennifer Bardsley (who read an early draft of this story and offered wonderful feedback)—thank you all. I'm so glad we're on this journey together! Thank you as well to so many of my fellow authors from our 2021 debut group for being a continual source of support and encouragement.

Thank you to the booksellers and librarians who continue to support my work, especially Heather Roney and Cara Perrion. And, of course, to my readers—thank you so much for taking a chance on my stories!

ABOUT THE AUTHOR

Photo © 2020 Meghan Kutz

Elissa Grossell Dickey is a former journalist who now works in higher education communications. Stories have always been a big part of Elissa's life—from getting lost in a book as a child to now reading bedtime stories to her own kids. She has shared her journey of living with multiple sclerosis through blog posts for the National MS Society. Elissa grew up in northern Minnesota and now lives in South Dakota with her husband and children. She is also the author of the novel *The Speed of Light*. Learn more at www.elissaadickey.wordpress.com.